ording to his file Rob Stevens lives on the Dorset
t with his wife and two young sons. He grew
Bournemouth before studying Engineering at
bridge University – a notorious MI6 recruiting
nd. Government documents list his occupation
rline Pilot', which would be the perfect cover for,
a spy undertaking frequent foreign assignments.
denies that he is a Secret Agent – which is exactly
what you would expect them to say.

Also by Rob Stevens

The Mapmaker's Monsters:
Beware the Buffalogre!

The Mapmaker's Monsters:
Vampanther Attack!

*Secret Team of Intrepid-Natured Kids
Battling Odious Masterminds (Basically)

ROB STEVENS

MACMILLAN CHILDREN'S BOOKS

First published 2011 by Macmillan Children's Books
a division of Macmillan Publishers Limited
20 New Wharf Road, London N1 9RR
Basingstoke and Oxford
Associated companies throughout the world
www.panmacmillan.com

ISBN 978-0-330-53024-8

1 3 5 7 9 8 6 4 2

A CIP catalogue record for this book is available from
the British Library.

Typeset by Nigel Hazle
Printed and bound in the UK by CPI Mackays, Chatham ME5 8TD

For Clare, Dylan and Charlie
again – always

Thank you to all the members of the squadron at RAF Wittering for kindly allowing me to fly their Harrier simulator. The experience left me in no doubt about the skill required to hover a jet aircraft, and full of admiration for the pilots who do it in the line of fire. I have had the pleasure of working with some top agents over the years and would like to thank them all for the back-up they provided, especially Julia, Becky, Zoe and of course Maddie and Clare. I am immensely grateful to my parents, my sister Amanda and brother Andrew for their tactical support and for always watching my six. Secret operatives Atkinson, Cook, Purcell, Redding and Schomberg provided invaluable intel on highly classified subjects, while Trisha and Keith offered crucial feedback on preliminary documents. Finally thank you to my editor, Emma Young, without whom this book would have been twice as long and half as good.

Chapter 1

Helen Highwater gazed across the Thames from her office in MI6 headquarters, swivelling her leather chair from side to side as she considered how to conduct her imminent meeting. Standing beside her, dressed in his customary tweed suit with his spidery arms crossed, was her Tech Branch Specialist, Holden Grey.

'I don't know what you're worried about,' he said, stroking his white, pencil-thin moustache with thumb and forefinger. 'You've been dealing with field operatives for years.'

'*They* were adults,' Highwater countered, tapping a silver pen against her teeth. 'Need I remind you that Agent X-ray is only fourteen years old?'

'I say we play it cool,' said Grey. 'Hip, even.' He

unfastened the top button of his shirt and loosened his knitted tie.

'I'm not sure that's a wise—' Highwater was interrupted by a knock at the door. Her sharply bobbed hair kicked outward as she spun her chair round. 'Come in,' she commanded.

Holden Grey quickly ruffled a hand through his hair and pushed up the sleeves of his jacket. 'Trust me,' he murmured, partly untucking his shirt. 'I think it's time to show Agent X-ray we're not too old to be down on the kids.' The door opened and the teenager approached the smoked-glass desk.

'Good afternoon, X-ray,' said Highwater.

'What's up, partner?' added Grey, holding up a fist as a salute.

'*Partner?*' the young agent sneered. 'What is this, like, the wild west or something?' Noticing Grey's dishevelled appearance, X-ray added, 'OMG, Mr Grey, have you been mugged or something?'

'No, no, nothing like that.' The old man affected a dismissive laugh. 'This is just me – being my casual, *groovy* self.'

'Groovy?' Agent X-ray repeated dubiously, as if reading some obscure Shakespearean text.

'Sit down, X-ray,' Highwater said sternly.

'Yeah,' Grey added. 'Like, just chill off for a while.'

'Er, I think you mean chill *out*,' mumbled the agent, dropping into the leather chair positioned opposite the desk.

'Oh, well.' Grey cleared his throat. 'I say tomato . . .'

Highwater glared at her colleague.

The clock on the desk ticked.

Agent X-ray looked absently round the office, taking in the plush black carpet, angular leather sofa and sleek grey walls adorned with colour-coordinated abstract paintings. The room was tastefully dressed with an assortment of vases in highly polished ceramic, and metallic vertical blinds were drawn back to reveal a stunning view of London.

'We have our first mission,' announced Highwater at last, persevering with her authoritative approach. 'There's been a disappearance. A young man in Norway has gone missing from his own bed. Local police are treating him as a runaway but we have information suggesting he was kidnapped.'

Agent X-ray's eyes narrowed. 'Is there any connection with—?'

'It's too soon to tell,' interrupted Highwater.

3

'For real,' Grey agreed, 'but we've got the green light on the go-ahead to investigate.'

'Do we have any leads?' asked X-ray.

'Affirmative,' stated Highwater.

Holden Grey grabbed a chair and straddled it backwards, trembling slightly as he lowered his ageing frame into the seat. 'We've just cracked a coded message on the Internet that foretold this latest kidnapping before it happened . . . obviously. It seems our mysterious kidnapper thought we wouldn't be smart enough to decipher his clue. Well, how wrong he was!'

'I'm not being funny,' X-ray sneered, 'but solving the riddle after the crime has taken place is about as useful as party poppers at a funeral.'

Highwater nodded as though she appreciated Agent X-ray's input but she was really thinking how much she missed working with grown-ups. At least adults *pretended* to respect her, unlike these kids who said exactly what they thought.

'In some ways you're right.' She frowned thoughtfully. 'The point we're making is that the Internet is so vast that identifying a code is usually much trickier than deciphering it. To be honest, the code itself is so simple even a child could solve it . . . no offence.'

Agent X-ray shrugged.

Highwater removed her rectangular spectacles and thought for a moment. 'Look, X-ray, this is serious,' she said grimly. 'I don't know what his intentions are but my instincts tell me we might have an EMU on our hands.'

'EMU?'

'Yes, Emu.' Highwater pressed her palms on to her desk and, leaning forward purposefully, whispered, 'Evil Mastermind Uprising.'

'So what's the plan then?' said Agent X-ray. 'Do we go and stake out his house or whatever?'

Holden Grey grimaced. 'The exact location of his precise . . . er . . . location is, presently at this moment in time, unknown to myselves – I mean ourself. That means we must monitor and filter the suspect website twenty-four-seven. Seven days a week. And that means round the clock.'

'Yeah, I know what twenty-four-seven means.'

Grey continued, 'Next time our Evil Mastermind brags about his impending crime we'll be one step ahead and stay right on his tail. Although, when I say "we", I do of course mean you, X-ray.'

Agent X-ray nodded.

'Naturally you'll need a partner,' said Highwater.

'What about Agent Hotel?'

Highwater shook her head. 'Unfortunately Agent Hotel will be spending the next six weeks in plaster following an injury sustained in the field.'

'The field?' Agent X-ray frowned. 'But this is our first mission!'

'Not that sort of field,' said Highwater wearily. 'The playing field. The silly boy broke his ankle playing football yesterday lunchtime. And Agent Kilo won't be available to us for months unless he's released from house arrest for exceptionally good behaviour.'

'House arrest?' Agent X-ray was horrified, imagining some sort of military coup in far-off lands.

'Yes, he's been grounded indefinitely for crashing his father's new BMW while showing off to his friends.'

'I didn't even know Agent Kilo had a licence.'

'He doesn't,' said Highwater with a snort of disapproval. 'In fact, with Agent Alpha suffering from chickenpox and Agent Uniform having her tonsils out we don't have a single existing agent who's eligible for this assignment.'

'I'll handle it then,' said Agent X-ray.

'Don't be foolish,' said Highwater. 'You know

agency protocol forbids underage operatives engaging in field ops alone. We will simply have to recruit a fresh agent.'

'Who?'

Helen Highwater stood, picked up two pieces of A4 paper and walked round her desk until she was opposite Agent X-ray. Handing over one sheet, she perched on the edge of the glass desktop and folded her arms. 'We ran SPADE again,' she said.

SPADE stood for Secret Potential Agent Data Evaluator – a computer program used by MI6 to identify people who possess the right skills and aptitude to make good future agents. The school records, SATS test results and sporting achievements of every child in the country were recorded alongside their medical records and genetic make-up. All the data was fed into SPADE, which analysed and quantified it before allocating each child a score from one to a hundred depending on their potential suitability for field ops.

'Ninety-eight,' said Agent X-ray, casually scanning the SPADE printout. 'Could do better.'

'Not much,' Highwater retorted.

At the top of the page was a photograph of a young boy with a lean oval face framed by a messy thatch of mousy hair. His shy smile revealed two front teeth with a slight overbite and his eager brown eyes peered keenly from behind small spectacles.

'He looks like a bookworm to me,' sneered Agent X-ray.

'Don't judge a bookworm by its cover,' laughed Grey.

'So why does SPADE rate him so highly?'

Highwater slid her glasses on and peered at her own copy of the printout. 'He has an impeccable school record and his SATS are exemplary. He is highly intelligent with a particular flair for lateral thinking, languages and verbal reasoning and he is potentially an expert at hand-to-hand combat, which might come in very handy if your cover gets blown.'

'It doesn't say anything here about any martial-arts training,' Agent X-ray interjected. 'I'm not being funny, but watching *The Karate Kid* doesn't make him a lethal weapon.'

'We have reason to believe that he is genetically predisposed to be able to look after himself,' stated Highwater. 'Besides which his father was a military test pilot and we know that he has inherited his piloting skills too. In fact my only reservation is based on his age.'

'I hate to break the bad news but all your agents are teenagers, you know,' said Agent X-ray.

'Exactly,' Highwater agreed. 'This one isn't. He's twelve.'

X-ray started to laugh but, realising that Highwater was serious, protested instead. 'That's crazy. You can't catch evil masterminds with babies.'

'SPADE says he's the best available.'

'Well, I say you'll be digging a deep hole for yourself if you use SPADE on this one.'

'Time will tell,' Grey mused, 'in the fullness of . . . er . . . time.'

'His youth may have certain advantages,' Highwater suggested. 'He probably won't be tempted by the sort of stunts that got Agent Kilo into trouble.'

'Whatever.' Agent X-ray shrugged. 'So what's his name, this new boy wonder?'

Highwater removed her glasses and smiled.

'Hunt,' she said emphatically. 'Archie Hunt.'

Chapter 2

Archie Hunt was struggling to stay awake. The afternoon sun was streaming through the classroom window and bathing him in warm yellow light while his teacher, Miss Moore, who was known as Moore the Bore, had been droning on about lizards or frogs or something for over an hour.

Archie allowed his eyelids to close – just for a moment – while he listened to his teacher's nasal monotone.

'Like many reptiles, lizards have a keen sense of smell which they use to detect the presence of any potential predators. Interestingly, they actually smell using their tongues.' The flat whine of Miss Moore's voice washed over Archie, gradually receding until it was no more than a faint hum, like a distant jet plane. His head began to nod.

Soon he was flying his own plane – soaring through the clear blue sky above. He was on a dangerous bombing mission, diving low over enemy territory, rocking his wings this way and that as he avoided enemy gunfire. Amidst the scream of his jet, the chatter of machine-gun fire and the drumbeat of explosions, he could hear mission control trying to contact him.

'Calling Mr Hunt. Come in, Mr Hunt.'

'This is Hunt,' he replied. 'Pass your message.'

'Will you be back with us soon?'

'Just as soon as I've taken out the enemy base.'

'Excellent. Will that be before or after PE?'

'PE?' Archie wondered. What was mission control talking about? But in that moment of reflection, the bombs faded away and his screaming jet plane evaporated. With a swelling sense of discomfort Archie opened his eyes.

Everyone in the class was looking at him. Some were wide-eyed with astonishment, others were grinning with malicious delight. Miss Moore was standing over Archie's desk, her lips pursed in an expression of disappointment.

'Now you've come back down to earth,' she said, 'I think you can safely put those wings away, don't you?'

As the whole class exploded with laughter Archie realised his arms were outstretched like a five-year-old playing planes. His cheeks burned furiously as he tucked his hands under his desk in case they should embarrass him again.

'Oh dear,' growled Harvey Newman, the class hard man, under his breath. 'It looks like Mr Goody Two Shoes himself is well and truly in the doghouse.' A handful of his cronies made a show of stifling their chuckles.

'I'm surprised at you, Mr Hunt,' said Miss Moore, placing her hands behind her back like a barrister cross-examining a witness. 'I hope, for your sake, you weren't actually *daydreaming* in my class?'

'No, Miss.' Archie did his best to sound surprised by the very suggestion.

'Good.' Miss Moore sounded so pleased that, for a moment, Archie thought he was off the hook. 'In that case,' she continued, 'perhaps you would be so kind as to remind the class what animals prey on lizards?'

Archie felt a rock drop into his stomach. 'Well . . . that would be . . . obviously . . .'

12

'I'm waiting.'

Miss Moore tapped her foot impatiently.

'If you can't give me an answer I'll have to conclude that you have been paying no attention whatsoever and refer the incident to Mr Head.'

Archie sighed. The headmaster, Head the Head, who was renowned for his merciless approach to classroom discipline, had once given a boy detention for a whole term for sneezing in assembly. Just as Archie was beginning to accept his fate he noticed his best friend, Barney Jones, who was sitting at the front of the class and holding up a sheet of A4 behind Miss Moore's back.

Surreptitiously Archie pushed his glasses up his nose and peered at the words Barney had scrawled on the paper.

'Five seconds,' barked Miss Moore.

'Birds of prey!' Archie blurted out with a mixture of relief and triumph.

'Yes,' Miss Moore conceded with grudging surprise. 'What else?'

'Most bigger animals like wolves . . . foxes and . . .' Archie squinted at the last word that Barney had squeezed into the bottom corner of the page.

'Coy . . . oats?'

'Excuse me?'

Quickly Archie realised his mistake. 'Coyotes,' he said hurriedly. 'I meant to say coyotes.'

'Correct,' Miss Moore said, studying him suspiciously.

Archie smiled innocently.

'OK, class,' continued the teacher. 'Get your textbooks out and turn to page two hundred and thirty-four.'

As she turned and strode to the front of the class Barney spun in his seat, screwed his cheat sheet into a tiny ball and pushed it into his rucksack.

'Thanks for helping me out with Moore the Bore,' Archie said as he and Barney walked along B-block corridor. The aroma of disinfectant and musty sweat filled the air. 'I owe you one.'

'Don't mention it,' said Barney, pushing a Bounty bar into his mouth. He was a tubby boy with tight curly blond hair and wide blue eyes that gave him an expression of permanent wonderment. 'I saw a fellow agent under interrogation and I acted. It's what I'm trained for.'

'Sure.' Archie smiled.

Barney spent his whole life playing a game in which he was an undercover agent, teachers were evil villains and some other pupils were double agents. He pretended his parents were his MI6 handlers and his bike was a supercar loaded with gadgets.

'I could see the Bore was about to break you and that would have compromised our mission,' Barney continued, speaking through one side of his mouth while chomping his chocolate bar on the other.

'Uh-huh.'

'So I sent you the coded message. It's basic trade craft.'

'The message wasn't exactly coded though, was it?' Archie laughed. 'It was just written quite small.'

'Exactly.' Barney grinned. 'I didn't want any enemy agents to decipher it.'

'Don't you ever get tired of pretending to be a spy?' Archie asked.

'Everyone needs a fantasy,' Barney conceded. 'You dream about being a pilot and I dream about being a spy. It's the same thing, isn't it?'

Archie hesitated for a moment. 'Yup,' he said. 'We're just a couple of dreamers.'

'Code red, code red.' Barney was looking towards the exit at the end of the corridor where Harvey Newman and a bunch of his mates were loitering. 'Enemy operatives up ahead.'

'Great,' sighed Archie. 'That's all we need – a run-in with Hardly Human.'

Barney studied his mobile as if it was a palmtop computer. 'Intel reports suggest suspects are prone to mindless aggression of the roughing-up variety and planning an imminent strike. Your orders are not to engage with the enemy. I repeat, do *not* engage.'

'What do you mean, "intel reports"?' asked Archie as they approached the group of thugs.

'It's short for intelligence rep—'

'I know what it's short for, you wally. I meant, "Where does your intel come from?"'

'I overheard him talking in the bogs,' Barney conceded. 'Newman got double detention for giving Miss Smith verbals. He said he's ready to pound someone.'

The gang blocked the corridor. 'Excuse us, please,' said Archie. 'Can we just get past?'

'Well, look who it is,' sneered Newman. He circled the two friends once then stood so close in front of

16

Archie that their noses were almost touching. 'All right, Hunt?'

'Hello, Hardly.'

Newman frowned. 'What did you just call me?' he demanded, grabbing a handful of Archie's shirt.

'I meant to say Harvey. Slip of the tongue, sorry.' Archie smiled amiably as Newman's eyes narrowed. He was a solid lump of a boy with pinkish skin and gingery blond hair cut into a flat top.

'If I find out that's some kind of smart-alec nickname then I'll mash you like a . . . like a . . .'

'A potato?' suggested Archie helpfully.

'You think you're so clever, don't you?' snarled Newman.

Archie shrugged. 'Not really.'

'Well, you're not the only one who can think up clever names,' Newman said. 'I'm going to start calling your friend here Fatty.'

'That *is* clever,' said Barney. 'Can we go now?'

'As for you, Hunt, I'm going to call you Four Eyes. You know, because you wear glasses and that.'

'Yes, I pieced that together for myself, thanks,' said Archie, absently adjusting his spectacles. 'Brilliant – well done you. Anyway, must dash.'

'Not so fast.' Newman put a hand on Archie's chest, stopping him in his tracks. 'What got into you in biology? You looked like such a weirdo.'

Archie shrugged. 'I don't know. Moore the Bore just seemed to be living up to her name more than usual.'

'Yeah, well, I was bored too. But I didn't pretend to fly round the classroom going, *"Come in, mission control, can you hear me, mission control?"*' For his impression of Archie, Newman adopted a high-pitched warble that made his cronies snigger. 'How come I get double litter duty for giving Smith a bit of lip and you get away scratch free for acting like such a clown? You were like that toy that thinks he can fly in that cartoon. You know, Buzz whatsaname. In fact, forget Four Eyes – I'm going to start calling you *Buzz*.'

Newman emphasised the last word by shoving Archie.

'You can go now, Fatty and Buzz,' Newman smirked, standing aside to let Archie and Barney pass.

The two friends exchanged glances then Barney pushed open the exit door.

'Bye, Hardly,' said Archie, stepping into the afternoon air.

'See you tomorrow, Buzz Lightwater.'

18

'You mean Light*year*, brainache,' Archie muttered under his breath.

'HEY!' Newman ordered. 'What did you say, Buzz?'

'Me? Nothing,' Archie said innocently. 'I probably misheard but it sounded like you just said Light*water*.'

'Yeah? And so what if I did?' Newman snorted.

'I think you meant Buzz Light*year*,' Archie said slowly.

'No I never,' Newman insisted, bunching his fists and frowning.

'My mistake.' Archie smiled pleasantly. 'So who is this Buzz Lightwater then?'

Newman studied Archie for a moment before turning to scan the expectant faces of his gang. Looking back he considered his options for a few seconds before replying with two simple words.

'Get them!'

Two of the bullies grabbed Barney, yanking his rucksack off his shoulder and tipping its contents on the ground before laying into him with their feet and fists. Meanwhile, Newman charged at Archie, who braced himself for the pain he was about to endure. Apart from being much slighter than Newman, he had never been in a fight in his whole life. But as the punches flew at his face Archie felt a strange sense of control come over him.

As though it was second nature to him, he skipped backwards, blocking or dodging every single blow. When there was a lull in Newman's onslaught Archie intuitively planted his left foot, leaned back and drove his right foot straight into his opponent's chest. To his amazement his kick lifted the bully clean off his feet, knocking him flat on his back.

Seeing Newman floored, his cronies forgot about battering Barney and scarpered immediately. Newman himself clambered hurriedly to his feet, jabbing his finger and warning Archie to 'look out next time' as he backed sheepishly into B block.

'Whoa! Dude!' Barney laughed. 'That was awesome! What got into you?'

Archie pushed his hands into his pockets and shrugged. 'I dunno,' he replied, his face pale with shock. 'It just, sort of, came naturally.'

'Well, just so there's no confusion next time,' Barney said, dabbing at his bloodied lip with a tissue while retrieving his James Bond lunch box, *Do not engage the enemy* translates into *Don't wind up Harvey Newman.*'

'Sorry,' said Archie, picking up a couple of exercise books and handing them to his friend. 'I thought it was some sort of code.'

'For what? Try and get us duffed up at all costs?'

Archie smiled weakly.

'M's going to kill me when she sees my coat,' said Barney, inspecting a tear under one arm.

'Tell your mum it was my fault.'

Barney smiled and shook his head. 'An agent never blows another operative's cover. Besides, it was worth it just to see you kick Harvey Newman's butt. You were like some sort of super-ninja-nerd. Seriously, where *did* you learn those moves?'

Archie clenched his hands in his pockets to stop them trembling. 'Honestly, I haven't got a clue.'

'Well, it was wicked.' Barney smiled. '*Totally* weird – but wicked.'

Blushing, Archie smiled. 'Are you sure you're OK?'

'I'm a bit shaken,' Barney admitted. 'But not stirred.'

Chapter 3

'You've got two bogeys in your six o'clock.'

Archie Hunt reacted instantly to the familiar voice in his headset, slamming forward both thrust levers and pulling the control column into his stomach. The jet aircraft responded immediately. It was a Dragonfly 600, a revolutionary business jet that boasted incredible aerobatic performance. Engines screaming, its nose reared up and it arced into an increasingly steep climb.

Archie glanced to his left, stifling a groan as the G-force pushed him into his seat. Far below, the surface of the Channel was sparkling in the afternoon sun as it lapped up against chalk cliffs and sandy beaches. When his torso was parallel to the horizon Archie checked

22

the stick forward and the jet powered vertically upward like a rocket piercing the clear blue sky. 'Yeeehaaah!'

The voice in Archie's headset was impassive. 'Don't forget you're not Captain Kirk, and you're not flying the starship *Enterprise*. Check your airspeed.' Archie scanned the two screens on the panel in front of him, comprising the aircraft's flight instruments, assimilating the information in a moment.

The Dragonfly's two jet engines couldn't sustain the vertical climb much longer. The aircraft was simply trading speed for height, like a cyclist freewheeling up a steep slope. Soon its momentum would run out and then the aircraft would simply topple out of the sky like a toy plane.

Pulling back on the stick, Archie kept the wingtips level as the aircraft looped on to its back. He dropped out of his seat and felt a momentary stab of panic before his shoulder straps snapped taut to arrest his fall. Hanging in his harness he shoved the control column forward to hold the Dragonfly's altitude and checked his instruments.

Glancing momentarily at the coastline above him, Archie felt his eyes bulging as the blood rushed to his head. Then, as he slapped the stick against his left thigh, the world spun round the aircraft's nose until the earth was beneath him once again. When the wings were level he centralised the controls, arresting the roll with a crisp jolt.

'Watch your airspeed.' The voice in Archie's headset was calm but firm.

Archie pushed the throttles forward but the plane's body angle was too steep, his reaction had been too slow and the aircraft began to wallow like a sinking ship. Suddenly the Dragonfly flipped on to its back, twisting to the left, spiralling like a corkscrew as it fell.

Archie knew the drill for spin recovery off pat and recited it in his head as the plane plunged towards the water. Forcing himself to adhere to the procedure, he relaxed his grip on the control column and extended his left leg against the rudder pedal. The aircraft's nose seemed to drop further as its rapid clockwise pirouette began to slow down. He glanced at the altimeter as he waited for the rotation to stop.

The Dragonfly had already dropped four thousand feet. It would take less than a minute to plummet the remaining ten thousand feet between him and disaster. Looking through the windscreen, he reckoned the world below was spinning more slowly but it was expanding at a frightening rate as it rushed up to meet him. Tiny details were emerging as if he was on Google Earth, zooming in on his point of impact. He could see the swell of the ocean and ripples on its surface and brightly coloured windsurfers skipping along in the breeze. All the time the plane was falling.

Seconds passed.

The aircraft tumbled another few hundred feet.

The plane had virtually stopped spiralling as the altimeter whipped through five thousand feet. Archie couldn't hold his nerve any longer and he hauled the controls into his gut.

'Wait for it,' urged the voice in his headset. But it was too late.

The air still wasn't flowing smoothly over the aircraft's wings and Archie's input only made matters worse. In a split second the world was spinning violently as the plane speared towards the earth in a tightening corkscrew.

'I have control!'

Breathless with terror, Archie watched as his father gripped the control stick between his knees. Richard Hunt was an ex-Royal Air Force test pilot who had flown countless combat missions over Iraq and the Balkans. After proving his skill and bravery at a young age he had been recruited to the SFS – the highly classified Special Flying Service – an elite squadron of fighter pilots trained to land behind enemy lines and carry out covert commando missions. While everyone knew tales about the daring missions carried out by the SAS, the SFS remained so secretive that only a handful of high-level government officials were even aware of its existence.

Archie knew that if anyone could save them, it was his father.

With arctic coolness, Richard Hunt centralised the controls and applied full left rudder. Then he started talking to Archie through the intercom in the sort of reassuring voice surgeons use when they're explaining an impending procedure to a nervous patient.

As his father commentated, Archie instinctively gripped his armrests and pushed himself back into his seat. The windscreen was filled with a terrifyingly close view of the sea, which would be pouring through their shattered canopy if they didn't pull out of their dive in the next fifteen seconds.

Richard continued, 'Fifteen hundred feet, rotation

26

rate zero, initiating recovery at twelve hundred feet.'

The sight of the unusual jet aeroplane tumbling earthward had caught the attention of a number of holidaymakers on the beaches of England's south coast. Some were frozen open-mouthed while others already had their camera phones poised, capturing the imminent impact, as they estimated the price they'd be able to demand from satellite news channels for their exclusive footage.

Just when everyone in the crowd was sure they were about to witness a horrific plane crash, the silver swept-wing jet began to recover. Swooping perilously close to the water, the aircraft drew gasps of wonder from its audience, almost skimming the waves before pulling out of its dive and climbing steeply away. As it headed skyward it completed an immaculate four-point roll, pausing briefly after each quarter-turn.

Archie exhaled long and hard.

'Sorry about that,' he breathed.

'We're still in one piece, aren't we?' Richard steered the plane inland.

The Dragonfly crossed the coast and descended into a wooded valley, like an insect targeting the crease of a sleeping rhino's skin. Dropping the undercarriage with the flick of a lever Richard banked hard right, carving a turn low over the vast chrome and glass house he shared with his son.

The aircraft Richard had flown in the SFS was the Harrier jump jet, a plane capable of hovering or executing a vertical take-off and landing by directing the thrust from its engines through controllable nozzles. Since leaving the SFS Richard had assembled a team of engineers capable of adapting the Harrier's vectored thrust technology to design the world's first Vertical Take-off and Landing (VTOL) private plane.

The Dragonfly was popular with millionaires, who liked the idea that it matched their helicopters' versatility while flying at five times the speed. Richard had used some of Hunt Aviation's handsome profits to fund a fleet of Red Cross Dragonflies, which were proving invaluable in providing swift medical care to people injured or endangered in remote war zones.

Archie brimmed with admiration as he watched his father coordinating subtle movements to achieve a rock-solid hover. Easing back the thrust levers, Richard finessed the controls and the Dragonfly began to descend vertically. Seconds later the aircraft's landing gear touched down and Richard taxied it towards his private purpose-built hangar.

When the engines were shut down Archie unclipped the canopy's red safety lever and slid the glass dome backwards along its rails. He felt devastated about the near catastrophe he had caused – angry with himself for messing up the spin recovery and ashamed that his father had witnessed his failure. Not only was Richard Hunt a test pilot of immense skill, he was the one person in the world whom Archie had always wanted to emulate and make proud.

Gripping the top of the windshield, Archie climbed from the cockpit and walked round the plane's sleek torpedo-shaped nose to meet his father. With his long gangly limbs, Archie was taller than most of his classmates and tended to slouch to compensate. His tousled hair gave him the appearance of someone who had just rolled out of bed but his brown eyes peered keenly through the rectangular lenses of his tortoiseshell glasses.

'I'm sorry about that, Dad,' he repeated, meeting his father's eyes. 'It won't happen again.'

'No.' Richard nodded as if to accept his son's apology. Archie looked up at his father, waiting for him to say something else – to offer some encouragement or praise to buoy his spirits. At last Richard ruffled his son's hair and said, 'Let's see what's for tea – I'm starving.'

Later that afternoon Archie was on Facebook when he got a new message from someone whose profile picture was a silver X on a red background. After reading it twice he grabbed his mobile and called Barney.

'What's happening?' asked Archie.

'Not much.'

'Listen, can you come over before school tomorrow?'

'Can do. What's up?'

'I just got this weird message on Facebook. I think you might be able to shed some light on it.'

Chapter 4

Barney stared at the computer screen in Archie's bedroom, his mouth hanging open slightly, as it had been for the last few minutes. He read the message out loud for the eighth time, his voice trembling with excitement.

'My name is Agent X-ray. You don't know me but I am a government operative. If you are willing to help your country in matters of national security, meet me at the corner of Ashdown Road and Cavendish Way at 8 a.m. tomorrow. Come alone.'

'You can own up now,' said Archie, gently shoulder-barging his friend.

'What do you mean?' asked Barney, taking his eyes off the screen at last.

'I'm on to you, Agent X-ray.'

'What? No! I didn't send that.'

'Promise?'

'I swear on my signed copy of *Silverfin*.'

'Well, if you didn't, who did?'

Barney's eyes widened. 'It could actually be from MI6,' he breathed.

'Sure, that's obviously the most likely solution,' said Archie dryly. 'But, just for argument's sake, let's work on the unlikely scenario that I haven't been contacted by an actual secret service spy. Who else could it be from?'

'What about Newman? He might be waiting on that corner with back-up – ready to get you back for the other day.'

'Nah.' Archie shook his head. 'Check the spelling.'

Barney looked back at the screen and nodded. 'I see what you mean – there's no way Newman could spell *government operative*.'

'I'd be surprised if he could pronounce it.'

Barney laughed and shoved the last quarter of a slice of buttered toast into his mouth.

'It's like watching a hyena devour a chicken. Or

whatever hyenas eat.' Archie pulled an uncertain face. 'Didn't you have breakfast before you left your house this morning?'

Barney bobbed his head from side to side and twirled a hand while he chewed up his mouthful, then said, 'Course I did. But that was nearly forty minutes ago.'

'No wonder you were getting hungry again. It's lucky you didn't pass out on the way over here.' Archie gestured at the monitor. 'I tried replying but it wouldn't let me.'

Barney nodded wisely. 'They've probably set up a number of ghost server nodes so they can't be traced. Standard secret service diversionary tactics.'

'Is that something that can actually happen or is it from one of your spy films?'

'No, it's real, honest,' Barney insisted earnestly. 'I saw it on *Spooks*.'

'If you say so.' Archie slung his rucksack over his shoulder. 'Come on. It's nearly quarter to and I don't want to miss my rendezvous with the mysterious Agent X-ray, do I?'

Archie strode purposefully along Cavendish Way, intrigued but half hoping he wasn't walking into some sort of ambush. His pace slowed instinctively as he neared the junction with Ashdown Road.

Suddenly someone grabbed his wrist from behind and pulled him into a rhododendron bush. He spun round to face his attacker, his pulse suddenly out of control.

'Barney! What are you doing?' he hissed.

'This could be an ambush,' whispered Barney. 'I suggest we covertly surveil the hotzone.'

Archie studied the street corner, which was deserted except for a young girl who was leaning against the street sign.

'I don't want to spoil your fun,' Archie murmured, 'but the zone in question doesn't look especially hot. And I don't think *surveil* is even a word.'

Barney responded by holding a finger to his lips and pulling Archie down to a crouching position.

The boys waited and watched in silence for ten minutes. No one else appeared except for an elderly lady walking a small dog, who crossed Cavendish Way and disappeared along Ashdown Road without pausing.

'It looks like the leopard has ceased stalking the polar bear,' whispered Barney at last.

34

Archie turned to him and frowned. 'What does that even mean?'

'It's code,' Barney said. 'You are the polar bear and whoever sent the message is the leopard. It means, "I don't think they're coming today,"'

'Why can't you just say that then?' asked Archie.

'What if we're overheard – or being bugged? If we use code we won't arouse suspicion.'

'You're right.' Archie smiled. 'After all, there's nothing suspicious about a couple of schoolboys cowering in the bushes talking about leopards and polar bears who, incidentally, live on different continents. I bet MI6 would recruit us on the spot if we weren't so darned elusive.' He stepped out of the bushes and glanced left and right. 'Polar bear to grizzly,' he said, laughing. 'You are clear to cease hibernation – the hunting season is over.'

Then he turned and sprinted as Barney broke his cover and chased him down the street.

Meanwhile, At A Secret Location Somewhere in Europe . . .

Chapter 5

A figure sat in a leather chair, dwarfed by a banked console that swept round him in a wide semicircle of dials, knobs and levers. Hunched over a keyboard, he tapped away frenetically, muttering conspiratorially to himself.

'Let's see who's going to be my next *volunteer*,' he mused. 'Who's going to sacrifice their own insignificant existence to benefit humankind? When I say *humankind* I do, of course, mean me. Although, to be honest, I'm only half human and I'm definitely not kind.' His shoulders began to rock as he suppressed a chuckle. 'In fact I'm quite *in*human and I'm positively despicable.' Unable to contain his merriment any longer he threw back his head and unleashed a volley of evil laughter, each burst louder and longer than the last, like someone revving a motorbike.

Eventually, wiping a tear from his one human eye, he looked round the room like a comedian expecting to feed off his audience's adulation. But the only other figure in the cavernous chamber was a young man who was in some sort of trance – and cocooned inside a tall glass cylinder. The villain's mirth was met with silence.

In a moment his laughter stopped and he sat back in his chair and sighed heavily.

'Well, no offence, Mr Ulrik, but you're not exactly the life and soul of the party.'

Two eyes stared out blankly from behind the glass.

'This reminds me of the days I had to share a lab with Malcolm Battersby – possibly the dullest man ever to walk the earth. It wasn't until a year after I'd secretly drugged him and given him a frontal lobotomy that people began to suspect he wasn't all there – which was true because half of his brain was in the laboratory under my house. Do you see what I did there? They thought he wasn't *all there* . . .' His body convulsed with amusement but the fit was short-lived. He sighed again and blew air through his mouth, making his

39

scaly lips flap. 'I might as well talk to myself for all the appreciation I get round here. It wasn't so bad when I had Pussy Galore to talk to but she had to go when my fur allergy flared up. I mean, it's almost impossible to stroke a cat menacingly while your nose is running like a snotty two-year-old's. And since we're on the subject, I can't imagine anyone round here ever stops to appreciate the effort I put in to dress the part.' He hooked a finger into the neck of his dark jacket and stuck out his hideously fat tongue as if he was choking. 'I'll have you know this bloomin' Nehru collar is killing me but I might as well slouch around in my PJs all day for all the good it does me.'

Silence filled the vast room.

'I don't know what you're looking so smug about anyway,' he sneered at his prisoner. 'I sent the world a pretty simple coded message that I was going to kidnap you but no one picked up on my sinister intentions, which is incredibly disappointing for both of us, although *possibly* more so for you. After all, what's the point of my being so deliciously brilliant if the rest of the world is too stupid to realise that something dastardly is about to happen?'

He bent over his keyboard and started to type, his

human eye staring intently at the screen while the other, a bulbous leathery orb, panned round jerkily.

'I'm just going to give the world one more chance to join in my little game,' he schemed. Sitting back to admire his message, he nodded smugly before pressing the 'send' key with an air of finality, as if he was firing a nuclear weapon. 'Come and get me,' he chuckled. 'If you're smart enough.'

Chapter 6

Barney was in his weekly chess club meeting so Archie had wandered alone across the school playground where he was sitting on an old bench, contemplating his Facebook message while he munched through his packed lunch.

He didn't share Barney's theory that MI6 might actually be trying to contact him but he had failed to come up with any alternative explanations. What if it really had come from Newman?

'Archie. Don't turn round.'

The voice came from over Archie's right shoulder. He stood up automatically and spun round to see a girl wearing jeans and a leather jacket. She was a bit older than him, with pale skin and black hair pulled back into a ponytail.

'Honestly,' she said, rolling her eyes behind her long fringe. 'Was the instruction "Don't turn round" too cryptic for you?'

'No,' Archie said defiantly. 'I just wanted to see who you were before I did what you said.'

The girl gave Archie a crooked smirk. 'That sort of defeats the object a bit, doesn't it?'

Archie shrugged. 'Who are you anyway?'

'Agent X-ray,' the girl whispered, pulling him behind the science block by the arm. 'You were supposed to meet me earlier.'

'Oh, that was you!' he said, remembering the girl he'd seen at the crossroads that morning. 'I didn't think you looked like a secret agent.'

'What do secret agents look like then?'

'I don't know . . .' Archie thought for a moment. 'I suppose if I knew what they look like, they wouldn't be very secret.'

'Clever boy.' As the girl laughed Archie noticed a single dimple on her left cheek.

'And you're a girl,' Archie added quickly.

'Brilliant.' The girl clapped loudly. 'With those powers of observation you'll do well.'

'Look, I don't know who you are,' Archie said

firmly, 'but I don't think for a moment you're a secret agent. I did come to the crossroads this morning but only because I was curious to see who was winding me up, so instead of waiting in the open I observed the meeting point discreetly.'

'I see.' The girl clicked her fingers. '*That's* what you were doing crouching in the bushes like a toddler playing hide and seek! Here's a little tip for you – even though you can't see anybody when you close your eyes, everyone can still see you.'

'You saw us?'

'Of course I saw you. And I could hear you. I could practically smell the crisps one of you was scoffing.'

'That was Barney,' Archie admitted sheepishly. 'He likes to keep his energy up.'

When the girl leaned past Archie's shoulder to peer round the corner of the science block, a waft of strawberry soap filled his nostrils. He turned to follow her gaze. About a hundred metres away a group of boys was crossing the playground towards them, passing a football among themselves.

'Listen, I haven't got time to chat,' said the girl. 'Those boys are coming our way and I can't be seen with you here. Just listen to this message.'

Archie nodded obediently, observing tiny toffee-coloured flecks in her blue eyes.

'Her Majesty's Secret Service needs your help.' The girl's voice was grave. 'MI6 has a brand new team of undercover kids ready to undertake covert surveillance missions. SPADE – the Secret Potential Agent Data Evaluator – has chosen you to join the team, to become a secret agent. It could be dangerous but you will be helping to protect your country. Think about it. When you have made up your mind, text the word *IN* or *OUT* to this number.'

The girl handed Archie a card with six digits scrawled on it.

'Why me?' he asked.

'To be honest, before I met you I thought the computer had made a mistake,' the girl admitted. 'But now . . . I'm sure of it. Anyway, I'm just following orders.'

'L-look,' Archie stammered. 'I'm really sorry about turning round . . .'

The girl held a finger to her lips. 'Memorise the number then destroy the card,' she instructed.

'Shouldn't it self-destruct in ten seconds?' Archie joked.

The girl didn't smile.

Archie blushed and cursed himself silently.

As the crowd of boys rounded the corner of the science block, Archie stood up straight and tried to look innocent – which only made him feel guiltier.

'Wassup, Nerd?' asked Josh Bellamy, tucking the football under one arm. 'What are you doing skulking round here?'

'He's probably doing something embarrassing,' suggested someone, 'like reading.'

Ignoring the jibe, Archie glanced round to see where the girl had got to, but she was gone – as if she'd disappeared into thin air like a twist of smoke. Maybe she really was Secret Service after all, he thought. Only someone with genuine MI6 training could vanish like that. Then one of the boys moved his head slightly and Archie saw the girl scrambling up a muddy bank about fifteen metres away.

'I know what you're up to,' laughed someone else. 'You were having a sneaky look at your plane-spotter's handbook, weren't you?'

'No,' said Archie defiantly. Momentarily he considered the wisdom of explaining that he was talking to an actual spy, then he grabbed a book from

46

his rucksack and held it up. 'I was just brushing up on my Spanish grammar.'

The boys laughed mockingly and pushed past Archie.

'See you around, Swot,' someone called over his shoulder and the other boys chuckled some more.

Archie stayed where he was and studied the card in his hand.

'So she said you should text the word "in" or "out" to this number?' asked Barney.

'Uh-huh.' Archie nodded.

'What do you think that means?'

'Well, it is quite a riddle,' said Archie earnestly, 'but I think I've cracked it. I have to text "in" if I want to be "in" the team and "out" if I'm "out".'

'Ahh.' Barney nodded sagely. 'The old straight-forward cipher trick. A classic double bluff.'

The boys were changing for their after-school swimming lesson and the excited chatter of twenty budding Olympians was echoing off the changing room's tiled walls. Barney studied the card the girl had given to Archie, running his thumb over the six digits and holding it up to the light.

'What are you looking for exactly?' asked Archie.

'A secret message of some sort – maybe a code. MI6 could be using the card as a cover to pass on some sort of information, like a microfilm.'

'The chances of this being from the actual MI6 are about as slim as a microfilm,' said Archie. 'It's got to be some sort of elaborate hoax. Somebody is waiting for me to send a text offering my services to MI6, then they're going to show it to the whole school and make my life a misery.'

'Who would want to ridicule you like that?'

'Barney, I'm not exactly one of the in-crowd,' stated Archie, snapping on his goggles. 'I love reading and learning, I don't play football, I don't answer teachers back and I have a slightly nerdy obsession with aeroplanes.'

'And you do look pretty geeky,' Barney added helpfully.

'Yes, thank you.' Archie laughed. 'I think most of the kids at this school would love to poke fun at me. An awful lot of them would like to poke a sharp stick at me.'

The changing room fell silent as the rotund figure of Mr Crawley appeared.

48

'This is supposed to be a swimming lesson, not a WI meeting,' he bellowed. 'Ten extra lengths of butterfly for the last boy in that pool!'

'I think there's still a chance you're being recruited by MI6,' Barney whispered as they scampered past their swimming coach.

'Think what you like,' Archie said, curling his toes over the edge of the pool. 'I'm not buying it.'

'He's not buying it,' Agent X-ray reported, slouching back in the leather chair in front of Helen Highwater's desk. 'He's going to need further persuasion.'

'I think you'd better take a look at this.' Highwater handed Agent X-ray a sheet of paper. 'It's a new message from our Evil Mastermind's website. It was posted at lunchtime but it's only just been decoded – Cipher Branch had to prioritise other tasks apparently.'

The girl scanned the text then looked up anxiously at Highwater and Holden Grey.

'There's a time for persuasion and a time for action,' offered Grey, folding his arms resolutely. 'And this is definitely one of those times.'

'Which?' asked Agent X-ray.

'Excuse me?'

'Which one is it a time for?'

'Do keep up, X-ray. It's a time for action.'

'We'll never get to him in time,' said Agent X-ray.

'We won't, but our boys in blue will,' Highwater stated.

'What are you going to do?'

'It's for his own protection,' Highwater said, picking up her phone. 'But I'm going to have Richard Hunt arrested.'

Chapter 7

'So how was swimming?' Richard Hunt asked, keeping his eyes trained on the winding road ahead.

'Fine,' Archie replied vacantly, fiddling with the stereo in his father's black Audi A5. Settling for Radio 1, he turned his head and watched the forest whip past the window.

'And school?' Richard tweaked the volume down a couple of notches. 'Anything exciting happen today?'

Archie wondered if he should mention the girl claiming to be an MI6 agent.

'Not really,' he said.

'What were you doing in maths?'

'Can't remember.'

'What did you get up to at lunchtime?'

'Nothing.'

'Have you given much thought to becoming a spy?' said Richard casually.

Archie jumped. He turned to look at his father, who was concentrating impassively on his driving. Did he know about the girl claiming to be from MI6? Maybe she was genuine after all, and his father had used his old military contacts to get him recruited. Dismissing this thought immediately, Archie desperately hoped his father hadn't sussed the embarrassing fact that he was almost certainly being picked on at school.

'What do you mean?' Archie asked innocently, trying to quell the note of panic in his voice.

'I've been interrogating you about your day for the last ten minutes and you've given absolutely nothing away.' Richard smiled briefly. 'I know plenty of hardened field agents who would have cracked by now.'

Archie beamed with amusement and relief. 'Sorry, Dad,' he said. 'There's just not much to report. I had double maths followed by double English, lunch on my own – without talking to anyone at all whatsoever – and in the afternoon I had French and double physics, then swimming. That's about it.'

52

Glancing at his son, Richard Hunt said, 'No more trouble from that Newman boy this week?'

'Actually . . .' Archie took a deep breath. 'The other day after school we did sort of have a bit of a . . . fight.'

'A fight!'

'I didn't start it. He was waiting for Barney and me after class with a gang of his mates. Two of them mashed Barney and Newman attacked me.'

'Are you OK?' Archie's father asked, concerned.

'Yeah, Dad. I'm fine,' Archie said. 'That's the weird thing. When Newman came at me it was as if some strange force took over my body – like I'd morphed into the Karate Kid or something. I blocked like a dozen punches, then I flattened him with this awesome kick. It was . . . a bit freaky actually.'

'Sounds like you need to be careful with your powers,' Richard said gravely.

'Powers?' Archie exclaimed. 'You make me sound like Clark Kent. All I did was knock over a bully.'

'Listen, Archie, the likelihood is that you have a natural flair for combat sports,' Archie's father said, toggling the gearstick into sixth.

'What are you saying?' Archie sniggered. 'That I was born to be some sort of ninja warrior?' He started karate-chopping an imaginary opponent. 'HiiiyAAH!'

'Sort of,' Richard replied with a mysterious shrug.

Archie looked at his father, whose eyes remained fixed on the winding road ahead. 'What makes you say that?'

Richard hunched his shoulders. 'I have my reasons. If this Newman kid comes after you again – and you really can't avoid it – don't think too hard. Just let your instincts guide you.'

Archie nodded solemnly then, stifling a chuckle, he said, 'OK, I will try to feel the force, Obi-Wan Kenobi.'

The car crested the brow of a hill and emerged from the shade of the forest into the dazzling glow of the late afternoon sun.

'Have you been flying today?' Archie asked at last, keen to move on from their weird conversation.

'I went up for about an hour – just some aeros for that scientific survey. They called this morning and asked if we could start the study a week early.' Richard held out his arm to show Archie the black rubber strap round his wrist. He had volunteered to take part in a two-week clinical study of the physiological effects of high G flying manoeuvres run by the RAF University, Cranfield. As well as the wristbands, which recorded his oxygen levels and blood pressure, he had a heart monitor strapped round his chest and his vital statistics were continuously being recorded and transmitted to his secure profile on the university website. 'I pulled four G at the bottom of the loop and negative three rolling off the top,' he reported, sliding on a pair of aviator sunglasses.

'And your old ticker held out OK?' Archie asked with mock surprise.

'So far so good,' Richard laughed, patting his chest.

'Are we still going flying on Saturday?' Archie asked.

'Actually, I wanted to talk to you about that.' Richard blew some air through his lips and paused. 'I don't think it's going to work out this weekend. It's better if we lay off the flying for while.'

Archie felt as if he'd been punched in the stomach. 'Is this because I messed up the spin recovery?' he asked weakly. 'I can crack it, I know I can. Just give me one more chance to show you I've learned from what happened the other day.'

'Listen, all I'm saying—'

'You think I'm not good enough, is that it?'

'If anyone ever found out about you flying the Dragonfly I could lose my licence – for good.'

'I know I let you down the other day but—'

'Look, I'm just saying we can't do it this weekend.'

'But you promised to teach me how to do a Cuban Eight.'

'Archie, you're not listening to me.'

'Mum always said a promise is a promise.'

Richard's jaw muscles flexed and he inhaled through his nose. 'Your mother would never have let me start teaching you in the first place, young man,' he said coldly.

Archie knew from his father's tone that their discussion was over. Since his mother had died three years ago he felt as if his craving for his father's approval was stronger than ever, and that his father had steadily grown more distant.

Archie blipped his window down a few inches and closed his eyes, allowing the cool air to buffet his face. Sulking, he sighed as loudly as he could – twice – thinking about the verbal exchange he'd just had with his father. His father hadn't actually agreed that Archie had let him down. But what stuck in Archie's

56

mind and twisted his gut was that he hadn't denied it either.

Then a wailing siren ripped through the tranquil evening. Richard Hunt glanced into his rear-view mirror while Archie turned in his seat to see through the rear windscreen. Flashing its headlights and approaching at high speed was a navy BMW with blacked-out windows and a blue light rippling along its dashboard.

'You've been busted, Dad,' said Archie, feeling a strange sense of triumph. 'How fast were you going?'

Richard checked his speedometer then all three mirrors. 'No more than fifty.'

Another blast of the siren made Archie turn anxiously in his seat. 'Er, I'm pretty sure they want you to pull over,' he observed, spying the BMW through the narrow gap between his seat and its headrest. The vehicle was now startlingly close, its front grille and bonnet out of view below the Audi's rear screen.

'Seriously, Dad,' said Archie, a note of concern registering in his voice. 'They really want us to stop.'

'I know, kiddo.' Archie's father dropped the clutch and toggled the gearstick into third. Then, with a final glance in his rear-view mirror, he floored the accelerator and the turbocharged Audi sped away from the BMW like a rocket.

'Dad! What are you doing?' demanded Archie as the force of the acceleration thrust him against his seat.

'Trust me,' said Richard, paddling his feet on the clutch and accelerator pedals as he negotiated a dipping right-hand bend at ninety miles per hour. 'I'll explain later.'

The BMW responded promptly and powerfully to Hunt's attempted escape. Within a few seconds it was right on the Audi's tail again, its siren screaming and lights pulsing.

Coordinating power with swift, aggressive turns of the steering wheel, Archie's father expertly negotiated a series of tight curves, sliding the Audi sideways through the bends like a professional rally driver. But when the road opened out into a long stretch, the BMW's superior straight-line speed was enough to close the gap between the cars.

'It's not slowing down!' Archie screamed.

Then, with an almighty metallic crunch, the BMW rammed the Audi's rear end.

'What are they playing at?' shouted Archie as his head jerked back against his seat.

'I don't know,' his father said grimly, fighting to stop the Audi's tail spinning out of control. 'But I'm not planning on hanging around to find out.'

The cars raced along, nose to tail, for a few terrifying seconds but eventually the Audi's superior manoeuvrability paid off and the BMW dropped out of sight in Richard Hunt's mirrors.

'Do you think we lost them?' asked Archie anxiously.

'I wouldn't bet on it,' his father replied, accelerating out of a corner and speeding down a straight cliff-top stretch.

Peering over the back of his seat, Archie spotted a pair of headlights pop over the brow of a distant hump. The BMW scorched over the tarmac like a missile and within a few seconds it had almost caught them up and, as before, showed no sign of slowing down.

'It's going to ram us again,' warned Archie, bracing himself in his seat.

But instead of barging the Audi from behind, the BMW swerved into the opposite lane and pulled up alongside it.

Suddenly the BMW cut across the Audi's path, nudging its nose sideways with the crunch of bending

59

sheet metal. Richard dabbed the brake pedal and waggled the steering wheel to keep the car straight. The BMW pulled over again and eased back on its speed, dropping back until it was level with the Audi.

'Why don't we just stop and explain that we weren't speeding?' pleaded Archie.

Richard shook his head. 'Trust me, that's exactly what they want us to do. Double-check your seat belt and sit back.'

The two cars raced over the tarmac at terrific speed, only inches apart. Within a few seconds the BMW had pulled ahead again and swerved suddenly to its left. This time it clipped the Audi's nose with a hefty thump and the cars ground together with a piercing screech, sending a plume of sparks spewing into the air. Richard tried to hold the Audi straight against the impact but its back end began to swing out. He spun the wheel frantically to correct it and the tail snapped into line – but only for an instant. As the Audi's rear swung out the other way, Archie's father spun the wheel back but there was nothing he could do to stop the vehicle spinning out of control.

From the moment the car began gliding sideways Archie felt as if everything was happening in slow motion. After a couple of seconds the Audi rotated into an elegant pirouette and the outside world started spinning round him as if he was on a merry-go-round.

Even when the car flipped on to its roof and the contents of the glovebox and the door pockets rattled around the cabin, Archie was overcome with an eerie sense of calm.

The Audi tumbled and twisted, bouncing from its roof to its side again and again. Archie was aware of metal bending and glass shattering and knew he was thrashing about in his seat but he felt no emotion in response to the carnage around him – it was as if he was watching the events play out on TV. He didn't notice his father's flailing hand punch the button on his seat-belt buckle, clicking it open.

By the time his airbag inflated Archie was unconscious so he was oblivious when the impact of another bounce twisted the car's chassis to such an extent that his passenger door popped open.

On the Audi's sixth violent, destructive revolution Archie's limp body was thrown clear of the vehicle, sailing five metres into the air before landing in a thick clump of cliff-top gorse.

On its seventh roll the car bounced over the edge of

the precipice, taking Archie's father with it. Its engine was still revving as it arced over the narrow beach far below and plummeted nose first into the sea beyond, spraying a sheet of water high into the air. In a matter of seconds the Audi filled with water, its nose bobbed downward and it sank without trace.

Chapter 8

Archie lay still with his eyes closed, wondering if he was alive or dead. His whole body was throbbing like one big bruise, his head was pounding and his left shoulder felt like someone was drilling a hole in it. I must be alive, he thought. Being dead can't possibly be this painful.

Slowly he opened his eyes, blinking hard a few times to encourage them to focus, and looked up at the sky – which, weirdly, was covered in polystyrene tiles. As he tried to turn his head a sharp spike of agony shot up his neck and jabbed at the base of his skull. Relaxing his neck muscles he slowly assessed his surroundings.

He was in a square room with white walls and a blue linoleum floor. There was a portable TV in one corner, a small chest of drawers and a tired-looking easy chair, angled to face the bed. He had a clip on the end of one finger, which was wired to an LCD monitor and a second screen was wired up to his chest.

The door opened and Archie's grandmother bustled in carrying a mug of tea and a copy of the *Daily Mail*. She looked weak and tired. Her skin was pale, almost grey, and the flesh beneath her eyes was puffy.

'Hello, Nan,' Archie tried to say, but no sound came out. He worked some saliva round his mouth, swallowed and tried again. This time his voice was a croaky whisper.

'Well, look who's finally decided to wake up.' Megan Hunt smiled brightly, setting down her mug and sliding her hand into his. 'How are you feeling, lazybones?'

'Achy bones would be more like it,' croaked Archie.

'You've had a nasty accident, love. You're in hospital.'

'That's a relief.' Archie winced with pain. 'I was thinking if this was my bedroom the new decorator must be rubbish.'

Archie's grandmother smiled, the wrinkles round her eyes forming deep creases. 'Do you remember what happened to you?' she said softly.

64

Archie gave a small nod. 'This police car wanted us to pull over,' he said, frowning.

His grandmother nodded. 'Christchurch Police Station had sent out a couple of officers to talk to your father but nobody seems to know what it was all about.'

'But Dad refused to stop,' Archie said, puzzled. 'They chased us for ages then they ran us off the road. I remember the car was rolling but after that it's all a blank. I told Dad to stop but . . .'

'He must have had good reason to keep going. He would never have acted recklessly, especially with you in the car. He loved you more than anything.'

Archie felt suddenly sick as his grandmother's hand tightened its grip on his.

'You mean *loves*,' he said urgently. 'You said he loved me but you meant *loves*, didn't you?'

As Archie watched his grandmother's eyes fill with tears he felt as if he was sinking.

'I'm sorry, Archie love,' she murmured. 'I'm so sorry.'

An hour later Archie was still staring up at the polystyrene ceiling tiles and trying to come to terms with the hideous news. It had been barely three years since his mother had been knocked down and killed in a hit-and-run accident, and life without her was something he was still dealing with. Some days were better than others but at some point every day he missed her so much that he felt like he might crumble on the spot. In those moments the thing that had kept him going was his father.

Part of Archie had felt that he had to keep going to secure his father's respect, while another part of him suspected his father needed someone to lean on just as much as he did.

Since his mother's death, Archie's father had become withdrawn and more serious, as if the responsibility of raising a child on his own meant that hugs and silliness were luxuries he rarely had time for.

Archie suddenly remembered the final cross words he had exchanged with his father, and the notion that his father had died feeling disappointed in him crashed down on him. He rolled agonisingly on to his side and eased his hands under his pillow. On the bedside table was his laptop and a pile of books and games that his grandmother had brought in for him.

His gran had told him that when he'd been thrown from his father's car some dense bushes had broken his fall. But the Audi had rolled over a cliff and landed in the sea. Police divers had inspected the car but his father's body had not been found so officials were working on the theory that it had been taken out to sea by strong tides.

As Archie stared blankly ahead he found himself looking at the monitor displaying the output from his heart, which was pulsing at a steady fifty-eight beats per minute. His father couldn't possibly be dead, he thought defiantly. If he could survive all those combat missions and assignments behind enemy lines there was no way a simple car crash would kill him. And what's more, his body still hadn't been found.

He couldn't believe his father was dead. He wouldn't believe it.

Then, as he stared at the trace of his own heartbeat, he had an idea and his pulse rate leaped immediately up to a hundred.

Ignoring the grinding pain in his joints, Archie pushed himself up into a sitting position and reached across to his bedside table. Sliding his computer from under the books he set it on his lap and opened it. The screen blinked into life and Archie's fingers danced over the keyboard.

Within a minute he was staring at the RAF University Cranfield home page. A few clicks later he was on a page entitled 'Physiological Studies in Aviation'. He was prompted for his email address and the keys purred as he typed in his father's address – then his fingers froze as he stared at the message on the screen:

Enter Password

He should have realised that all the data gathered for the study would be protected. 'How about this?' he mumbled, typing the word *Dragonfly* and clicking the submit button.

A boxed message popped up on the screen in red lettering:

Sorry, the details you have entered
have not been recognised.

Archie bit his lip. Then he typed his own name into the password field but the same message appeared – and again when he entered *Lara*, his mother's name. A host of famous people he knew his father admired such as sportsmen, explorers and aviation pioneers received the same blunt refusal.

Changing tack, Archie typed in a selection of significant dates such as his father's birthday, his birthday, his parents' wedding anniversary, the date of the first moon landing, the numbers of all the squadrons his father had ever belonged to. When that failed he combined dates and names in countless combinations, with capitals, without capitals, with the numbers first and last. In desperation he tried flying terminology. *Ailerons, loop, horizon*. All rejected.

Archie sat back against his crisp white pillows and let out a long breath. He could feel a coating of sweat on his skin as he stared at the blinking cursor, utterly bewildered and defeated. Just as he was about to close the laptop he noticed some small font at the bottom of the screen.

Click here for password hint.

Feeling a rush of hope he clicked on the prompt and held his breath as he read his father's clue.

I keep it up my sleeve.

Archie immediately knew what the hint referred to.

His father had often told him how he'd fallen head over heels for his mother when they'd met at university. Walking home late one night with some of his friends, Richard Hunt had passed a twenty-four-hour tattoo parlour, which seemed at the time to offer the perfect opportunity to prove to Lara how serious he was about her. When she saw the tattoo the next day, Archie's mother had joked that it was a touching gesture but that she'd prefer a bunch of flowers next time.

Archie's father had spent the next twenty-five years feeling slightly embarrassed by the permanent reminder of his youthful impulsiveness – the word *Lara* inscribed for evermore within an image of a heart on his upper arm.

Archie smiled to himself as he typed the word *heart* and tapped the enter key.

This time there was no rejection message and four charts flashed on to the screen. Eagerly, he scanned the information in front of him. The top three charts' vertical axes were labelled Blood Pressure, Oxygen Saturation and Pulse Rate, while they all had a common horizontal scale labelled Time. The fourth chart, which could be overlaid on to any of the others with the click of the mouse, was a plot of G-force versus time, which Archie guessed was fed by the flight data recorder on his father's Dragonfly.

As he scrolled across the graphs he could see that his father's pulse had been elevated for a period of about an hour the previous morning, which corresponded to some spikes on the G-force chart ranging from plus four to negative three. His heartbeat had returned to a normal rate in the mid-50s shortly after that flight and had remained in that region until 4.49 in the afternoon – when he'd been driving Archie home from his swimming lesson.

Archie realised that the sudden jump in his father's pulse must correspond to the time the BMW had begun harassing them. Using his forefinger on the trackpad, he dragged the chart across the screen so that the data recorded after 5 p.m. was displayed.

His father's pulse had remained steadily high for a period of nearly six minutes, after which it had dropped sharply to a rate of only twenty beats per minute – the time the car went into the sea, Archie reckoned. He could hardly bear to scroll further across the screen, almost unable to bring himself to look at this cold scientific representation of the moment his father's life had been snuffed out.

As he slid the time scale to the left Archie felt his own heart thumping inside his bruised ribcage. His father's pulse had continued to drop, reaching a low of thirteen beats per minute and remaining there for sixty seconds. Glancing up the screen, Archie saw that his blood oxygen levels were also frighteningly low at this moment.

But then, incredibly, his father's pulse had begun to recover. Within five minutes it was back at fifty beats per minute and his blood oxygen levels were up to eighty-five per cent and still climbing. A quick scan across the chart showed Archie that his father's vital signs had remained strong well past midnight, when the signal had been lost.

This could mean only one thing, Archie thought, realising his hands were trembling. His father was still alive!

Chapter 9

Detective Constable Flowers wore a permanent frown of concern as he listened to Archie's theory, nodding occasionally and leaning forward to study the graphs on the boy's laptop computer. Archie's grandmother had ushered the police officer into his room shortly after he had made his discovery and insisted on talking to the authorities.

When Archie had finished his explanation DC Flowers gave him a smile that was probably meant to appear kind but simply came across as patronising.

'Firstly can I say how sorry I am for your loss,' he said in an emotionless monotone.

'Have you been listening to anything I just said?'

Archie demanded. 'I haven't suffered any loss. My father is still alive.'

'It's perfectly normal for someone in your position to feel this way, Archie,' Flowers continued flatly. 'The normal response to such traumatic news is shock followed by anger followed by a rejection of the facts, which is the emotion you are currently experiencing, at this moment in time. Soon you will come to accept the situation and finally your healing process can begin.'

'Look at the website,' Archie snapped. 'My father's heart was still beating after midnight.'

'Please try and calm down, Archie. I understand you're angry – you have been through an awful lot in the last twenty-four hours.'

'Of course I'm angry,' Archie retorted. 'You're treating me like I'm crazy.'

'You're not *crazy*, Archie.' DC Flowers smiled condescendingly. 'You're just a little confused.' Then, to show he was taking Archie's concerns seriously, he squinted studiously at the website. 'I can't help noticing that your father presently has no vital signs which, in my professional experience, would indicate that he has sadly deceased.' Flowers made a glum face but Archie could tell it was no more than an afterthought.

'That's because the website isn't picking up a signal any more,' Archie explained, exasperation raising his voice an octave. 'He's probably just taken off his chest and wrist straps.'

'That is one explanation,' Flowers said dubiously. 'However, owing to the lack of vital signs, the official line of enquiry will continue to focus on an altogether more plausible set of circumstances – i.e. the nature of your father's death.'

'Just because there's no heart-rate signal doesn't mean there's no heart rate,' Archie argued desperately. 'I mean, there's no readout for your pulse on the website either but that doesn't mean you're dead, does it?' he asked, adding under his breath, 'Except from the neck up.'

The police officer digested the idea with a confused frown.

'Of course I'm not dead,' Flowers said at last. 'I am clearly alive and well and sitting right in front of you. Your father, however, is none of the above and I think it would be better for all concerned if you started to accept his loss.' Flowers jerked his head and glanced sideways as he spoke, motioning towards Archie's grandmother, who was standing by the doorway.

As he studied his gran's face, scored with anxiety, it occurred to Archie that she was in as much pain as he was. She was facing the prospect of losing her son and he was suddenly overwhelmed with sympathy for her. Realising that his attention was on her, she forced a bright smile on to her lips.

'You believe me, Nan, don't you?' Archie implored.

His grandmother approached and brushed his hair from his forehead with her hand. 'I think we have to trust the police to carry out their investigations,' she said kindly.

'But what about the evidence?' Archie asked shrilly, jabbing the computer screen with his finger.

'I'm sure this nice police officer will include your theory in his report,' she said, glaring at DC Flowers, who nodded his concurrence. She continued, 'I shall be requesting a copy of the report to make sure he is true to his word. Meanwhile, if he has any more questions he can speak to you at home.'

'Home?' Archie repeated hopefully.

His grandmother nodded. 'I've just been speaking to your doctor. He said you've had a miraculous escape but you've no broken bones or internal injuries – just some nasty bruises. So he's discharging you – *provided* you promise to take it easy for a week or so.'

Archie nodded obediently. 'OK, Nan.'

Realising he had been dismissed, DC Flowers closed his notebook and stood up, put his hat on and pulled its peak low over his eyes. When he reached the doorway he stopped and turned round. 'I wish you a speedy recovery, Archie,' he said. 'And rest assured we will find the culprits responsible for this terrible accident.'

'That shouldn't be too hard,' Archie sneered. 'Even for you.'

'Excuse me?' queried Flowers. 'Would you care to elaborate as to the meaning of your implied suggestion?'

Archie had gingerly swung his legs over the edge of the bed and was wiggling his toes on the cold floor. 'Well, it was one of your cars that rammed us so I suppose all you have to do is check the police log to see who was driving,' he said, true anger setting in.

Flowers looked momentarily stunned, then his expression softened.

'I'm sure I'm not speaking out of turn when I tell you that you have been misinformed,' he recited. 'The car responsible was not a constabulary vehicle.'

Archie's grandmother stopped folding clothes and turned to look at the policeman. 'But I was told a police car had been sent to question Archie's dad.'

'That's right,' said Flowers. 'A patrol car was sent to apprehend Mr Richard Hunt on the afternoon in question. It arrived at his home address at four thirty-two p.m., but the officers received no response when they knocked at the door. Concluding no one was at home, they returned to Christchurch police station at five p.m. and filed their report to that effect.'

Archie looked open-mouthed at his grandmother for a moment before turning to DC Flowers. 'So the car that ran us off the road wasn't a police car?'

The police officer shook his head. 'No.'

'But it had flashing lights and a siren,' Archie protested.

'We believe the occupants were posing as members of Her Majesty's constabulary in the hope of tricking your father into pulling over. After reviewing footage from traffic cameras along the route of the chase, we have ascertained the vehicle in question had a foreign number plate. We are working on the theory that this fact alerted your father to their subterfuge and a high-speed chase then ensued thereafter.'

'Why?' Archie asked, clutching a fistful of his tangled hair. '*Why* did they want us to stop?'

'We believe their motive was the unlawful apprehension and detention of a person or persons against his or her will.'

'You mean . . .' Archie gasped, then his voice failed him.

Flowers nodded grimly. 'That's right, Archie,' he said. 'They were planning to kidnap your father.'

Chapter 10

'Kidnap?' exclaimed Barney before sinking his teeth into a Twix. 'Why would they want to kidnap him?'

Archie sat back in his desk chair, swinging the seat from side to side and gazing out of his bedroom window. 'All sorts of reasons,' he sighed. 'My dad's pretty wealthy so they might have been planning to demand a ransom, or it might have been a political protest by someone who has a problem with the Red Cross Dragonflies. There's even a chance terrorists targeted him because of his military record – who knows.'

Barney, who was sitting cross-legged on Archie's bed, stared at his lap and shook his head. 'Unreal,' he muttered, still chewing. 'Un-real.'

Archie picked up a model of a Tornado F3 from his desk and examined it. 'I'm more interested in finding him alive than working out who's responsible,' he said. 'Unless I can figure out how he survived, no one will believe that it's possible.'

'He probably found an air pocket inside the car,' Barney suggested. 'Or maybe in the Air Force he'd been trained to put his body into a state of hibernation or something while he was underwater? Suspended animation – that's what they call it. I saw this old spy film once called *Our Man Flint* . . .'

'It's pointless though, isn't it?' Archie sighed bitterly. 'The police have decided he's dead and there's nothing I can do to change their minds. Maybe they're right anyway.'

A heavy silence filled the room.

Archie spun his chair round to face his desk and began jabbing his keyboard with sullen disinterest. As a mark of respect Barney tried to chew his last bite of Twix without making any noise but then he spoilt everything by crinkling the wrapper noisily when he pushed it into his pocket.

For a long while Archie punished his keyboard and Barney studied the room and neither said a word, then –

'Hey,' Archie exclaimed, pushing himself upright on the arms of his chair. 'Come and look at this!'

Barney planted his feet on the floor and heaved himself up, sending a shower of biscuit crumbs on to the carpet.

'Wassup?' he asked, looking over Archie's shoulder at his Facebook page.

Archie flicked the computer screen and pushed his chair back to allow Barney to read the new message for himself.

From – Agent X-ray
We have information about your father's situation. We can help you if you help us.
16 Stour Gardens, 13.00 hrs.
Come alone.

'Do you think it's for real?' Barney asked, having read the message for a third time.

Archie held his hands out wide. 'Who knows?'

'I mean, it seems a bit too straightforward, doesn't it?' Barney mused. 'I'd have thought the real MI6 would have disguised their message to avoid suspicion.'

82

'What, like "The eagle will nest with the mongoose before hunting a badger"?' Archie suggested, trying not to smile as Barney nodded earnestly in response. 'Maybe it's one of those double bluffs you mentioned the other day?'

Barney's eyes narrowed. 'You might be right.'

Archie jumped up from his chair. 'Well, there's only one way to find out – come on, we've only got an hour.'

'Where are we going?' Barney asked.

'Try and keep up,' Archie called from halfway down the stairs. 'Sixteen Stour Gardens.'

It was a warm, muggy day and Archie could feel the perspiration gathering on his forehead as he pedalled his bike up the long, steady incline towards Kings Park, the housing estate where Stour Gardens could be found. Barney was trailing about 200 yards back, puffing and protesting with equal vigour.

Approaching number sixteen, Archie dismounted at speed and hit the ground running, allowing his bike to topple into a hedgerow. His finger hovered over the doorbell for a second. He was probably about to initiate an embarrassing ordeal that would haunt him

83

for the rest of his schooldays. But if there was even a sliver of hope that this was for real – that Agent X-ray might help him find his father – then it was a chance he had to take.

He rang the bell and waited.

Chapter 11

Archie heard footsteps approaching from the other side of the door and took a couple of steps back, as if those extra few inches might offer him some sort of protection from the imminent verbal onslaught. He could see a figure through the pebbled glass panel in the door and he caught his breath as the latch clicked and the door swung open.

Standing in the doorway and wearing an expression of disdain was the girl Archie had met in the school playground. She was wearing a black T-shirt with the words Green Day across the chest, skinny black jeans and Converse boots.

'Hiya,' said Archie.

'You're late.'

Archie glanced at his watch. 'Only by a couple of minutes,' he commented breezily.

The girl fixed him with a cold stare. 'In undercover operations a couple of seconds can be the difference between life and death,' she said darkly.

Archie swallowed and nodded. 'Sorry.'

The girl lifted herself on to her tiptoes and craned her neck to scan the street over Archie's head. 'Well, at least you came alone,' she said drily. 'That shows you have a very basic ability to follow simple instructions. Our success depends on your aptitude to keep things to yourself. Discretion is our watchword. Do you think anyone could have followed you here?'

'Absolutely not,' Archie replied.

Suddenly there was an almighty screech of brakes and Barney skidded to a halt on the pavement outside the house.

'There you are!' he exclaimed wheezily. 'You could've waited for me – it's not easy cycling up hills with my heavy bones.' Then, noticing the girl in the doorway, he added, 'And you must be the mysterious Agent X-ray? Archie's told me everything about you.'

The girl arched an eyebrow accusingly at Archie.

He adjusted his glasses and gave her a sheepish smile. 'Oh, I wouldn't say I've told him *everything*.'

Agent X-ray ushered the boys into the house and closed the front door.

'Listen, motormouth,' she said to Barney. 'The basic idea of undercover ops is that we don't announce ourselves to the whole neighbourhood, OK?'

'Understood,' Barney answered with a salute. 'Good idea to switch to codenames, by the way. I was just wondering if there's any chance I could be something like Nightfox instead of Motormouth?'

With an exasperated sigh the girl turned and marched down the narrow hallway. 'You'd better follow me,' she said over her shoulder. 'We'll let the boss decide what to do with you.'

As the boys tagged along, Barney tapped Archie's arm with the back of his hand to get his attention. 'Don't worry,' he whispered. 'I'm sure you'll get a codename soon.'

Archie cast his eyes around the house, which was a small semi-detached decorated with floral prints and frilly curtains.

'So are we supposed to believe this is MI6 headquarters?' he said cynically. 'I mean, it's very *convenient* that it's only a couple of miles from my house, don't you think?'

The girl turned round. Dropping one hip and folding her arms she huffed irritably. 'No, this isn't MI6 HQ. Obviously. It's a safe house, OK? They use it to hide witnesses and foreign operatives from enemy assassins and stuff. And no, it's not a *coincidence* that it's close to your house. We have safe houses all over the country – there's probably one within a few miles of everyone's house. Now, does anyone else have any *clever* questions?'

'Yeah, I've got loads,' announced Barney keenly.

'Somehow that doesn't surprise me,' the girl replied, catching Archie's eye.

Thinking he detected the faintest of smiles on her lips, Archie suddenly started laughing much too loudly. 'That's really funny,' he wheezed.

The girl frowned.

'Dude, what's the matter with you?' asked Barney.

'Nothing,' Archie replied, wondering why his stomach was fluttering.

The boys followed the girl to the bottom of a flight of stairs where a wooden door blocked their path. As he watched her type a series of digits into a keypad, it occurred to Archie that this was an awful lot of trouble to go to just to make fun of him. Nevertheless, as the girl swung the door open he was prepared for a chorus of jeers from whoever was in the room beyond.

Chapter 12

To Archie's relief and surprise there was no explosion of ridicule to greet their arrival, just the faint whirr of computer cooling fans. As the girl closed the door, Archie noticed that it was constructed from steel and six inches thick, the wooden veneer on the outside preserving a facade of suburban normality.

For the first time Archie considered seriously the prospect that Agent X-ray might actually be who she claimed to be. With a sense of nervous excitement he stepped into the room and looked round the vast underground chamber.

The walls and ceiling were made of smooth concrete and the floor was clad in black marble. Low lighting was provided by a combination of spotlights and steel anglepoise lamps. A bank of computer terminals lined one wall, each one scrolling through endless websites apparently at random. On another wall hung eight flat-screen TVs, all muted and tuned to a different twenty-four-hour news channel.

At one end of the room was a large desk constructed of chrome and glass, on which stood two flat-screen computer monitors and a slender wireless keyboard. Behind the desk sat a woman Archie guessed to be about forty to forty-five – pretty old anyway. She had short dark hair and wore a black suit over a grey blouse. Her thin lips were tinted by plum-coloured lipstick and a gold chain draped from her horn-rimmed spectacles.

Standing behind the woman, with his back to the room, was a gangly man in a tweed suit who was wearing headphones over his untidy white hair. He was totally engrossed in a programme showing on yet another TV. Archie could see the man was watching re-runs of *MTV Cribs*, a programme that gave the viewer a look inside the extravagant homes of celebrities. Archie recognised the Brazilian footballer Caesar Romario gesturing to his huge mountainside swimming pool that overlooked a glistening ocean below.

The presence of adults dispelled Archie's doubts

once and for all and he felt a surge of adrenalin. 'This isn't a wind-up,' he whispered. 'They *must* be MI6.'

'Copy that,' Barney squeaked. 'Looks like some sort of splinter cell to me.'

When the girl approached the glass desk the woman looked up from her work.

'Ah, Agent X-ray,' said the woman. 'And who do we have here?'

'This is Archie Hunt,' said the girl. 'And his . . . friend.'

'The name's Jones,' Barney drawled. 'Barney Jones.'

The woman looked them up and down and cleared her throat like a judge about to pass sentence. 'Sit down, both of you.' Her unnatural smile came as an afterthought.

Archie and Barney lowered themselves into the two chairs in front of the desk. The girl stood to their side.

'My name is Helen Highwater,' the woman announced sternly. 'I am the Initiative Commander of an MI6 project to recruit, train and run kids as undercover surveillance agents in matters of national security.'

Archie thought he heard a faint yelp of pleasure escape from Barney's lips.

'You have already met our Computer Technician and Data Analyst, Agent X-ray.' Highwater gestured to the girl; her expression remained unchanged but she lifted her chin almost imperceptibly. 'Next, allow me to introduce you to our very own Tech Branch Specialist. He had been retired for some considerable time but fortunately for us he's agreed to pick up his, er, scientist's tools to join our brand new operation.' Spinning her chair and gesturing at the man behind her with a flourish, she announced, 'This is Tech Branch Specialist Holden Grey.'

Everybody waited in silence for the man to react but he didn't flinch. Instead he remained transfixed by the TV, mumbling something over and over to himself. Each time he gave the words new emphasis and stretched the vowels in different directions as if trying to master the pronunciation of a foreign phrase.

'The *pool* is well fierce, isn't it? Tha pool is *well* fierce, innit? Da poo-al eez well fee-arce, innit?'

Huffing loudly, Highwater picked up a remote control from her desk and, aiming it at the offending screen, killed the picture. Removing his headphones the man spun round, his pale blue eyes wild with glee.

'I'm terribly sorry, I didn't realise we had company,' he said. His voice was crisp and enthusiastic but modulated by the warble of advancing years. Turning to the boys he added, 'Yo, dudes,' and shot them with his index fingers.

'This is Archie Hunt and Barney Jones,' Highwater announced.

'And I'm Holden Grey.' The man approached the desk with a limp. 'Welcome to our cot.'

Archie and Barney looked sideways at each other.

Agent X-ray sighed wearily. 'Er – you mean welcome to your crib,' she corrected. 'Besides, I think the whole MTV vibe is a bit over their heads.' She jabbed a thumb at Archie and Barney. 'You might have more luck with some CBeebies jargon.'

'What is up?' Grey asked, pronouncing each syllable clearly. 'I mean, wassup, brothers, I mean bros?'

Archie shrugged. 'Er, not much. Sir.'

Barney shook his head eagerly.

'OK, introductions over, let's get down to business,' Highwater said brusquely. 'For years we have used a computer program called SPADE – the Secret Potential Agent Data Evaluator – to identify individual children

94

with the necessary attributes to make excellent field agents at a later date, i.e. when they are adults. SPADE quantifies the school record, medical history, genetic pedigree and sporting achievements of every child in the country and assigns them a score from one to one hundred according to their potential suitability for field ops. Your score was very impressive, young man.'

'You're too kind,' Barney grinned.

'Not you, sport,' Highwater snorted. 'Him.'

'Me?' Archie asked incredulously.

'Please can you check mine too?' Barney beamed.

Peering through the spectacles perched on her nose, Helen Highwater typed Barney's name into the SPADE database and waited for his score to be displayed. Grimacing, she sucked sharply on her teeth then smiled apologetically. 'Well, I'm sure you have plenty of potential, Mr Jones,' she said, 'but field ops is not where your strengths lie. Perhaps we'll give you a call if we're ever looking to start our own circus?'

Through the corner of his eye Archie saw Barney's whole body sag as if he was physically deflating.

'Well, Mr Hunt?' Highwater demanded. 'Do you have anything to say?'

Archie thought carefully about his options then said, 'Is this some kind of joke?'

'Oh, Mr Hunt,' Highwater said wryly. 'I've learned the hard way that National Security is no joking matter.'

As she spoke Helen Highwater was thinking back to the recent MI6 policy meeting when the Director General had asked Team Leaders for suggestions on how to improve operational surveillance techniques. As an Assistant Team Leader the question hadn't even been addressed to her, but for some unfathomable reason she had chosen to fill the awkward silence that followed the DG's request with a joke.

'Well, given that ninety per cent of surveillance entails hanging around and scrutinising people, then we ought to get kids to do it,' she had quipped. 'I mean, nobody gives a second thought to a group of teenagers loitering on the street and eyeing up every passer-by, do they? That's all kids seem to do these days.'

There had been a couple of stifled titters. Highwater's direct boss, Hugh Figo, whom she secretly called Huge Ego, had scowled at her disapprovingly. The DG had looked pensive and for a moment Highwater had been concerned that she had insulted the most powerful man in MI6 until he'd boomed his one-word response. 'Brilliant!'

'Excuse me?' Figo had blustered.

'It's about time we started to think outside the box, man,' the DG had enthused. 'Who's going to suspect a kid of being an MI6 agent? Nobody.' The DG had a habit of answering his own questions. 'Kids can nose around and explore wherever they like. And what if they do get caught? It'll just be put down to youthful exuberance. It's a superb idea!'

The DG had got so carried away that he had appointed Highwater Initiative Commander and promised her promotion to Head of Surveillance, two grades senior to Figo, if her idea proved a success. That was the point at which she should have politely declined the DG's invitation, but she had been enjoying the look of utter horror on her boss's face so much that she'd accepted the role just to spite him.

'What about my dad?' Archie asked, bringing Highwater back to the present. 'Your message said you've got information about him.'

'Come this way,' said Highwater.

Followed by Holden Grey, Helen Highwater led the boys to the bank of computer terminals where Agent

X-ray had taken a seat at a smooth white desk with a white keyboard and mouse on it.

Highwater turned to face Archie and Barney, gave them a cursory smile that was so brief she might have just been stretching her cheek muscles, and began. 'With the dawn of the Internet almost anyone in the world can publish whatever they wish.'

'That's right.' Holden Grey gestured to screens with his almost telescopic arms, and said, 'Any of these social networking sites – you know, Twitbook or Facetweet or whatever – gives a platform for anyone to communicate with millions of people all over the world. MI6 Cipher Branch annually spends tens of thousands of man hours every year filtering the world wildlife web for any potentially sinister communications. Our sophisticated mainframe computers scan thousands of web pages every minute, looking for any one of hundreds of tagged words as well as highlighting unusual patterns or repetitions of words or letters.'

Highwater allowed the boys a moment to watch the filtration process on the screens before continuing. 'If the computer senses some kind of suspicious activity it will be flagged and a Cipher Branch agent – a

98

codebreaker – will be assigned the task of analysing the site for any hidden messages.'

While Archie listened in awed silence, Barney was nodding knowingly, as if to confirm the accuracy of Highwater's information.

She continued, 'Following certain leads, we have reason to believe that a particular individual is plotting to undermine the very fabric of our society.'

'For actual,' Grey chimed in. 'His activities threaten to . . . threaten . . . the national security of our nation.'

'A little over a week ago the Cipher Branch computer program flagged the following message on someone's Facebook page.' Highwater nodded to Agent X-ray who tapped a few keys, displaying the same short paragraph on every monitor.

> 4pm – I respect any Scandinavian who chooses to champion a cause that will sadly but inevitably go nowhere. I am missing many old friends from chapters of my own past. But nobody's home will be safe, at my triumphant eternal midnight.

'I'm sure you will agree,' Highwater asserted, 'this is somewhat bizarre but not necessarily sinister?'

Archie shrugged. 'I guess.'

'However, if we isolate every fourth word, we get a more chilling message altogether . . .'

Agent X-ray tapped some more keys and a single line of text appeared on the screens.

Scandinavian champion will go missing
from own home at midnight.

Highwater fixed the boys with a sombre stare. 'I can confirm that at approximately midnight on the night this message was posted, a young Norwegian biathlon champion disappeared from his family residence and has not been heard from since.'

Archie nodded thoughtfully. 'How come the MI6 computer was suspicious about this guy's profile in the first place?'

'Well, it's a highly sophisticated program that filters all sorts of parameters using algorithms and language pattern templates.' Highwater cleared her throat. 'Plus, the individual in question calls himself Doctor Doom.'

'And it picked up on something as subtle as that?'

Archie mumbled. 'Computers are so clever these days. Where would national security be without them?'

'Many of Doctor Doom's posts talk about revenge and retribution,' Highwater continued, ignoring Archie. 'Cipher Branch reported their findings to my boss Huge – I mean *Hugh* – Figo and he assigned the investigation to our division.'

'I suppose your colleagues in the Norwegian Secret Service are working up some intel?' said Barney in a slightly strange American accent.

'Negative.' Highwater removed her glasses. 'As far as they're concerned this is a simple case of a runaway. But the young man in question – Mr Henry Ulrik – has joint Norwegian and British citizenship so it's up to us to find him.'

Holden Grey nodded sagely. 'AKA this baby's in our court now.'

'Excuse me,' Archie interjected, raising his hand. 'I'm really sorry Mr Ulrik is missing and I don't want to be all me, me, me or anything – but what does all this have to do with my dad?'

Helen Highwater slid her glasses back on and smiled briefly. 'I'm glad you asked me that,' she said. 'Take a look at this.'

Chapter 13

X-ray's fingers danced over the keyboard and a new paragraph appeared on the monitors.

'This update was posted on Doctor Doom's page two days ago,' said Highwater.

'The day of the car crash,' Archie whispered to himself as his eyes eagerly scanned the post.

> *3pm – Very few police have the will power to take the necessary care. Too many of them will hunt selfishly on this and every afternoon.*

Falteringly Archie announced the hidden message, reading every fourth word, 'Have – to – care – them –

on – afternoon?' He frowned and cocked his head. 'That doesn't make any sense.'

'Guess again, Einstein,' said X-ray without looking up from her keyboard.

'Barney?' Highwater said invitingly. 'Any ideas?'

Barney pinched his chin thoughtfully and said, 'From my experience I'd guess our mark is using a classic helical substitution cipher, or perhaps a cross-numerical progression code?'

Highwater looked at him blankly. 'OK,' she said. 'Does anyone have any ideas that actually make sense? Archie?'

Archie said nothing for a moment because his mind was racing. This new message had been posted at 3 p.m., which meant . . .

His blood chilled as the hidden meaning became clear. In a voice that was barely audible he read the message.

'Police will take care of Hunt this afternoon.'

'Bravo,' said Grey, adding quickly, 'I mean kuoros.'

'No,' said Agent X-ray through gritted teeth, 'you actually mean kudos.'

'So somebody was planning to kill my father?' Archie felt anger bubbling in his veins. 'How soon did you decode this message?'

'Only about half an hour before the accident,' said Highwater. 'We didn't relocate to this safe house until yesterday so we were still in London at the time. We sent a uniformed unit to your home but they were too late to intercept your father.'

'Typical of the plod,' said Barney wearily. 'If you want a job done right you've got to go with Tactical Armed Response.'

'We have reason to believe things are not as straightforward as they at first appear,' said Highwater. 'Agent X-ray will explain.'

The girl spun her chair round to face the boys. As she addressed them she kept her head tilted slightly to one side so that her fringe hung across half of her face. 'Firstly we believe the phrase "take care of hunt" in the original message is ambiguous,' she mumbled, like a teenager who's been forced to propose a toast at a family function. 'It could mean, you know, to kill, or bump off, or ice or whatever. But it might just mean "taking care of business".'

'In what way?' asked Archie.

'In this case we think it meant they wanted to pick up your father.'

'You mean kidnap?'

X-ray nodded. 'Sort of. We don't think the chase and the accident were in the kidnappers' plan. Things just went a bit Pete Tong when your dad saw through their police disguise and kept going. We accessed some satellite images of the crash site and they clearly show that in the seconds following your old man's car making like a submarine, someone else jumped into the sea from the cliff. We reckon the kidnappers were trying to rescue him.'

'And did they?' Archie demanded urgently.

'We don't know for sure.' Agent X-ray pursed her lips. 'The satellite was being repositioned to spy on some foreign students suspected of plotting to bump off the Queen. It was only luck that it caught any of the action at all.'

'He must have saved him though,' Archie said brightly. 'You see, my dad was wearing this heart monitor to help RAF Cranfield with a study they're doing—'

'Yeah, we know all about the scientific study,' Agent X-ray interrupted, displaying the university website on one of the wall-mounted monitors. 'We bugged your hospital room so we heard what you told DC Flowers. We accessed your father's vital statistics to check for ourselves and we agree with you.'

'You think he's alive?' Archie beamed.

'We're pretty sure he is,' said Agent X-ray with just a flicker of a smile. 'Or at least he was at just gone midnight the night before last.'

'That's brilliant!' Archie turned and high-fived Barney. Then he noticed that Highwater and Agent X-ray weren't smiling.

'That's the good news,' said Highwater grimly. 'Unfortunately there's some bad news too.'

Chapter 14

'The bad news, Mr Hunt, is that while your father is alive,' Grey chipped in, 'he's still in very hot water without a paddle.'

Archie grimaced as he tried to decipher the elderly man's metaphor.

'In simple terms,' Highwater added, glaring at her colleague, 'we are working on the theory that the man who kidnapped your father is planning to carry out some sort of experiments on his captives in order to further his despicable plan to take over the world. In short, we are dealing with an Evil Mastermind Uprising.'

Barney nodded, the corners of his mouth turned down as if this was exactly the scenario he had expected.

Archie began to feel weirdly woozy, as if he was immersed in glycerine. It was as though reality had somehow become mixed up with some strange spy fantasy. 'Evil Mastermind Uprising. Is that, like, an official term?'

'I'm afraid so,' Highwater stated coldly. 'We use it only in the very gravest circumstances when an individual of exceptional intelligence demonstrates he has both the intention and the wherewithal to instigate a fiendish plot designed to destabilise the balance of world power.'

'In short, he's a well nasty gangster, isn't it?' added Grey.

'And what exactly is he going to do with my father?' Archie asked faintly.

Highwater nodded knowingly. 'I'm afraid, young man, that our theory as to Doctor Doom's objectives is highly classified information. I can't tell you any more unless you agree to sign the Official Secrets Act and accept the terms of the MI6 Undercover Agents Disclaimer. And this is the point at which I must ask Mr Jones to leave.'

Archie looked at Barney, who gave him a tight-lipped smile and a nod of encouragement.

'OK, I'll sign,' Archie said.

'Excellent.' Highwater produced a welcoming smile.

'But only if Barney's on the team too.'

Highwater's face froze. 'I'm sorry, Mr Hunt, this isn't some after-school club. You don't get to join because your friend's a member.'

'But Barney knows everything there is to know about spy stuff,' Archie insisted.

'I *have* seen every single James Bond film at least five times,' Barney offered timidly, 'even *Die Another Day*. I've read all the Young Bond books over and over – and I got through the whole Alex Rider series in one week. I never miss an episode of *Spooks* or *Alias* and I even watched *The Bourne Identity* when my parents thought I was doing my homework. I can recite all the dialogue from *Mission Imposs—*'

'This is all very . . . impressive,' Highwater interrupted, holding up a hand, 'but how does your slightly fanatical interest in spy fiction qualify you for a place on our team of highly skilled agents?'

Barney blew out his rosy cheeks and rolled his eyes, searching the ceiling pensively.

'Well, Mr Jones,' Highwater said, 'I think your silence speaks volumes, don't you?'

'What about a profiler?' Archie blurted out.

Highwater and Barney turned to face him. 'Profiler?' they echoed.

'Yeah,' said Archie. 'Barney must know all there is to know about evil masterminds. I bet he could give you a pretty accurate insight into this Doctor Doom's methods and motives.'

'Well, OK,' Highwater agreed. 'This should at least be entertaining if nothing else.'

'We've already worked up a pretty detailed profile,' Agent X-ray volunteered, opening a beige folder. Highwater took the folder from the girl and turned to Barney.

'OK, Mr Jones. If you can tell me five key points about Doctor Doom's evil plan then you can join the team. If not I'll have to show you the door. Do we have a deal?'

Barney nodded earnestly and swallowed hard. 'Let me see,' he said, scratching his armpit nervously. 'Well, you're obviously dealing with a highly intelligent person.'

'I think the term *mastermind* sort of gives that away,' Highwater sneered.

'But he's also arrogant because he's taunting you

110

by leaving clues on the Internet,' Barney suggested falteringly. 'He thinks he's too clever to get caught – like he's playing cat and mouse with you. What he's doing is showing the world that he can outsmart the entire Secret Service.'

'Thank you, Mr Jones,' Highwater barked then after a breath she added more calmly, 'What was the point you were making?'

Barney stuck out his bottom lip. 'Just that he thinks he can't be found out, as though he's God or something.'

'God complex,' confirmed Highwater, marking a tick in her folder.

Encouraged by his success, Barney allowed himself to theorise more freely. 'Any self-respecting mad scientist lives in a secluded lair on a deserted island or inside a volcano or, I don't know, perched on the side of a cliff.'

'Reclusive, check,' Highwater remarked, ticking her folder again. 'What about his motives?'

'Revenge,' Barney answered automatically. 'These guys are always after revenge of some sort. He wants to punish the people, or the country, that he feels wronged him. Greed is always a factor too. He's probably plotting something that will destabilise the political balance and make him so rich that he will achieve world domination, a bit like that dude in *Point Blanc*.'

'World domination,' announced Highwater. 'That's three. Two more and you're in. Any thoughts about his method?'

Barney scratched his head and exhaled pensively. 'Well, he's bound to have some evil creation brewing. He's kidnapped a sporting champion and Archie's dad, who was an all-round high achiever, so it's probably something involving cloning or gene selection . . . that's it!' Barney clicked his fingers in triumph. 'He's going to extract genes from his captives and combine them somehow to make a genetically superior monster or creature that he'll clone and take over the world with.'

Archie shook his head and sighed, thinking Barney had just blown his chances. But to his amazement Highwater marked another tick on her folder. 'Creating a super-being, check,' she said. Then, tapping her pen on her teeth, she said, 'So far so good, Mr Jones. One more correct supposition and you're in, although I have to warn you I can't accept a wrong answer at this stage.'

Barney studied the ceiling again. Seconds ticked by.

'OK, Mr Jones.' Highwater closed her folder. 'Time's up. Close but no cigar. I trust you can show yourself out.'

Barney took one last, lingering look round the secret underground MI6 ops centre then began to shuffle reluctantly towards the door.

'I don't get it,' Archie said, sadly watching his friend edge out of sight. 'If you know this much about Doctor Doom then shouldn't you have a pretty good idea who he is?'

'We've run the evidence through our database,' X-ray mumbled from behind the slanted curtain of her fringe. 'We've used different electronic filter tags, adjusted the parameter tolerances and played with all sorts of data-funnelling algorithms. Every time it comes up with one possible suspect.'

'And . . . ?' Archie demanded impatiently.

'. . . and, he's your evil enemy,' said Highwater.

'Of course he's my enemy,' Archie retorted. 'And he's obviously evil.'

'No – that's his name,' Agent X-ray explained disdainfully. 'Professor, Yuri, Villenemi. Pronounced "Yu-ree Vill-enemi".'

'That figures,' Archie replied. 'Sounds like your average evil genius to me.'

'Professor Villenemi worked as a chief government research scientist until about four years ago,' explained Highwater, 'when it was discovered that he had been secretly experimenting on human embryos. He was conducting illegal experiments into genetic modification and human cloning with a view to selling the results to terrorist groups. When he was found out he went on the run. MI6's top agent was tracking him down but Villenemi killed her in cold blood.'

'This doesn't stack up.' Archie shook his head dubiously. 'Why has MI6 given us – I mean you – such an important case?'

Highwater smiled as though it was a question she had expected. 'Mr Ego – that's Mr Figo – believes this is our opportunity to demonstrate our true worth,' she said with a conviction she didn't feel.

Highwater rightly suspected that her boss was highly sceptical of any real link between the ramblings of Dr Doom and the apparent runaway teenager in Norway. Figo believed the Internet was so vast you could generate thousands of hidden messages if you analysed every possible pattern of words and letters, so any connection between the blog and the events in Norway was probably coincidental.

He had assigned the case to Highwater because he was confident that, after weeks of Internet monitoring and field surveillance, her team of fledgling agents would find no concrete evidence. Following their embarrassing failure in their maiden assignment, Figo was sure that any talk of Highwater leapfrogging him on the corporate ladder would be brushed under the carpet.

'So he wanted to give your kids a chance to prove themselves? That's cool,' Archie commented, removing his glasses to polish them on his hoody. Replacing them, he continued, 'But now you've identified Villenemi as the main suspect – and if this Villenemi is really as dangerous as you say and has already killed an MI6 agent – then surely this isn't the time to let us play at being spies? Surely the whole of MI6 should be concentrating on nailing this man?'

Agent X-ray looked uncertainly at her superiors then mumbled, 'They don't believe our theory, though. They say Villenemi can't be the bad guy.'

'How come?' Archie asked.

Highwater's leather chair squeaked as she shifted her position.

Agent X-ray inspected her hair for split ends.

There was a long pause before Holden Grey spoke. 'Well, according to *official* records,' he said sceptically, 'the SAS smoked him two years ago.'

'What do you mean?' Archie asked.

'I mean they blew up his secret lair – with him in it,' Grey confessed. 'DNA analysis was used to identify Villenemi from his charred remains.'

Archie blinked at the three MI6 agents and frowned. 'Sorry if I'm being a bit thick, but . . . doesn't the fact that he's dead sort of eliminate him from your enquiries?'

'We are fully aware that our mission faces certain challenges, Mr Hunt,' Highwater added.

Archie snorted. 'What, apart from the fact that your only suspect is dead?'

For a moment an uncomfortable silence descended, then a mumbled suggestion came from the other side of the room.

'Or he *wants* you to believe that he's dead.'

Everyone turned to see Barney's round face poking out from round the corner.

'I thought you'd been asked to leave,' Agent X-ray sneered.

'The door is locked,' Barney offered, pointing awkwardly at the exit. 'I didn't want to interrupt.'

'Would you care to explain your remark, Mr Jones?' Highwater ordered.

Barney looked momentarily surprised, then stepped round the corner into full view. 'I mean that Villenemi could have faked his own death. Well, it's classic anti-surveillance spy craft, isn't it?' He shrugged and scratched his head.

'Not really,' Highwater corrected. 'Ducking into a shop doorway or getting off a train at the last minute is classic anti-surveillance spy craft. Faking your own death is pretty fanciful stuff.'

'Oh, OK.' Barney sounded downbeat. 'It's just that double-oh six did it in *Goldeneye*.'

'Excuse me?'

'Alec Trevelyan, who was played by Sean Bean, was double-oh six.' Barney threw his palms wide as though this was basic information that everyone should know. 'He faked his own death while on a mission with Bond in a Russian weapons factory. With MI6 believing he was dead, he was free to go off and become the head of the evil Janus syndicate.'

Studying Barney, Highwater tapped a pen on her

teeth. At last she said, 'And how would you explain the DNA match in the burned-out lab?'

Barney rolled his wide eyes skywards and took a couple more steps into the room. 'He's a genetic scientist, isn't he?' he remarked, his tone bordering on exasperation. 'He'd probably cloned himself or spliced his genes with one of his henchmen or something. All I'm saying is it wouldn't be hard for a brilliant genetic scientist to duplicate his own DNA and plant it in some other tissue in order to fool the authorities into believing he's dead.'

Highwater looked enquiringly from Holden Grey to Agent X-ray. Both responded with a cautious nod.

'When you put it like that, it does sound pretty basic.' Highwater scribbled hastily in her beige folder. 'Good work, Mr Jones. We've only just reached a similar conclusion ourselves.' She continued to scribble feverishly.

'Does that mean I'm in?' Barney's cheeks were blooming.

'We can evidently use someone with your unique expertise,' Highwater stated, extending a hand for Barney to shake. 'Welcome to the team.'

Beaming, Barney resumed his position next to Archie, who gave his shoulder a congratulatory punch but was clearly lost in his own thoughts.

The information Archie had been given was a bittersweet revelation. Yes, his father was probably still alive but, if so, he was to be used as a guinea pig in some bizarre scientific experiment.

'I'm sure you have plenty of questions that I'd be happy to give you answers to,' said Highwater, studying Archie.

He didn't know where to begin. How would Dr Doom's experiments affect his father? Were there any leads as to the whereabouts of Doom's laboratory? Once it was located, how would they go about overpowering the evil mastermind and rescuing his hostages? Archie wanted to interrogate Highwater on every tiny aspect of her plan but, overwhelmed with a strange mixture of relief and anxiety, he found that he couldn't speak.

'I have a question,' Barney piped up.

'Yes, Mr Jones?' said Highwater.

Archie smiled, grateful to his friend for stepping in to establish the facts on his behalf.

'Do we get any cool gadgets?' asked Barney.

'Gadgets?' echoed Archie, bewildered.

'Yeah, gadgets,' said Barney defensively. 'In the movies undercover agents always get a bunch of cool gadgets at the beginning of the mission. And there's always one gadget with a really random but specific function that just so happens to be exactly what the agent needs to get out of a tight spot when he's inside the baddie's lair.

'And while we're at it, we need a name for the agency,' Barney gabbled excitedly. 'Some sort of cool acronym like PANTHERS or something.'

'Wicked, innit?' bluffed Grey. 'What do the letters stand for?'

A faint pinkish hue bloomed in Barney's round cheeks. 'I dunno,' he mumbled. 'I just thought it was a cool name.'

'Correct me if I'm wrong,' sighed Highwater, 'but the general idea of an acronym is that each letter is an initial of the title.' She enjoyed her sense of superiority for a long moment before continuing. 'Now, before you go into the field I will need you both to sign a disclaimer. It's simply a formality—'

'What about the gadgets?' demanded Archie, annoyed at the way his friend had been dismissed. 'You

120

did say you'd answer all our questions.'

'Ah yes.' Highwater clicked her fingers as if the subject had momentarily slipped her mind. 'The gadgets.'

Chapter 15

Her heels tick-tocked on the marble floor as she led the way to the opposite end of the room where a long workbench was cluttered with dismantled radios, butchered computers and the insides of numerous household appliances. Holden Grey snatched a white lab coat from a wall-mounted hook and pulled it on as he followed.

Archie, Barney and Agent X-ray tagged along and they all gathered round the table.

'OK, guys,' said Grey, his pale eyes twinkling. 'Let's cut the business and get straight down to the chase. I'm about to brief you on the equipment I've developed for your secret undercover mission.'

Archie could sense Barney tense up with excitement

as Holden Grey turned to pick something up from the countertop behind him. When Grey turned back he was holding a black plastic block between the thumb and forefinger of both hands.

'This,' he announced in a reverential whisper, 'is what I call the Portable Communication and Image Transference Device.'

Archie studied the object, which was about the size of a pack of playing cards. 'What does it do?' he asked.

Grey smiled proudly. 'This innocuous looking item has the capability of providing telecommunications from anywhere in the world.'

Agent X-ray groaned.

Archie and Barney exchanged confused looks.

'So,' said Archie tentatively. 'It's a bit like a . . . telephone?'

Holden Grey smiled triumphantly, holding up a single finger. 'Except that unlike ordinary phones this device has its very own inbuilt power source and needs no physical connection to any existing telecoms network. It's completely wireless.'

'So it's a *mobile* phone?' Agent X-ray offered.

Archie slipped his own mobile out of his pocket and

held it up. 'Like this one?' Grey took it off him and compared it to his much bulkier invention, hefting the two devices in his hands.

'Well I never,' he muttered. 'Quite extraordinary.' He handed Archie's phone back before continuing. 'However, *my* innovation possesses a brilliant secret feature. One simple movement and . . .' With a mysterious glint in his eye, Grey slid back the fascia of his invention. 'Hey presto, the device transforms into a video camera capable of recording up to sixty seconds of black and white footage which can easily be transmitted back to HQ by plugging the handset into any personal computer. Now tell me, Mr Hunt, can your device do *that*?'

'Actually it can record up to ten minutes of colour video,' Archie said apologetically. 'And it can send the film instantly as a text message or email attachment without plugging into anything.'

'How very extraordinary. Where did you get it?' Grey enquired with intrigue.

'It's my father's.'

'Ah yes – he did his fair share of special ops in his time, didn't he?' Grey squinted thoughtfully. 'Do you know if he picked this up from MOSSAD or the KGB?'

Archie shrugged. 'I think it's from the Carphone Warehouse.'

'Goodness me,' exclaimed Holden Grey, with a bemused chuckle. 'It's amazing, isn't it? You turn your back on technology for twenty years or so and all of a sudden you're out of date. Next you'll be telling me video recorders are obsolete.'

Archie shuffled nervously. 'Actually . . .'

'I'm only joking, Mr – I mean, homie!' Grey winked at him. 'I may not know too much about mobile phones but I couldn't cope without my Sky+ box. I'll have you know I've never missed an episode of *Antiques Roadshow* yet. And I've heard *The Eggs Factor* is heavy too. I must watch that some time – I do love a nice cookery programme.'

'You mean *The X Factor*.' Agent X-ray smiled. 'And it isn't exactly about cooking – although, come to think of it, it is full of turkeys.'

Helen Highwater interrupted sharply. 'Perhaps we could get back to the matter in hand?'

Holden Grey placed the phone on the table in front of him and patted his chest with both palms. At last his eyes lit up and he produced a pen from inside his jacket pocket, handing it to Barney who examined it eagerly.

'Let me guess.' Barney pointed it towards a blank wall, repeatedly clicking the button with his thumb. 'It fires tiny bullets, doesn't it? Or little tranquilliser darts?'

'We're too young to carry firearms,' Agent X-ray pointed out. 'Government rules.'

'Oh,' said Barney, disappointed. Sniffing the point of the biro, he asked, 'Is the ink actually poison? No? Invisible then – we use it to write secret messages giving you updates on our progress?'

Holden Grey shook his head. 'It's just an ordinary pen,' he explained, his brow furrowing in confusion. 'I thought you were about to sign that disclaimer.'

Barney smiled gratefully but his cheeks had lost their eager swell.

'Have you got anything else we might need, Mr Grey?' asked Archie, feeling sorry for his friend. 'Anything at all?'

'Let me see . . .' Holden Grey rubbed his chin. 'The only other thing I've got is this.' Opening what looked like a lunch box, he produced a Mars bar.

'Oh, I'm not hungry, thank you,' said Archie.

'Speak for yourself,' said Barney, grabbing the chocolate bar.

He pinched the top of the wrapper with both hands

and was just about to tear it open when—

'STOP!' bellowed Holden Grey.

Barney relaxed his grip on the sweet wrapper and everyone waited in stunned silence.

'That's no ordinary chocolate bar,' explained Grey, breathing heavily after his outburst. 'I've been experimenting by lacing chocolate with various chemicals in order to make it a doubly lethal secret weapon. I'm trying to perfect a poison that is as deadly as cyanide to anyone who consumes it and also releases a toxic substance into the air that will immobilise anyone whose DNA contains the evil gene.'

'The evil gene?' questioned Archie.

Grey nodded. 'Oh yes. As you've seen, I haven't exactly stayed at the cutting edge of comms technology but I've been spending my retirement studying the genetic make-up of history's most barbaric individuals. Attila the Hun, Vlad the Impaler, Ivan the Terrible – you name it – they all had one thing in common. They all possessed the evil gene.'

'So this chocolate bar will kill anyone who eats it,' marvelled Barney, turning the Mars bar over in his hands. 'And immobilise any really bad guys in the vicinity?'

Holden Grey's smile dropped. 'Actually no,' he said. 'It's still very much a work in progress. What you hold in your hand is a prototype chocolate bar laced with a substance that has the same toxic qualities as a powerful insecticide. In addition, when the bar is bitten into it releases canine pheromones into the atmosphere.'

'Wow,' Barney grinned. 'So if, say, we were being attacked by killer bees *and* surrounded by some really ferocious cats, then . . . this is exactly the gadget we'd need?'

'Precisely,' said Grey. 'The insecticide would kill the bees and the canine pheromones would repel the cats.'

'Is that the sort of situation many agents find themselves in?' asked Archie pointedly.

'It's bound to happen all the time,' Agent X-ray mumbled.

Holden Grey puffed out his cheeks as he considered his response.

'You never know,' suggested Barney. 'Anything could happen.'

'Exactly,' agreed Grey gratefully. 'You never know when the Toxic Chocolate Stinkbomb will come in handy.'

'OK. Thanks, Mr Grey.' Archie smiled uncertainly

128

and took the Mars bar from Barney, slipping it into the pocket of his hoody.

'Stinkbomb?' said Barney. 'That's a brilliant name. We could use it for the agency too.'

'Dear oh dear, Mr Jones,' sneered Helen Highwater. 'It really is no good choosing exciting words if the initials don't mean anything.'

Spurred on by his friend's discomfort, Archie's mind spun into action. 'They do though,' he insisted.

'They do?' asked Highwater.

'They *do*?' whispered Barney.

Archie smiled. 'Of course. S.T.I.N.K.B.O.M.B. stands for Secret Team of Intrepid-Natured Kids . . . Battling Odious Masterminds, erm . . . Basically.'

Helen Highwater replayed the phrase in her head a few times before proclaiming her verdict. 'Not bad. Not bad at all.'

'It's insane,' Grey added. 'And by that I mean I like it.'

'Wicked,' smiled Agent X-ray.

'STINKBOMB,' mused Archie with a smile. 'Watch out, Doctor Doom, we'll get right up your nose.'

Chapter 16

Highwater ushered Archie and Barney back to the other end of the converted cellar, where they both signed the Official Secrets Act and the MI6 Undercover Agents Disclaimer.

'So basically,' Archie surmised, sliding his completed forms back to his new boss, 'if we blab that we're undercover agents then you'll deny all knowledge of us?'

'Exactly,' said Highwater with a cold smile. 'Then we'll have you killed by MI6 assassins.'

Archie and Barney stared into Highwater's flint-grey eyes.

'K-k-killed?' repeated Archie after a few seconds.

Highwater's mouth curled into a wicked smile.

'Kidding!' she chuckled. 'That's just a little bit of Secret Service humour to help you to relax.'

'That's very funny,' Barney wheezed, adding a nervy laugh.

Archie blew a lungful of air through his lips. 'I don't know about Barney but I've never felt more relaxed.'

'We couldn't have you killed even if we wanted to,' continued Highwater. 'Not without mountains of paperwork anyway. But if you did try and out us we'd have you diagnosed as pathologically delusional by a government doctor and have you *permanently* institutionalised – somewhere peaceful and clean like the Falklands.'

Barney began to chuckle again but, realising Highwater wasn't joking this time, pretended to cough instead.

'From now on, for the purposes of any future communications via unsecure lines, we will no longer use any names. Archie, your designator will be Agent Yankee and Barney, you're Agent Zulu. Agent X-ray's real name is Gemma Croft but you are to stick rigidly to designators unless ops specifically require otherwise. Everyone calls me Icy.'

'Perhaps you could try smiling more often?'

suggested Archie with a cheeky grin.

'I.C., not Icy,' Highwater barked. 'It stands for Initiative Commander.'

'Oh right,' said Archie, adding under his breath, 'I think I was right the first time.'

'So what happens now?' asked Barney eagerly. 'I'm guessing we'll go dark on the comms until the Cockerel crows that the Golden Eagle has laid another egg when we'll RV on the QT?'

'I have no idea what you just said. But I'm monitoring Doom's website so we'll let you know as soon as we need your assistance,' said Gemma.

'And in the meantime? We just carry on as if none of this ever happened?' Archie demanded, holding his palms upward.

'Precisely,' said Gemma.

'I get it.' Barney winked conspiratorially. 'We go back to pretending we're just a couple of ordinary schoolboys.'

'You were never *ordinary* schoolboys,' said Gemma. 'Ordinary suggests a level of popularity you two could only aspire to.'

Gemma led Archie and Barney back upstairs and

stood at the front door, watching the boys walk down the footpath.

Halfway to the pavement Archie turned and asked, 'I was just wondering, how did MI6 recruit you?'

'Seriously, Yankee,' she hissed, scanning the street, 'could you say that any louder?'

'Sorry,' Archie whispered.

Gemma's expression softened. 'It was no big deal really. I've always been into computers. One day I just hacked into the Police mainframe computer. I'd been snooping around for weeks before they traced me.'

'Did you get into trouble?'

'Not really.' Gemma allowed herself a fleeting smile of triumph. 'They said they'd let me off if I showed them how I'd done it. Then they offered me a place in this new agency so here I am. It was a no-brainer.'

'That's so cool,' Archie cooed, immediately thinking his words sounded lame.

'I'm so excited we're actual agents!' Barney called from the pavement, immediately clapping a hand over his mouth. Then he whispered, 'It's unbelievable.'

'You know what?' Gemma scanned the street once more and smiled coldly. 'I couldn't agree more.'

Back At That Secret Location (Remember, The One That's Somewhere in Europe)

Chapter 17

A squat figure was peering over his banked console at his freakishly tall and painfully thin visitor.

'So nobody tried to intercept you?'

The strangely skinny man unfolded his immensely long arms, which seemed to have at least two elbows each. He pushed back his cap with a twiggy, hairy finger and shook his shiny, elongated head. 'Nobody, Mr Doom.'

'DOCTOR!' shrieked the small man. 'DOCTOR Doom.' Then with chilling cordiality he continued, 'Really, Antony. How many times must I remind you?'

'Sorry, Mr – I mean Doctor Doom.' The skinny figure adjusted his stance and cleared his throat. 'No one physically tried to stop us but we did hear something of interest on our police scanner . . . A squad car being dispatched to the Hunt residence around the time of the intercept.'

Dr Doom's human eye glinted. 'I see,' he purred, steepling his fingertips together thoughtfully. 'So maybe someone *is* paying attention to me after all. Perhaps there *are* some people in the world intelligent enough to understand and marvel at the genius I am about to unleash?' He threw his head back and the first ripple of malevolent mirth burbled in the back of his throat. Antony looked on nervously.

'So.' Dr Doom laced his fingers together and stretched his arms out in front of him. 'If you managed to decipher my last riddle then let's see how you do with this one.'

Antony watched his boss typing feverishly on his keyboard for a few seconds then, uncertainly, asked, 'Sorry, Misterdoctor Doom, were you talking to me?'

'No,' Dr Doom answered sweetly, 'I wasn't. I doubt, dear Antony, you could unravel a ball of wool, never mind untangling my fiendishly clever clues. I am sending a message to whoever tried to warn Hunt of your imminent arrival – challenging them to see if they're clever enough to save Mr Schumaker.

Somebody out there has picked up the gauntlet and my little game of cat and mouse is—'

'What gauntlet?' Antony asked.

'It's an expression, you fool,' spat Doom. 'I've told you before, please don't interrupt me when I am giving my explanatory evil monologues.' Doom's eye swivelled skyward in exasperation. 'Now where was I . . . ? Oh yes, *somebody* out there has picked up the gauntlet and my little game of cat and mouse is about to get interesting. *Very* interesting indeed.' He was about to throw his head back again, but stopped. 'In the interests of expediency, let's assume that at this point I laughed, you joined in, and we both cackled about my genius together. That will be all.'

Doom's fingers rattled on his keyboard for a few more seconds before he noticed Antony was still loitering in front of him. One of his exceptionally long, wiry arms was raised like a schoolboy waiting to catch his teacher's attention.

The evil villain's shoulders drooped. 'If you're waiting to ask about the cat and the mouse, the answer is no. They are not real either.'

'Oh.' Slowly Antony lowered his hand and turned, skulking towards the exit with long, loping strides.

'Just one more thing, Antony,' Dr Doom said casually, lightly resting his mismatched hands on his computer keys. 'When you went to intercept Hunt, am I right in concluding that you chased his car off the road, resulting in Richard Hunt sailing into the sea inside his vehicle? While his son could not be found and is presumed to have been thrown clear?'

'Erm, that's right.'

One side of Dr Doom's mouth stretched into a broad smile. 'Thought so,' he said warmly. 'Oh – one very final thing. Could you take a couple of steps to the left for me? Thank you.'

Immediately Doom yanked a lever then pressed a button next to it. Antony instinctively glanced at his feet.

Three sounds followed in quick succession. First there was an emphatic *'shuck'* like the sound of someone putting their palm over the nozzle of a vacuum cleaner. Then came the pneumatic *'swish'* of sliding doors before a deep liquid *'ploosh'*!

Dr Doom grinned at the dark cloud billowing on one of the screens mounted on his desk. Calmly he reached out and flicked a small switch then leaned towards a microphone.

'Hello, is that the Clone Zone?' he asked. 'It's Doctor Doom here. Listen, I need you to grow me another Antony and I need it in twenty minutes. Is that understood?' Pause. 'Excellent. I'm afraid the last one rather dropped himself in it.'

Chapter 18

Archie and Barney were sitting in Archie's room, snacking on sandwiches and two tall glasses of cold milk Archie's grandmother had prepared for them. They'd cycled back from the safe house in stunned silence and hadn't spoken since getting to Archie's.

'We're MI6 agents, you know,' said Archie at last.

'I know!' Barney beamed. 'STINKBOMB agents, to be precise.'

'How's your sandwich, Agent Zulu?'

'That's classified, Agent Yankee. I could tell you but I'd have to kill you!'

'Gemma's pretty cool, don't you think?' Archie said, trying to sound vaguely bored by the topic. 'I mean, she's not like other girls we know or anything.'

'Of course she's not,' Barney laughed. 'She's an MI6 secret agent for starters.'

'I suppose.' Archie studied his glass before taking a slurp of milk. 'But apart from that, she's just quite, I dunno, cool.'

'How do you mean?'

'Well, hacking into the police computer is pretty cool.'

'True.'

'And the way she dresses – the jacket and that – is cool.'

'I guess.'

'Have you noticed that funny dimple she gets . . .' Archie stopped himself. Suddenly feeling the overwhelming urge to swallow he slowly raised his eyes to meet Barney's.

'Let me guess,' Barney said, grinning. 'The dimple is cool too?'

The boys were interrupted by the sound of Archie's phone chirping the theme from *Star Wars*.

Archie was slouched back on his bed so Barney pushed across the room on the chair's castors and picked the phone up off the desk.

'Hello?' he said, rolling a bite of sandwich into his

cheek like a hamster. 'Archie Hunt's phone. Oh, hi, Gemma.'

There was a lengthy pause before Barney spoke again. 'Sorry. Yes, Agent X-ray. It was a momentary lapse in agency protocol. It won't happen again . . . That's affirmatory.'

Archie watched his friend's eyes open steadily wider as he listened to the handset. Finally he said, 'Copy that – message received and understood. Over,' before ending the call and tossing the phone on to the bed.

'We've got to get online,' he announced, spinning to face the desk. 'We've got a code blue on the suspect. Looks like the cheetah is about to snare its next mouse.'

Barney bit his bottom lip and hunched over the keyboard, typing feverishly. When Dr Doom's page appeared on the screen both boys sat in silence and read the latest message.

I will select my next volunteer where a secretive cave dweller hangs around with someone whose achievements are out of this world – 12071600

143

Archie let out a long breath. 'I haven't got a Scooby Doo what he's on about.'

'Agent X-ray said Doom must have changed his cipher on this one. It's classic evil mastermind behaviour. He's sort of taunting the authorities while still keeping us guessing,' said Barney, with a knowing look.

'Well, how are we supposed to crack it if we don't know how the code works?'

'Agent X-ray told us not to bother trying to solve it anyway,' Barney said, before glugging the last of his milk.

'How come?'

'She said it was far too complicated for us to work out and we should let the professionals do the thinking.'

'She said that?' said Archie, his blood fizzing with anger. Suddenly the importance of what they were doing jolted him into action. His father's life was at risk and it was in his power to help. It was as if someone had lit a fuse inside him and he could practically feel the synapses in his brain firing as he channelled all his attention into solving the riddle.

'OK, let's think about this,' Archie muttered. 'A cave dweller could be an animal of some sort – a bear or a

144

salamander or even some kind of sea creature which might live in an underwater cave . . .'

The boys stared at the walls for a long while. Barney popped open a packet of crisps and started munching.

'There must be millions of creatures that live in caves,' he sighed, spraying cheesy crumbs into the air.

'Maybe we're thinking about it too literally,' Archie offered, wiping some crisp spray off his cheek with the back of his hand. 'What if it's not an animal at all? Who else lives in a cave?'

Barney shrugged. 'A caveman? Ooh, I know, Captain Caveman!'

As he excitedly pronounced each C, more globules of soggy potato rained over Archie.

'I'm not sure I'd describe Captain Caveman as secretive exactly.' Archie paused, picking a morsel off his glasses. 'What about Batman, though? He was pretty secretive and he lived in a cave.'

'I think you've cracked it, Agent Yankee.'

'Well, it's a possibility,' Archie said. 'Let's see if it fits with the rest of the clue. Let's see . . . Whose achievements are out of this world?'

'Anyone who's really successful,' Barney suggested. 'Actors, sportspeople, rock stars – tons of people. How are we supposed to pick a name out of thin air? It's impossible.'

For a few moments both boys slouched in front of the computer, staring at the screen in silence. Then Archie's back straightened.

'Unless . . .' he said, leaning across Barney and tapping something into the computer, '. . . Doom is referring to someone whose achievements are *actually* on another planet.'

'Like E.T.?' Barney suggested.

'Could be,' encouraged Archie, adrenalin pumping round his body. 'Who else goes outside this world to achieve their goals?'

'Astronauts,' Barney beamed, starting to enjoy the challenge.

'Exactly!' said Archie. 'And who's the most famous astronaut in the world?'

Barney clicked his fingers triumphantly. 'Armstrong. Neil Armstrong!' he proclaimed, then a frown puckered his forehead. 'But I'm not sure the Caped Crusader ever met Neil Armstrong.'

Archie's fingers were a blur on the keyboard. 'The clue doesn't say they meet each other,' he pointed out. 'It says they *hang around with* each other.'

'Same difference, isn't it?'

Without taking his eyes off the computer screen Archie shook his head. 'I think Doom chose his words very carefully. What jumps out at me is that we're not talking about actual people, obviously, but we might be talking about pictures, or portraits. And where might you find paintings of, say, Batman and Neil Armstrong?'

Realisation relaxed Barney's frown. '*Hanging around a gallery?*'

'Exactly.' Archie grinned and pushed his glasses up the bridge of his nose. 'The Atomic Gallery in Hamburg, to be exact.'

'How do you know that?'

'Easy.' Archie shrugged modestly. 'I just Googled the words *gallery exhibition Batman* and *Neil Armstrong* and this came up.'

Archie pointed about halfway down the screen of search results and Barney leaned forward to read the text.

ATOMIC SALON **GALLERY**

Glashuttenstrasse 19 HAMBURG

. . . showing an **exhibition** of portraits of

20th century icons including

147

Marilyn Monroe, **Batman**, Muhammad Ali, James Bond and **Neil Armstrong** . . .

'That's awesome.' Barney grinned. 'You'd better let Gemma know you've done her job for her.'

'I know,' said Archie, grabbing his mobile. 'We haven't got much time.'

'What do you mean?' asked Barney, a baffled frown creasing his face again.

Archie pulled up Dr Doom's blog and tapped the eight-digit sequence beneath his riddle.

'Twelve, oh-seven, sixteen hundred,' read Barney. 'What is that, a telephone number or something?'

Archie shook his head. 'It's a date and time,' he explained, waiting for his call to be answered. 'Twelve, oh-seven means the kidnap will take place on the twelfth of July and sixteen hundred is the designated time for the snatch.'

'Four o'clock today?' Barney glanced at his watch. 'But that means we only have . . .'

He looked at Archie, his jaw slack with despair.

'That's right.' Archie nodded grimly. 'We've got less than two hours.'

Chapter 19

'So you're saying it's going to happen at sixteen hundred hours?'

'Four o'clock, yes.'

'And that's this afternoon?'

'Yes.'

'Well, that doesn't give us much time, does it?' Highwater's statement almost sounded like an accusation.

'That's what I've been trying to tell you,' Archie said, managing to stay calm. It had been a long phone call during which Highwater and Gemma had forced him to explain each stage of his thought process. 'I was thinking we should contact the German authorities and inform them that a crime is about to be committed.

They could get a team of agents down to the gallery and catch Doctor Doom in the act.'

The next voice Archie heard was Holden Grey's. 'Yo, Yankee. A.S.I. Grey witcha.'

'Er . . . hello, Mr Grey.'

'Hear me now,' Grey continued. 'FIY, our Spooks ain't tight enough with the Polizei Posse for us to drop a beat and expect them to boogie. Do you feel me?'

'Let me make a phone call,' Highwater said, coming back on the line. 'I'll call you back in five.'

While Archie waited for Highwater to ring back he instructed Barney to find out the scheduled departure and arrival times of every commercial flight from the UK to Hamburg that afternoon. When his ringtone sounded again he stepped out of his room on to the landing to answer it.

'Yankee, this is I.C.'

'What's the score?' asked Archie.

'I've reported your theory to my immediate superior.'

'And?'

'He wants to give Cipher Branch some time to corroborate your findings before he calls in a foreign agency.'

'Time?!' Archie yelped. 'We haven't got any time. There's an hour and fifty-one minutes before Doctor Doom kidnaps another innocent person and we need to do something – now.'

The reality was that the Hamburg Polizei would not respond to STINKBOMB's new intelligence. Hugh Figo had been so determined Highwater's fledgling agency should fail that he'd assigned it a pitifully low security clearance level, rendering it virtually powerless. Any information coming from the agency would be ignored unless its priority was boosted by verification from Figo himself.

Archie waited to hear Highwater's Plan B but all that came from her was a series of noises intended to convey annoyance.

'Listen,' he said, feeling his frustration boiling over. 'At exactly five minutes to four call Hamburg Police and report a crime at the Atomic Salon Gallery.'

'But the kidnap won't have happened by then.'

'The police won't know that. It doesn't have to be a kidnap, it could be an assault or a robbery or anything – we just want the cavalry to arrive as the abduction is taking place.'

'Good idea,' said Highwater with a note of surprise.

'I'm going to try and get to the gallery,' Archie continued. 'Barney's checking timetables online now. If there's a flight from Bournemouth in the next twenty minutes we might make it.'

Muffled by some amplified rustling, Archie heard Highwater speaking to someone else with her hand over her mouthpiece.

'X-ray can't get there in time,' she announced. 'She's checked the flights and nothing leaves any London airport until three thirty this afternoon.'

'Oh well,' said Archie, 'we'll send you both a postcard.'

'Listen, Yankee,' said Highwater with cold authority. 'I am not happy with you and Zulu going into the field alone. But it must be done. Remember, you are not to engage the enemy under any circumstances. Your role is surveillance only, do I make myself clear?'

'As a bell. I've got to go,' said Archie and he ended the call.

He went back into his bedroom where Barney was frantically working the keyboard.

'Come on,' he said, pulling on his A&F hoody. 'We'll have to take a plane asap.'

Barney thrust himself back in his chair and threw

his hands up. 'There aren't any Bournemouth flights,' he sighed. 'The quickest route for us would be flying via Amsterdam and we'd still miss the snatch by about three hours.'

Archie leaned across his friend and opened his desk drawer, grabbing a pile of euro notes. 'These'll come in handy,' he muttered. 'Now, where did I put my rucksack?'

'Archie!' said Barney loudly. 'Did you hear me? There aren't any flights we can catch that will get us there in time.'

Archie looked at his friend and allowed a smile to tweak the corners of his mouth.

'I didn't say we're going to *catch a flight*,' he said. 'I said we'll have to *take a plane*.'

153

Chapter 20

Three minutes later Archie and Barney rendezvoused at the front door of the house. Barney had been to the kitchen and filled the rucksack with provisions for their mission while Archie had spent the short period on the iMac computer in his father's study.

'Ready?' asked Archie.

Barney beamed and shrugged. 'Whatever you've got planned, I'm ready.'

'Nan!' Archie called as he opened the door. 'I'm just going out with Barney – I'll see you later.'

'All right, love,' came the distant reply. 'You two be careful now.'

Archie slammed the font door behind him and led Barney along the wide gravel path that swept through the grounds of his home. Two hundred yards from the house the path split in two. A short distance straight ahead stood the front gates of the Hunt estate leading on to the main road, but Archie took the path that branched off at ninety degrees, towards a large copse of fir trees. The gravel guided the boys through a narrow gap in the trees, which concealed a flat lawn that was about half the size of a football pitch. A large silver structure with a curved roof stood at the far corner of the grass square. The wall of firs hemmed the quadrangle on all four sides, hiding the building and its setting from public gaze.

Archie led Barney across the grass and they paused at the door of the silver building.

'Your dad's hangar?' puzzled Barney. 'What are we doing here?'

'You'll see,' said Archie, typing a six-digit code into the security keypad. With a soft mechanical purr the door slid to one side, revealing the sleek, shark-like silhouette of the twin-engine jet plane inside.

'There she is,' smiled Archie, flicking a row of four wall-mounted switches at once. 'The Dragonfly.'

Within a few seconds the four overhead strip lights flashed and buzzed into life, reflecting like go-faster stripes on the aircraft's elegant brushed-aluminium curves.

Archie placed a hand on the plane's nose as if it was a racehorse then he ducked down to inspect its tyres. Standing upright he briskly circled the machine, allowing his hand to trail along the swept-back leading edges of its wings and gently spinning the blades of its two turbines.

'Er, what are you doing?' asked Barney, a note of impatience filtering into his voice.

'Pre-flight checks,' said Archie, stepping into the foothold in the fuselage just below the pilot's seat and pulling himself up.

'Pre-flight?' echoed Barney. 'Don't tell me this thing can fly itself to Hamburg?'

Twisting a bright red latch on top of the glass dome that encompassed the entire cockpit, Archie smiled. 'Of course it can't fly itself,' he laughed, sliding the canopy open. 'I'm going to fly it. Jump in.'

Archie stepped into the cockpit and sat in the soft leather seat. He fastened his three-pointed lap straps and began preparing the plane for take-off, sweeping his hands over the instrument panels, pushing buttons and flicking switches.

156

'Are you coming or what?' he asked Barney, who was still standing at the doorway, his mouth slightly open. 'I'm going to be ready to take off in about two minutes and I'd really like you to come with me.'

Still in a daze, Barney skirted the Dragonfly's rounded nose and hoisted himself up on the right-hand side of the cockpit.

'So you can actually fly this thing?' he asked, sliding into the seat next to Archie.

'Pretty much,' Archie replied, taking a USB stick from his pocket and pushing it into a port on the plane's navigation computer. 'My dad started showing me the ropes a couple of years ago.'

'Funny you never mentioned it.'

The USB stick contained the flight plan to a small airfield called Finkenwerder, situated just ten miles south-west of Hamburg's main airport. Richard Hunt had visited the airfield regularly because many of the Dragonfly's components were assembled there.

Archie's phone started ringing again.

'Hello?'

'Yankee, this is X-ray. I've done some digging around in the Atomic Salon gallery's electronic records. They have a large party of kids from South London booked in this afternoon. They're on a joint field trip. The two schools are called Saint Peter's and Saint Joseph's. I thought it might provide you with a neat cover story if you need it.'

'Thanks. Listen, I have to go. My plane's about to leave.'

'OK. Good luck.'

Archie hung up and slipped the phone into the pocket of his hoody.

'Seriously . . . how come you never told me you were learning to fly?' asked Barney, gazing round the cockpit in wonderment like a kid at Disneyland.

'I wasn't allowed to.' Archie flicked two switches, opening the fuel valves and initiating the engine start sequence. 'My dad could have lost his licence if the CAA had found out he was letting me take the controls.'

A high-pitched whine echoed round the hangar as the two turbines accelerated to 10,000 rpm and the bittersweet aroma of aviation fuel filled the air. Archie pulled on his shoulder straps and slotted them into their circular buckle then, placing his headset over his ears, he adjusted the boom mic so that it was about an inch from his lips.

Flicking on the intercom, Archie spoke into his microphone. 'How do you read?'

'Wow, an intercom – cool.' Barney adjusted his mic. 'Reading you loud and clear, over.'

'So, are you ready for our first mission, Agent Zulu?'

Pale-faced, Barney smiled bravely and gave a thumbs up. 'Game on! Over.'

Archie released the Dragonfly's park brake and the plane rolled forward, gliding out of the hangar and bouncing gently on the grass as it taxied into the centre of the square field. Holding the plane steady on the toe-brakes Archie ran through his pre-take-off drills from memory.

'Er . . . Archie? What did you mean when you said you can "pretty much" fly this thing, over?' Barney asked with a sudden forcefulness that suggested he'd been bottling the question up for some time.

Archie smiled. 'Like I said, when we went flying my dad let me do practically all the handling. I can do a wicked loop, a flick roll – all sorts. There's only a handful of manoeuvres I've never quite managed on my own.' He gripped the control column in his left hand and began to ease the thrust levers forward with his right.

159

'What sort of manoeuvres, over?' demanded Barney urgently.

'Oh, I don't know,' Archie said evasively. 'Recovering from a spiral dive is really tricky.' He slid a lever backwards, directing the engines' thrust vertically downward through the four controllable nozzles. Meanwhile he continued to ease the thrust levers forward, tentatively increasing the power output from the engines.

'Anything else, over?' Barney badgered.

The whine from the engines was now more like a scream and the whole aircraft was vibrating with the immense force building beneath its wings. Archie felt both exhilarated and terrified, like a rodeo rider sitting astride a wild bull that was about to be let loose.

'Well?' Barney persisted.

'OK, OK . . . there's also . . . well, I've never *actually* done the take-off myself,' Archie admitted.

'You what?' shrieked Barney. 'Over!'

A wave of anxiety hit Archie, washing away his determination. Barney was right. What was he thinking? He couldn't fly the Dragonfly all the way to Germany on his own! Even hovering the plane was outside his capabilities, never mind the delicate business of climbing away from the tight landing pad without crashing into the wall of fir trees. As if waking from a thrilling dream, Archie realised that his plan had been impossibly fanciful. He would have to go back to the house and inform Highwater they'd been unable to get to Hamburg in time.

But just as he had decided to close the thrust levers, the Dragonfly leaped into the air.

Chapter 21

'WHOA!' cried Archie as the plane rose and lurched forward.

Instinctively he pulled the stick back, and the plane shot backwards. Fifty feet off the ground, the Dragonfly was reversing at a terrific rate straight towards the hangar.

'Watch out, over!' screamed Barney.

Reacting quickly, Archie pushed the stick forward.

The plane continued powering backwards.

'I don't suppose this thing has bumpers, over?' Barney yelped, looking over his shoulder at the approaching hangar.

Holding his breath, Archie waited.

The Dragonfly's nose bobbed downward, and with

its tail no more than six inches from the hangar roof the plane came to a motionless hover. A moment later it started to edge forward, slowly at first but picking up speed rapidly. Soon it was careering towards the trees ahead.

The memory of his previous outing in the Dragonfly flashed through Archie's mind – his father taking over to rescue the plane from certain disaster. His hands froze on the controls. I can't do this, he thought. I can't fly this thing on my own.

'WE'RE GOING TO DIE! . . . OVER.'

Barney's terrified wail interrupted his thoughts.

Taking off some power, Archie desperately kicked in some rudder and snapped the control column to the right. The plane pirouetted and lurched sideways, its right wing dropping as it swooped.

'We're going down,' Barney gabbled, staring at the lawn racing up towards him. 'Archie! If you don't do something sharpish it'll all be over, over.'

Centralising the control stick to lift the wing, Archie pushed the thrust levers forward until they hit the stops. The engines responded with a tremendous roar and slowly but surely the Dragonfly's descent slowed. Only yards above the ground it hovered briefly then started to climb, as if bouncing on an invisible trampoline.

'We're going to hit the trees!' Barney yelped. 'We're not going to make it over, over.'

'We'll be OK,' said Archie, not daring to move the controls. He'd realised that hovering the Dragonfly was like keeping a ball bearing balanced in the middle of a smooth plate. Now that he had the jet under some sort of control he didn't want to upset its balance if he could possibly avoid it.

Both boys watched in silence as the aircraft listed towards the treetops.

Barney squeezed his eyes shut, while Archie remained transfixed by the ragged green wall that stood between them and clear blue sky.

'Hold tight!' Archie instructed.

There was a harsh scraping and snapping sound as the Dragonfly's undercarriage crashed through the foliage – then it was clear.

Neither boy spoke for a moment.

'Did we make it?' asked Barney, his eyes still screwed tightly shut. 'Is it all over, over?'

'Course we made it!' Archie laughed with sheer relief. 'We're off to a flying start.'

Barney opened one eye and tentatively peered round then, satisfied there was no immediate danger, he opened the other. 'Is it normal to crash into the trees on take-off? Over.'

Archie shrugged. 'I was just hedging my jets.'

'It's funny – I'm normally a nervous flyer,' Barney said. 'So I'm surprised I stayed so cool. I guess at times like that the agent in you just takes over, over.'

'Cool? Oh sure.' Archie fought to hide his smile. 'Which film was it again, when James Bond screamed like a girl, "We're going to die"?'

'I was just providing you with a real-time worst-case scenario.' Barney sulked. 'Over and out.'

'Well, we can relax now,' Archie replied, his pulse slowly returning to normal. 'From now on it's going to be plane sailing.' He eased the nozzle lever forward, gradually returning the Dragonfly to normal flight mode. The aircraft accelerated to three hundred knots as it speared through the sky.

Archie dialled a frequency into the plane's VHF radio and clicked the transmit switch.

'London Control, this is Hoverbird zero one,' he said, trying to sound authoritative. 'We're climbing to altitude six thousand feet, currently overhead

Christchurch harbour and requesting airways clearance.'

'Good afternoon, Hoverbird zero one.' Archie found the air traffic controller's calm tone strangely reassuring. 'Route direct to Southampton VOR to join the Upper November eight-six-six to Brookman's Park then as filed. Climb flight level two, two zero.'

Archie read back his instructions and banked the aircraft hard left to head for the Southampton radio beacon.

'Next stop Hamburg,' he said. 'Let's take in a gallery – and stake out some bad guys.'

Chapter 22

As they cruised over Amsterdam at thirty thousand feet, Archie was getting the feel of the plane and starting to enjoy the sense of exhilaration he got from being in command. Barney was getting hungry.

'Zulu to Yankee,' Barney announced excitedly into his intercom. 'Come in, Yankee, do you read, over?'

Archie looked at his friend who was no more than two feet away. 'Uh, I'm right here, Barney,' he said. 'Of course I read you. What is it?'

'Zulu to Yankee, would you like something to eat, over?'

'Barney,' Archie explained gently, 'you don't have to keep saying "over".'

'Roger, wilco and copy that, over.' Barney was

167

frowning earnestly. 'I say again – would you like something to eat, over?'

'What have you got?' asked Archie.

Barney pushed his face into the open rucksack on his lap. 'Mars bars, Twix, Dairy Milk, Jaffa Cakes . . .'

Archie smiled. 'Have you filled that entire bag with chocolates and biscuits?'

'Negative, over,' Barney said, sounding offended. 'I brought two packets of crisps, over.'

'That's what I call a balanced diet. Twix then, please.'

'Roger that. One Twix coming over, over.'

As Archie bit into his chocolate bar the clipped accent of the German air traffic controller came into his headset. 'Hoverbird zero one, descend to flight level one hundred, fly direct to Lima Bravo Echo.'

Archie repeated the instructions then chopped the power and lowered the aircraft's nose two degrees, putting the Dragonfly into a glide descent towards Hamburg.

Passing ten thousand feet the details of the landscape below were beginning to emerge. The rectangles of green, brown and yellow that covered the flat countryside developed different textures that seemed to breathe in the gentle easterly breeze. The cars that dotted the straight grey autobahns were beetling along, carrying the residents of northern Germany about their daily routines. And ahead, beyond the shimmering silver swathe of the river Elbe, lurked the buildings of Hamburg – shrouded in a pale haze.

Archie clicked his transmit switch and spoke to the controller. 'Radar, Hoverbird zero one request.'

'Go ahead, Hoverbird zero one.'

'We'd like to leave controlled airspace and continue visually for some general handling before landing at Finkenwerder.'

'That is approved, Hoverbird zero one. Remain outside controller airspace at all times, not above five thousand feet.'

'What's going on, over?' asked Barney, swallowing the last of his snack. 'I thought we were going to Finkenwerder, over.'

Archie pursed his lips and shook his head. 'If we land at an airfield we'll have to deal with customs and passport control. I have a feeling they might have a problem with me flying this plane on my own.' As he spoke he glanced at the digital clock on the Dragonfly's instrument panel. It was three fifteen.

'Our only chance is to find a landing site close to the gallery.'

'When you say "landing site" . . .' Barney probed, 'what exactly do you mean, over?'

Archie shrugged. 'Some sort of field, I suppose.' As he spoke he pushed the plane's nose down and, reaching across the centre console, switched off its transponder. He glanced at his friend. 'Get ready – we're going in under the radar,' he said. Switching off his radio he added, 'And we're going dark on comms.'

For a moment Barney looked terrified, but then his cheeks reddened as he broke into a wide grin. 'Sweet,' he said. 'Over.'

Archie pulled the thrust levers back to slow the plane to two hundred knots as they crossed a motorway running north to south, parallel to a railway line. Just to the east of the track was a small housing estate, beyond which Archie spotted a large rectangular field.

He slowed the plane to one hundred and forty knots and, extending some wing flap, positioned the aircraft about a mile to the south-west of the landing site.

'OK, wish me luck,' Archie gulped, gently easing the nozzle lever backwards.

'We're all counting on you, over,' said Barney.

By the time Archie had fully engaged 'hover mode' and the aircraft's forward momentum had dissipated, the plane had drifted to the far end of the field. Gently Archie tweaked the control stick backwards. The plane's nose bobbed up a few degrees and it began to reverse while Archie peered downward over his shoulder to judge his position.

When the wings were over the middle of the field he nudged the stick forward briefly, before holding it neutral.

The plane hung motionless, two hundred feet in the air.

'We're hovering!' Archie laughed. 'We're actually hovering!'

'Brilliant,' said Barney. 'Now put us down – we haven't got time to hang around.'

Very slowly Archie eased the thrust levers back a short way, freezing his hand when he felt the aircraft start to descend. Looking ahead, he watched the lush grass rising to meet him, as if he was riding a glass elevator down to the field. A moment later there was a jolt as the undercarriage hit the ground.

'Welcome to Hamburg.' Archie's front teeth

protruded over his bottom lip as he beamed with relief. 'I hope you enjoyed your trip. Please take all your personal belongings with you when you leave the plane.'

He taxied the plane to the edge of the field and swung it under the overhanging bough of a large beech tree before cutting the engines and shutting down all the aircraft systems.

Archie stepped out of the cockpit and jumped to the ground. Opening a small hatch on the plane's rear fuselage that contained three Gortex bags, he removed the one labelled 'Jungle' and tore it open. The other two bags were labelled 'Desert' and 'Urban'.

'What's that?' asked Barney.

'A camo' cover,' Archie said, shaking out a large green net festooned with canvas leaves in various shades of green. 'Come on – help me throw it over the plane. We have to be quick.'

The Dragonfly's standard spec included three camouflage covers designed for different environments. The Red Cross used them in the field and they'd been included as a bit of a gimmick for private owners.

Archie and Barney stretched the mesh out and hurriedly draped it over the jet plane. When they had finished the aircraft's distinctive silhouette merged with the trees and hedges behind it, rendering it invisible to all but the keenest observer.

A minute later Archie and Barney were sprinting across the field towards the edge of the housing estate. Finding themselves on Kirchdorfer Strasse, they headed north towards the city.

'What's the time?' Barney wheezed, lagging ten yards behind Archie.

'Quarter to four,' Archie replied.

'We'll never make it.'

Archie reached a T-junction and scanned the road in both directions. 'Taxi!' he yelled.

A cream Mercedes pulled up next to the kerb and both boys jumped in, sliding across the black leather seat.

'Guten tag,' said Archie. 'Aus Glashuttenstrasse, bitte, der gallery Atomic Salon.'

173

Chapter 23

The taxi dropped Archie and Barney outside number nineteen Glashuttenstrasse and pulled away.

The Atomic Salon gallery was a narrow building in the middle of a tall terrace of shops and restaurants. Hanging in the window was a collage of iconic faces, including Batman and an astronaut who Archie assumed was Neil Armstrong.

'Bingo,' he said, glancing at his watch. 'And we've still got five minutes to spare. Let's go.'

Barney grabbed Archie's arm and pulled him back.

'What's up?' Archie asked.

'We need to brief the op,' Barney whispered, scanning the street furtively.

'Oh, right,' said Archie. 'Here's the plan. We go in.

We look around pretending to admire the paintings, and when someone gets kidnapped we try and get a good look at the bad guys.'

Barney had already started shaking his head before Archie was even halfway through his idea. 'Negative,' he muttered. 'Before we go active we need to establish our entry point and exit strategy.'

'Well, I don't know about you,' said Archie, glancing at the gallery and back to Barney. 'But I was sort of planning to use the front door – for both.'

'In and out through the main door, copy that,' Barney said with an air of faint disappointment.

The door was locked so Archie pressed the buzzer. After a short wait it was opened by a tall man with a shaved head and a large tummy that strained against a tight pink T-shirt.

'Guten tag,' Archie said in an obviously English accent, adding slowly. 'Can we come in?'

'Membership cards, please,' the man whined, twirling an outstretched hand towards the boys. Anticipating the likely response, he stepped forward, as if to plug the entrance with his tummy. 'Vee are having a friends and invited guests day at the gallery. If

175

you are not members then I'm afraid you cannot enter herein.'

'No worries,' Archie replied, thinking on his feet. 'We're from Saint Peter's school, yeah? We just want to catch up with the rest of our class.'

The man tilted his head back while he considered the boy's claim, his eyes widened and his nostrils flared.

'This I vill have to check,' he said at last. 'You vill vait here.'

The door closed and the boys watched through the window.

'Man, he's bringing a teacher over,' Archie groaned.

'We're toast,' muttered Barney.

Before the boys had a chance to formulate a plan, the door swung open and the man gestured to them with a flamboyant sweep of his arm. 'Here they are.'

A woman with frizzy grey hair and ruddy cheeks looked at them inquisitively.

'Hello, Miss,' Archie said brightly.

'Er, hello,' the woman answered with a frown. 'What are you doing here, boys?'

While he tried to think how to answer the question Archie smiled angelically at the lady. Perhaps used to

176

asking unanswered questions, the teacher tried another. 'Are you from Saint Joseph's – in Mr Jenkins's group?'

'Yes, Miss,' Archie replied.

'And you've finished your tour already?'

'Yes, Miss,' Barney piped up. 'It was hilarious fun.'

'The war museum was hilarious fun?'

'He means we learned a lot about the sacrifices people made during the war,' Archie offered. 'Anyway, the two of us went to the loo and when we came out our group had left. Luckily we remembered your group was coming here.'

'I see,' the teacher said curtly. 'Naturally I'll have to talk to Mr Jenkins about this matter.' Feeling the need to justify her ignorance she said to the man from the gallery, 'We're on a joint trip with forty kids from another school, you see. How on earth they expect us to learn everyone's name . . .'

The man said nothing but his eyes and nostrils expanded while his lips tightened.

'So, what are your names, boys?' asked the woman.

'Erm . . .' Archie's eyes flicked to the painting in the window. 'I'm Armstrong.'

'And you?'

Barney paused before answering. Sensing what was

going through his friend's mind Archie gave him a narrow-eyed glare, but there was no deterring Barney, who raised one eyebrow and said, 'The name's Bond.'

'If you say so,' the teacher said wearily. 'All right, Armstrong and Bond, come in and join the rest of the year group – and for heaven's sake don't get lost again.'

'No, Miss,' the boys mumbled as they entered the gallery.

The teacher rolled her eyes at the man. 'Kids!' she exclaimed.

Apart from the throng of schoolchildren sprawled across the room, a handful of adults were scattered around the gallery, studying the collection of paintings, sketches and cartoons that filled every available inch of wall space.

Archie and Barney positioned themselves at the far end of the school group, frowning appreciatively at the pictures on display as they tried to discreetly assess everyone else in the room.

Perusing one wall was a smartly dressed elderly couple. Further along a young couple, wearing denim jackets and carrying motorbike helmets, were admiring

178

a portrayal of David Beckham as a saint, complete with gold-leaf halo.

Three people were looking at the display on the opposite wall. Judging by his posture and size, one was a teenager with the hood of his grey sweatshirt covering his head. Next to him stood a young man with a ponytail and straggly beard, the sleeves of his orange fleece pushed up to show his strong sinewy arms. The third character wore a black leather trench coat belted tightly round his impossibly small waist, the collar turned up to meet the baseball cap on his head. He was clutching a polythene bag in one hand and holding a chocolate bar in the other.

'Man, I'm starving,' Barney groaned.

'Let's try and concentrate on the mission,' Archie whispered. 'We've got about thirty seconds.'

'Well, I'm not sure who the target is,' Barney replied, 'but that couple in denim look well dodgy. I mean, you have to ask yourself what they're doing carrying those helmets.'

'It's a long shot but maybe they came on a motorbike,' Archie whispered. 'Like the one parked outside?'

Barney glanced through the window and saw a petrol blue Yamaha 950 tourer standing next to the kerb. 'Boy, they're good,' he whispered knowingly. 'The fox is going to stalk the ugly ducklings and see if they're really swans.'

'Right-oh,' said Archie. He watched Barney cross the gallery and stand unnaturally close to the female biker.

Sensing his presence, she turned and asked sharply, 'Kann ich ihnen helfen?'

Cheeks glowing, Barney smiled innocently and said, 'Na, ich just looken aus die picturos.' As the couple edged away from him Barney turned and gave Archie a furtive thumbs up.

'Way to keep a low profile, Barney,' Archie muttered to himself. Turning to take in his surroundings, he felt a strange sense of unease creeping up his spine. Something wasn't right, but he couldn't for the life of him pinpoint exactly what it was. It was as if he was looking at a photograph that was slightly out of focus.

Once again he studied each person in the room, his stomach tightening with the growing feeling that he was missing something obvious.

'The bag!' Archie said aloud as the blurred picture pulled into focus.

The plastic bag carried by the skinny figure in the leather trench coat bore some nondescript green writing. The words were all creased up because he was clutching the bag by its neck but in a flash Archie had just realised that the scrunched-up letters spelled the words Bure Stores – the name of the newsagent less than a mile from his father's house. The brightness of the bag's coloured lettering suggested it had probably been pulled off the roll at the checkout within the last seven days. What were the chances of this man having been to Archie's local shop less than a week ago? Either it was a pretty unbelievable coincidence, or he was looking at the person who'd run his father's car off the road a couple of days ago. Archie didn't believe in coincidences.

His heart racing, he spun on his heel and saw instantly that his suspicions were correct.

'Barney!' he yelled. 'Look!'

Barney turned and followed his friend's pointing finger towards the front of the gallery. The figure in the grey hoody was holding the door open while the skinny guy in the black trench coat was backing out on to the street. And he was dragging the bearded man in the orange fleece with him!

181

No one else had noticed what was happening. Realising he was the only one who could stop the kidnap, Archie rushed for the door. Immediately Barney followed but he was still at least fifteen metres away.

Nimbly Archie sidestepped a teacher and weaved between two pupils. But then he was engulfed by a group of schoolkids.

All he could do was watch as the skinny man abducted the target. One exceptionally long leather-clad arm was clamped around the bearded man's chest, the other over his mouth to stifle his protests. The figure in the hoody followed them through the door, which slammed shut behind them.

'They've got him!' Archie despaired as he broke through the crowd. 'Right from under our noses.'

'Why didn't anyone stop them?' Barney gasped.

Archie nodded to the two bikers who were facing the door, smiling and clapping politely. 'They think it was some kind of show, like a play or something.'

'Oh yeah, that famous play *Man Kidnapped from Gallery*.' Barney sighed. 'We need to call this in to IC.'

Archie looked thoughtful for a moment.

'Or . . . we could go after them ourselves,' he suggested. 'Come on!'

Chapter 24

Archie pelted across the tiled floor, yanked open the gallery door and rushed out on to the pavement where the two kidnappers were manhandling the bearded man along the street. The victim was bucking and thrusting furiously but the man in the trench coat had a vice-like grip on his torso. The hooded youth was holding the man's ankles together and wrapping duct tape around them. The victim's wrists were also bound tightly with tape.

As Archie started running towards the car he heard Barney exiting the gallery behind him.

'Do not engage,' Barney wheezed. 'I repeat, do not engage.'

But Archie was sure the kidnappers were the same

people who had run his father off the road and he had only one thing on his mind as he sprinted along the pavement.

'Stand down, Agent Yankee,' Barney puffed half-heartedly, before throwing his hands up in despair and joining the chase.

When Archie reached the kidnappers they were bundling their victim into the back seat of a BMW parked fifty yards from the gallery.

'Let him go!' he shouted, grabbing the hooded youth's arm and pulling him off his captive's legs.

The figure turned and squared up to Archie, who intuitively dropped to a crouch and jabbed his right fist into his opponent's stomach, doubling him over. Immediately Archie swung his leg in a horizontal arc along the ground, sweeping the kidnapper's feet from under him and knocking him flat on to his back.

Watching from a distance, Barney's mouth fell open. 'Where *did* he learn to kick butt like that?'

Leaping over his prostrate adversary, Archie threw himself at the other kidnapper from behind, clinging to his black leather coat like a wildcat attacking an antelope. The man's shoulders felt eerily wiry under Archie's grip. Ignoring the boy grappling with him he concentrated on bundling the bearded man into the BMW before closing and locking the door. Only then did he stand upright, lifting Archie's feet a metre off the ground. With a small but powerful flick of his shoulders he swung Archie off his back, grabbing one wrist and one ankle as the boy tumbled towards the pavement.

Barney watched in horror as the tall skinny figure swung his friend back and forth a couple of times before effortlessly tossing him away as if he were no heavier than a sack of rubbish. Archie's arms and legs flailed helplessly as he sailed into the air before coming down hard on the pavement about twenty feet away, grunting loudly as the impact punched the wind out of his lungs.

'Hey!' Barney yelled, rushing to help Archie to his feet.

The tall skinny man strode towards Barney with a jerky gait, as if he was walking on stilts. By now the youth in the hoody had recovered from Archie's attack and he too approached the boys, walking with a teenage hip-hop limp.

Archie and Barney stood shoulder to shoulder, considering the double trouble closing in on them.

'I don't like the look of the tall guy,' muttered Barney. 'His head's way too small and his legs have got too many joints.'

'And he's freakishly strong,' added Archie. 'Not to mention creepily wiry.'

As Archie spoke the teenager's hood slipped back, revealing a wide, flat head that appeared to be covered in rotting scales. His bulbous eyes stared unblinking from either side of his skull while his fat-lipped mouth opened rhythmically into a perfect circle.

'As for him,' said Archie, his pulse racing out of control, 'there's definitely something fishy about that guy.'

The two muggers stalked towards the boys.

Archie raised his hands in readiness, while bouncing lightly on the balls of his feet. 'Come on then, Fishface.'

'Yeah, come on then, Stickman,' goaded Barney, but with much less conviction.

Nobody moved for a moment then suddenly the fish-like boy rushed Archie, throwing a barrage of punches.

Archie responded without thinking, springing backwards to keep some distance from his attacker.

His arms were no more than a blur as he reacted to the flurry of punches coming at him, frantically thrashing his hands in front of his face. Only when there was a lull in his attacker's advance did Archie realise that he hadn't been struck once.

Driven by sudden confidence, Archie rallied with an onslaught of his own. As if his arms were being controlled by some unseen ninja he threw three, four, five stiff, straight blows that connected with his opponent's body, driving him backwards across the pavement. When the fishy kid attempted his own counter-attack, Archie stood his ground, allowing the mugger to come within striking range before retaliating. Planting his left foot, he leaned back then fired out his right leg like a piston that drove into his enemy's solar plexus, leaving him curled up on the ground, gasping for breath.

'Where did that come from?' Barney asked, his eyes bulging with amazement.

'I've no idea!' Archie laughed, staring at his own hands as if he'd never seen them before. 'I just relaxed, I suppose. Let my instincts guide me – just like my dad told me to do.' To underline his newfound expertise, Archie unleashed another flurry of punches to warn off the wiry guy, finishing with a spectacular jumping back-kick. When he landed he looked up to see that his enemy was no longer lurking. Thinking he had scared the stickman away he turned, laughing and panting, to enjoy Barney's reaction, then a tide of utter terror engulfed him.

The stickman had Barney by the throat, holding him at arm's length three feet off the ground in a frightening display of his strength. Barney's face was deep purple and his eyes were swollen. A strangled choking noise escaped sporadically from his gaping mouth. His feet were kicking wildly but Archie could tell his friend's fight was fading.

Chapter 25

Emitting the sort of scream you might expect from someone being dunked in a bath of boiling water, Archie sprinted across the pavement and launched himself at Barney's attacker.

'Haaaiii-yyaaahh!'

Driving one knee upward to propel himself as high as possible, he leaned back so that his body and legs made one straight horizontal line. Like a human torpedo, Archie speared through the air. His aim couldn't have been sweeter and his feet hit his opponent's upper torso with immense force.

'Ooooff!' He felt as if he'd just launched himself against a brick wall. His joints crumpled, his knees buckled up to his chin and he fell stunned to the floor.

Only when Archie lay groaning at his feet did the strange mugger acknowledge his presence, turning his head briefly and stooping to get a close look at him.

Staring up from the ground, Archie caught his first glimpse of the face hidden beneath the peaked cap and turned-up collar – and what he saw chilled his bones to their marrow.

The man's head was covered in glossy orange skin and horribly deformed, as if it had been squashed and stretched into an elongated egg shape. What looked at first glance like a dollop of frogspawn on either side of his enemy's head Archie quickly realised were two clusters of tiny eyeballs, each one staring menacingly at him. Protruding from the creature's cuff was a segmented orange arm that was no thicker than a broom handle and covered in thorny white hairs. At its extremity the limb split into two pointed digits that were wrapped around Barney's neck with lethal force.

'Wh-what are you?' Archie stammered.

Two hooked fangs protruded from the end of the strange man's bullet-shaped snout and clashed together like pincers. 'Your worst nightmare,' he growled.

'I've had worse nightmares than this,' Archie bluffed. Trying to reverse along the pavement on his bottom he quickly considered his options. His only hope was to distract his enemy from his goal. 'The other night I dreamed I'd turned up naked for French. Now *that* was scary.'

The stickman appeared confused for a moment as he pondered Archie's dream and, just for a moment, relaxed his grip on Barney's throat. As Archie had hoped, this allowed the blood to flow freely to his friend's brain once again.

Suddenly Barney sprang to life, slipping the rucksack off his shoulder. It was surprisingly hefty due to the supplies he'd loaded for the journey and he swung it round at arm's length, bringing it crashing against the skinny man's head. The blow made little impression on the powerful mugger – apart from knocking his cap off – while the contents of the bag, which had been left unzipped, exploded into the air before raining down on the pavement in a junk-food shower.

The stickman stared at Barney, two hairy antennae standing upright on his smooth skull and twitching eagerly in the air.

'Hey, Baldy!' called Archie, jumping to his feet and waving his hands in the air. 'Don't waste your time on him. Come and get me.'

Instantly the odd-looking man released his grip on Barney, who dropped to the ground like a bag of cement, and turned to face Archie.

'Yikes,' muttered Archie, glancing left and right. 'I was only trying to distract you – I didn't expect you to take me seriously.'

Archie backed away as the strange creature strode towards him, his mandibles thrashing together hungrily. Then a peculiar expression crept over the man's face, and he dropped to his knees. Ripping open a packet of Maltesers that had fallen from Barney's bag, he tilted his head back and poured in the chocolate balls, munching and swallowing the whole lot in a second. Frantically the mutant crawled a few yards on all fours before tearing open and devouring a Bounty and a Mars bar in quick succession.

Archie watched with bemusement as the freakish stranger scrabbled about on the ground, scavenging for sweets with the desperate hunger of a stray dog. Freed from the paralysing stranglehold, Barney had regained consciousness and clambered to his feet.

'Hey, Buster,' he called defiantly. 'Keep your weird feeler-type hands off my sweets.'

Only as the villain turned and scurried away to

retrieve a far-flung chocolate bar did the perfect plan of action formulate in Archie's mind. In a flash he communicated its essence to Barney.

'Run for it!' he yelled.

Fifteen seconds later Archie was a hundred yards down the street, pumping his legs and punching the air. Behind him he could hear the wail of approaching sirens but it was too late for the Polizei to help. As he rounded a ninety-degree corner into a side street he glanced back up Glashuttenstrasse to check that Barney had followed his lead safely.

The good news was that the stickman was still on all fours shovelling sweets into his mandibles and Barney was just a few yards behind Archie. The bad news was that the boy with the fish face had recovered from Archie's karate kick and was now a few yards behind Barney. And closing in fast.

Chapter 26

'Hurry!' Archie hollered. 'He's right behind you!'

Archie slowed down just enough to allow Barney to catch up with him before speeding up again. Not daring to check their tail, the boys pelted to the end of the side street and took a right. Immediately Archie grabbed Barney's sweatshirt and pulled him behind a parked car.

For what seemed like an hour the two boys crouched behind the vehicle as their breathing subsided, their backs pressed against its metallic grey flank. At last Archie turned and raised his head slowly until his eyeline was just above the car's bonnet.

'I think we lost him,' he whispered tentatively. 'Whatever *he* was.'

'Copy that,' replied Barney, squinting over the car. 'It looks like the mice have slipped through the, er, net . . . We're the mice, by the way.'

'Yeah, I gathered that,' Archie replied, keeping his eyes trained on the street corner. His head was spinning as he tried to come to terms with the weird characters he'd just fought. 'I don't know what we've got ourselves into but those guys were freaks,' he panted. 'The tall one looked like some sort of *insect* or something.'

'I know,' Barney added. 'And that guy chasing us was a real *fish out of water*.'

'Very good,' chuckled Archie.

'It's sort of espionage humour,' explained Barney. 'Spies always crack a joke when they've outsmarted a bad guy.'

'Really?' Archie asked sceptically. 'When you say spies, I take it you mean . . .'

'James Bond,' Barney admitted sheepishly, adding, 'and Alex Rider does it sometimes.'

'Oh well, in that case . . .' Archie thought for a moment. 'We may have given him the slip but I bet there's plenty more fish in the sea.' As he spoke an unpleasant salty aroma wafted into his nostrils.

'I know what you mean.' Barney sniggered. 'Shouldn't he be in *school* anyway?'

'Mind you,' Archie smirked, 'when I'd finished with him he was *battered*.'

'Maybe he was fighting you just for the *hake* of it,' said a timid, slurpy voice behind them.

Archie and Barney froze for a moment before exchanging expressions of silent surprise. As one they slowly turned round, their hearts drumming hard in their chests.

'Whoa!' Archie exclaimed, understanding the source of the odd smell he'd detected. Barney grabbed his sleeve and squeezed his arm.

Standing just a yard away from them, his bulbous eyes trained on the corner of the street and his mouth making a circular hole in his scaly head, was the fishy-looking creature.

'I don't think he's coming,' he whispered. 'I think we've given him the slip.'

'Right,' said Archie uncertainly. 'Just as a matter of interest . . . who are you running away from?'

The boy took his eyes off the street and looked at Archie. 'Anybody,' he said with a dismissive shrug.

'Anybody?' Archie repeated.

196

'Whoever,' the fishy kid suggested vaguely. 'I don't really know, to be honest. I only legged it because you screamed, "Run for it." It seemed like a sensible thing to do at the time – especially with that weird gangly guy on the scene. I didn't like the look of him at all.'

'You were with him,' said Barney.

'Who?'

'The weird gangly guy.'

'There was a weird gangly guy?'

'Yeah.' Archie pushed his spectacles up the bridge of his nose. 'We were running away from both of you.'

'Really?' The strange boy sounded genuinely hurt. 'Why would you run away from me?'

'Er, because you attacked me?' Archie countered.

'You started it. I might have a terrible memory but I remember that clearly. You grabbed my arm and when I turned round you knocked me to the ground.'

'That is true,' Archie admitted guiltily. 'Sorry – but I only did it because I *thought* you were going to attack me.'

'Why would you think that?'

'Oh, I don't know,' said Barney harshly. 'Maybe it had something to do with the fact that you were bundling an innocent man into the back of a car?'

197

The boy looked horrified. 'What man?'

'The dude you and the weird gangly man dragged out of the gallery,' said Barney.

'What gallery? And who's the weird gangly man?'

Archie could see that the more questions he and Barney fired at the scaly-skinned kid the more confused and distressed he became. There was more to him than met the eye, Archie was sure. So he suggested going to a cafe to get something to eat. A short distance away they found an Italian restaurant where they sat at a table in the corner and ordered three pizzas.

'We haven't been properly introduced,' smiled Archie. 'I'm Archie and this is Barney.'

Barney raised a hand but didn't look up from his Four Cheese Pizza with extra cheese.

'Hi.' The fishy boy nodded from deep inside his hood, which he had flipped over his head as he'd entered the building.

'What's your name?' Archie probed gently.

'They call me Finn.'

'Who's they?'

'I dunno. Everyone.'

'Why did you come to Hamburg?'

198

'I don't remember, exactly.' Finn sighed and hung his head. 'There's this kind of professor, or whatever, who lives somewhere . . . else. He sends us all over the place.'

Archie gave Finn an encouraging smile. 'And why did he send you here?'

'I'm not exactly sure. I get so confused, you see. Collect something, I think.'

'Something or someone?'

'Can't remember,' Finn said angrily. 'I can't remember much at all since . . .'

Archie noticed that Finn was struggling to cut his food but the cutlery was slipping in his stubby, scaly fingers. He saw with a shock that Finn's hands were covered in scalloped flaps of skin, some of which hung loose in clumps.

'I can't be bothered eating this with a knife and fork,' Archie announced, tearing off a chunk of his pizza and taking a bite. 'It's much more fun to rip it up.'

Frowning, Barney looked up from his plate. 'Hey, you're the one who's always telling me not to eat with my fing— Ouch! Why are you kicking me?'

Archie ignored his friend's protests and smiled at Finn, who nodded gratefully and tore a piece off his pizza.

'Do you remember what happened to you?' Archie ventured at last.

'Not really,' Finn said bitterly. 'I was one of his experiments. He mixed me up with a fish – you know, genetically.'

'Why?' asked Archie, appalled.

'Part of his evil master plan, I suppose. Now I'm a really strong swimmer and I can breathe underwater – but I've literally got the memory of a goldfish.'

Archie said nothing and concentrated on not looking too shocked. He ignored Barney, who was silently mouthing, 'He's one of Doom's mutants!'

'And I'll tell you something else,' Finn added, licking stringy mozzarella off his fingers. 'I've got a memory like a goldfish too.'

'How long is your memory?' Archie enquired. 'Minutes? Seconds?'

'Depends,' said Finn, pausing to suck milkshake through a straw. 'I forget most things instantly – people, events, places. Sometimes I sense I've been somewhere before but the details will be hazy. Occasionally someone will say something and a whole load of memories come back to me but generally it's a case of "out of sight, out of mind".'

200

'So life's full of surprises?' Archie smiled grimly.

'I still get a shock every morning,' Finn said sadly. 'I go to the mirror in the bathroom and I see this hideous face for the first time.'

'What's this evil scientist called?' Archie probed.

'Which evil scientist?' Finn said blankly.

'If we can't find him we'll be doomed,' Archie commented, choosing his words carefully.

'Doctor Doom!' Finn announced. 'He's a professor experimenting on animals and people to research his evil plan to take over the world or something. He genetically crossed me with a fish. Now I'm a good swimmer but my memory's really short.'

Archie raised his eyebrows as if hearing Finn's revelation for the first time.

'Does Doctor Doom have any more genetic experiments in the pipeline?' Barney asked. 'Is the guy you nabbed from the gallery going to be crossed with a frog or something?'

Finn sat back and pressed the heels of his hands against his forehead. 'I don't know. I suppose so. Probably. Oh gosh, how did I get into this mess? I should have refused to help but I'm so easily influenced. I don't know right from wrong most of the time.'

'Don't worry,' Archie said resolutely. 'Everything's going to be OK. And, just for the record, we're the good guys.'

Archie excused himself from the table and followed the signs to the restaurant's toilets. Inside the Gents he locked himself in a cubicle, took out his mobile and dialled the number for STINKBOMB's Emergency Agent Recovery Unit, which Highwater had given to him.

'Hello?'

'SEARU?' Archie whispered.

'No, young man, I'm afraid you've got the wrong number.'

Archie rolled his eyes. 'Mr Grey!' he hissed. 'It's Agent Yankee.'

'Yankee,' Holden Grey exclaimed with surprise. 'Why didn't you say so?'

'I didn't expect to speak to you,' Archie explained. 'I thought this was the dedicated secure line to SEARU . . .'

'Searu . . . ?' Grey repeated slowly.

'Yes,' Archie said, lowering his voice even further. 'STINKBOMB's Emergency Agent Recovery Unit.'

'Oh, Sear-*u*!' Grey stressed the last syllable as if Archie's incorrect pronunciation had misled him. 'Yeah,

202

this is it, sure. I was just engaging in a little counter-espionage bluffery, in case you were the November Mike Echo, or enemy to you and me. It's the sort of advanced field ops procedure you'll learn about when you've mastered the basics.'

'So SEARU is just you?' Archie's voice was weak with disappointment. 'I thought it was a whole team of specialists.'

'No, of course it's not just me,' Grey laughed. 'IC and Agent X-ray are both here too and we make a pretty good team, even if we say so myselves.'

'Not exactly a crack team of SAS commandos though,' muttered Archie.

'What's the current situation, as we speak right now?' Grey enquired.

Archie cupped his hand over his mouth as he whispered into his mobile. 'The kidnap went down at four o'clock, as predicted. Two of them snatched this guy from the gallery and bundled him into a black BMW.'

Archie heard Holden Grey relating what he'd just heard to the others in the room. The sound of static rustling – as if someone was wiping the receiver – was followed by a moment of silence. The next voice Archie heard was Highwater's.

'Yankee, it's IC. We'll evaluate the mission in detail when we meet but, briefly, did you get a good look at the suspects?'

'Yup.'

'Is that all you've got to say?' Highwater snapped.

'Well, you said "briefly".' Archie sighed. 'OK, there was a tall skinny guy who was like an ant-man or something but had superhuman strength and another one who's half man, half fish.'

'All right, Yankee, I can do without your sarcasm, thank you,' said Highwater sternly. 'And, presumably, you followed orders and maintained your cover at all times during the operation?'

Archie rolled his eyes skyward as he considered his response. 'Well, I'm not sure if I would say "at all times", exactly.'

Highwater groaned. 'What makes you think they suspected you weren't ordinary art lovers?'

'Oh, I don't know, it's more of a gut feeling than anything,' Archie said evasively. 'I mean, I had a sort of fight with one of them and the other one nearly throttled Barney but it's hard to pinpoint at what stage *exactly* we'd properly broken cover.'

'You engaged them in a street brawl?' Highwater's

204

shriek pierced Archie's ear, causing him to yank his mobile away from his head.

'They started it,' Archie mumbled.

'This is not the playground, Agent Yankee.' Highwater's voice was now scarily quiet. 'We will discuss your behaviour another time. Right now we need to get you and Zulu to a safe house.'

'And Finn,' Archie interjected. 'He was one of the bad guys – but now he's a good guy. Actually, I think he always was a good guy – he just gets easily confused on account of having a goldfish brain. Anyway, I think he might be able to help us find Doctor Doom if we can jog his memory somehow.'

There was a long pause before Highwater spoke.

'I hope for your sake you are not treating this whole adventure as a joke,' she said calmly. 'In a few minutes you will receive a text message giving you the address of a safe location. Go there and sit tight until we contact you.'

'Got it,' Archie whispered.

'Oh, and Agent Yankee?'

'Yes?'

'Do try not to cause any more trouble.'

★

By the time Archie had joined Barney and Finn at the corner table, his mobile had bleeped twice, alerting him to an incoming text message:

Intercontinental Hotel
Rooms booked under David Zaster
Housekeeping will come at 10.00hrs to clean up mess

Archie read it once to himself then quietly to Barney and Finn.

'We'd better get the bill,' he suggested, attracting the waitress's attention.

'I don't get it,' said Barney, one side of his top lip curling up. 'Why are they sending housekeeping round? I mean, how do they even know we're going to mess up the room?'

Archie turned to his friend, his eyes wide with disbelief. 'I don't believe it,' he said, grinning. 'All this time you've been imagining coded messages everywhere you look and when you finally get a real one, you take it at face value.'

Barney cocked his head to one side, his face frozen in a confused snarl.

'I think housekeeping is code for STINKBOMB,' Archie whispered. 'And I think the mess they're referring to is the one we made of our surveillance mission.'

'Yeah, I knew that,' insisted Barney, a touch of pink seeping into his cheeks. 'I just wasn't sure if you knew it, that's all.'

'Sure.' Archie placed a few notes on the table with the bill and anchored them down with a pepper mill. 'Let's go.'

207

Chapter 27

Less than five minutes later Archie, Barney and Finn were in a taxi, on their way to the Intercontinental Hotel. Archie assumed that the freakish gangly man was by now well on *his* way to Dr Doom's hideout with his latest hostage, but nevertheless he had made absolutely sure the coast was clear before venturing out on to the pavement.

Inside the expansive hotel lobby Archie approached the sweeping reception desk, admiring the view of the lake through the plate glass windows while he waited to be served.

'Guten tag,' he said to the wide-eyed receptionist. 'I have a reservation in the name of Zaster – D. Zaster.'

As he spoke he realised the hidden meaning of

his false name and his heart drummed harder in anticipation of his official mission debrief.

The room key – a plastic card – was produced with brisk efficiency and Archie, Barney and Finn rode the lift to the tenth floor. Reaching their room, Archie was just about to slide the keycard into the locking mechanism when Barney placed a hand on his wrist.

'Wait!' Barney hissed, pressing his back and head against the wall next to the door. 'You open the door – I'll go in first. On three.'

'OK, whatever,' Archie said. 'One . . . two . . . three.' He slid the card into the slot below the doorknob, turned the handle when the green light flashed and pushed the door open.

Barney leaped into action, swinging through the doorway and throwing his back against the wall adjacent to the door of the en suite. Archie watched in amused silence as his friend felt blindly behind him for the bathroom door handle, his head twisting from side to side as he scanned the short entrance hall. Locating the knob, he turned it slowly before flinging the door open and throwing himself into the bathroom. Archie heard a succession of noises, which he identified in turn as a toilet seat being lifted, a shower curtain being aggressively swished back and a mirrored cabinet being yanked open – closely followed by the tinkle of a number of complimentary toiletries tumbling into a sink.

'Clear!' Barney yelled before emerging from the en suite and slamming his back against the side of the wardrobe.

Having stormed the closet – coming off second best to a selection of coat hangers – Barney edged along the wall and charged round the corner into the main body of the room. Archie and Finn waited in the corridor, listening to the sound of bedding being slung around and drawers being snatched open, punctuated by Barney shouting, 'Clear!' before tackling another inanimate object.

Some minutes later Barney reappeared in the doorway, his hair plastered to his head in tight, moist curls. 'I've secured the premises,' he panted, giving them a thumbs-up sign. 'The room is clean and unoccupied.'

'Great stuff,' said Archie, stepping through the doorway. 'Although I'm pretty sure that's how most hotel rooms come these days.'

★

Archie, Barney and Finn ordered cheeseburgers and Coke on room service and watched a film on the hotel pay-per-view channel. Just before going to bed Archie sent his grandmother a text message to say he was spending the night with Barney – which, he told himself, wasn't a *total* lie. He volunteered to sleep on the sofa bed and he lay awake thinking about the events of the last few days and listening to the snores of the other two.

It still didn't feel quite real. Who would have thought he would ever be an MI6 agent on the trail of an evil villain? When he imagined what Harvey Newman would say if he found out about his secret life he couldn't help but smile to himself.

But his amusement faded quickly when his thoughts turned inevitably to his father. Imagining him inside a giant test tube being filled up with acid or wired up to a machine while running on a giant wheel like a lab rat, Archie's stomach twisted into angry knots and his hands squeezed into fists of frustration.

More and more unanswerable questions crowded his head. How many genetically mutated monsters had Dr Doom made to research his ultimate creation? How exactly did he plan to take over the world? Was there really any chance Finn would be able to help them find the mad professor before it was too late?

Archie tossed and turned, unable to shake the thought that his impulsive actions at the gallery might have alerted Dr Doom that STINKBOMB was hot on his tail. Deep down he knew Finn's almost non-existent recall would prevent him from offering any substantial leads as to Doom's whereabouts.

Archie lay awake long into the night considering his plight. If Doom decided not to broadcast any more clues as to his intentions or whereabouts then STINKBOMB had no chance of preventing him from carrying out his twisted endeavours. And Archie would have no hope of saving his father from Doom's evil clutches.

The Now-Familiar

Secret Location

Somewhere

in Europe . . .

Again

Chapter 28

'So, let me get this straight, Antony,' mused Dr Doom, studying the rucksack he was holding. 'Two kids chased you out of the gallery and tried to stop you grabbing Mr Schumaker?'

The gangly figure slowly nodded his bullet-shaped head. 'I got hold of the chubby one but the other one gave Finn a good hiding.'

'Then you let the "chubby one" go?' Doom raised his human eyebrow in curiosity. 'How did that come about?'

Antony hesitated. 'He dropped that backpack.' Each word was followed by a long pause as he considered his next one carefully. 'I thought it might prove useful . . .'

'. . . So you dropped the boy and grabbed the bag?'

'Y-e-s,' Antony replied hesitantly.

'Then our two do-gooders ran off, Finn went after them, and you haven't seen any of them since?'

'Correct.'

'I'm slightly puzzled, Antony, as to what you thought would be so interesting about a rucksack full of empty chocolate wrappers?'

Antony concentrated on something on the ceiling.

'But wait – what have we here?' Doom said, looking more closely at the bag. 'There's a name in this rucksack, and not just any old name. It seems our little vigilante is none other than Archie Hunt. It looks like he's trying to track down his poor old daddy. Isn't that sweet? Don't you think, Antony?'

'Sorry?' asked Antony, who had been so busy trying to look innocent that he hadn't been listening.

'I said, "Sweet!"' huffed Doom.

'Oooh yes, please,' Antony replied eagerly, a long string of drool bouncing from his chin.

Luckily for him, Dr Doom was already too wrapped up in his own scheming thoughts for the misunderstanding to register. 'If young Mr Hunt wants to find his daddy then let's give him a run for

215

his money. Taking over the world is *so* much more rewarding when someone is actually on your tail.'

Antony was concerned. 'What if he gets in our way though?'

'Don't be so preposterous,' replied Doom, his shoulders rocking gently. 'Doctor Doom is much too brilliant to be outsmarted by a mere *child*. One more sample is all I need before initiating my ultimate creation.'

'Have you identified a victim?'

'Oh yes,' Doom chuckled wickedly. 'It's in the bag.'

Chapter 29

The following morning breakfast was ordered to the room. As Barney devoured cereal, a full English, toast and pastries, Finn watched Sky News.

When a human-interest story about a skateboarding dog came on Finn laughed so hard that fat tears rolled down his cheeks. Fifteen minutes later, when the loop of daily news had been completed, the item about the dog was screened again – and once again Finn was doubled up with laughter.

'I have a feeling there might be a funny story in a minute about – oh, I don't know – a skateboarding dog,' Barney mused.

When the Jack Russell appeared on the screen for the third time, Finn's mouth widened into its characteristic circle. 'How did you know that was coming?' he asked in wonderment. But before Barney could answer, the dog's antics had reduced Finn to helpless giggles once more.

Archie, who had woken first and immediately connected his phone to the hotel's wireless broadband, checked Dr Doom's blog for the twentieth time. Disappointment pulsed through him as he saw that Doom still hadn't posted anything since the art gallery clue. Just as he was closing his Internet browser his phone bleeped twice, but before he could read the incoming text there was a knock at the door, accompanied by a female voice.

'Housekeeping!'

Barney checked the spyhole in the door before opening it just long enough for three people to enter the room. Helen Highwater strode in first, wearing a black suit and carrying a clipboard – looking every inch the hotel housekeeper recording which rooms had been serviced. Holden Grey entered next, wearing the drab navy overalls of a hotel maintenance man. He was followed by Gemma, dressed in a plain grey nylon smock and white mop cap and pushing a large trolley.

218

Archie couldn't help smiling at his fellow agent's disguise.

'Don't say a word, Yankee,' she warned, her eyes narrowing.

'What?' Archie held his hands up. 'I think you look fantastic. I mean – you know – your *disguise* looks fantastic. I wasn't saying . . .' Archie's voice tailed off and his cheeks reddened.

'I'm happy to see you too,' Barney offered. 'In fact you've *maid* my day.'

'Shut *up!*' Agent X-ray grabbed a towel off her trolley and tossed it at him.

'OK, that's enough!' barked Highwater.

'IC is right, guys,' said Grey. 'You all need to make like cucumbers and that means, er, take a cool pill.'

Highwater turned to Archie. 'As for you, Yankee, I'd have thought you'd be on your best behaviour after the dog's breakfast you made of yesterday's surveillance mission.' Her mouth suddenly twisted with disgust as she turned and noticed the strange bulbous-eyed character laughing hysterically at the TV. 'Who on earth is that?'

Grey added, 'And what in the name of Fifty Percent is the matter with his skin?'

'That's Finn,' Archie explained. 'I tried to tell you about him on the phone! Doom genetically crossed him with a fish. He was with this other guy at the gallery who was like half insect or something – one of our friendly evil maniac's more aggressive creations.'

'The insect dude was super-strong too,' Barney piped up. 'He held me off the ground with one arm.'

Highwater eyed Barney up and down, mentally estimating his weight. 'That is *unbelievably* strong,' she remarked.

'Why would Doctor Doom be genetically mixing people with other species like fish and insects?' Gemma mused. 'Maybe *Finn* can shed some light on matters?'

Finn flinched on hearing his name. 'Sorry? Oh, hello.'

Archie explained that the three new arrivals were all members of a government agency tasked with capturing Dr Doom before he completed his mysterious plot.

'Have we met before?' asked Finn, his eyes fixed on Gemma.

She shook her head. 'Er . . . no. We just got here.'

'You met Barney and me yesterday,' Archie explained, placing a reassuring hand on Finn's shoulder.

'IC, Agent X-ray and I arrived this morning,' Grey

220

explained. 'We're going to help track down Doctor Doom.'

'Did you say Doom? I think I might have met him before,' Finn offered uncertainly.

'Can you remember where?' Archie enquired, but Finn's attention had already been grabbed by events on the TV screen. 'Finn!' Archie snapped.

Finn's head whipped round to face him. 'Hmm?'

Archie took a deep, calming breath. 'Can you remember where you met Doctor Doom?' he asked evenly.

'Met who?'

Archie flinched slightly. 'Never mind.'

Highwater walked to the window and stood for a moment, gazing at the cool blue lake below before speaking.

'Agents Yankee and Zulu,' she said sternly, 'can I speak with you both?'

Archie felt his heart pounding as, followed by Barney, he approached his boss.

'Yesterday's mission . . .' Highwater said, as if announcing the title of a poem she was about to recite. The two boys nodded contritely. 'What a complete shambles. I might have been willing to overlook your

221

disobedience had you managed to secure a useful witness but instead you have enlisted the help of a smelly halfwit with a nasty dose of psoriasis.' Archie opened his mouth to protest but Highwater was in full flow, white saliva gathering at the corners of her mouth as she ranted. 'Thanks to your antics, today's papers are full of the details of the kidnapping of a promising young mountain climber from an art gallery. There's also an appeal from the Hamburg police for two witnesses, who were seen brawling with the suspects, to come forward. What was I *thinking* sending you two on such an important mission? What made me *think* that kids could actually do the job of fully fledged agents? What on earth were you *thinking* engaging Doom's henchmen in broad daylight?'

It was a moment before Archie realised the last of Highwater's questions wasn't rhetorical. In fact, she was angrily awaiting an answer. 'Oh . . . well, that was my fault. I saw this guy being kidnapped and I thought . . .'

'Yes?'

'Well, I thought I might be able to rescue him.'

'And what about the integrity of our mission, Agent Yankee?'

'What was I supposed to do – just stand by and watch him being kidnapped?' he asked plaintively.

'Yes,' Highwater shrieked. 'That's *precisely* what you should have done.'

'What if they were going to kill him?'

'So be it.' Highwater's eyes were like flint behind her glasses – cold and hard. 'National security could potentially hang on the success of this mission. That is more important than the fate of any individual – whether they be a record-breaking mountaineer or indeed your father. Is that clear?'

Both boys studied their trainers and nodded.

'Once you two have been delivered, Agent X-ray will escort Finn to the airport to board an RAF Hercules bound for Northolt airbase. In the fullness of time he will be thoroughly debriefed by a team of medical specialists.'

'When you say we'll be delivered . . . ?' Barney probed.

Highwater peered over her spectacles at him. 'In ten minutes some local police officers will respond to an anonymous tip-off from yours truly that I will make when I leave this room. They will come and take you and Yankee down to the station and question you about yesterday's events. My sources tell me there are already whisperings within the local Polizei that you two are something to do with MI6. If they find out MI6 has been running covert ops – and I use the term in the loosest possible sense – in their back yard without permission we could have a diplomatic disaster on our hands. We need to nip this in the bud. Am I making myself understood?'

'Er . . . yes, ma'am,' Archie and Barney chorused.

Highwater continued, jabbing her finger at each of the boys in turn. 'You have to convince them that you are just two tourists caught up in a random street crime. If they ask you anything about the secret service just act dumb. Which shouldn't be too much of a stretch. If you cooperate you'll probably be freed in about four or five hours.'

'Won't they be suspicious that we haven't got any passports or ID?' Archie asked.

Highwater shrugged. 'Tell them the bad guys stole them or you lost them or something. Actually, tell them anything you like but don't mention MI6 or STINKBOMB and whatever you do don't mention my name. When they're done with you they'll despatch you to the British Embassy. I'll collect you there later when the coast is clear and I've finished my business.'

'Where are you going?' Archie asked.

'Me? I shall be on a conference call explaining to the DG and Huge Ego . . . I mean Hugh Figo . . . why my agents were brawling in the street when they were supposed to be engaged in covert surveillance.'

Holden Grey nodded to Gemma. 'We're about to leave you in the capable hands of Agent X-ray's, erm, hands. She will remain undercover and guard this room from the outside until the Polizei come knocking.'

'What about Finn?' said Archie.

'He'll be undercover too.' Gemma smirked and patted the giant laundry basket she'd wheeled in. 'Actually, he'll be under *bed* covers – and towels or whatever. Our priority is to get Finn back to HQ for a thorough debrief without the German authorities knowing we were ever here.'

Followed by Grey, Highwater marched across the room, pausing when she got to the door. 'And if I hear that you haven't followed orders to the letter you'll find yourselves on a plane to the Falklands quicker than you can say "Livin' la Vida Loca".'

The two adults left the room, closing the door

softly behind them. Gemma stared at Archie and Barney.

'Wow!' Archie sighed, forcing a nervous laugh. 'What is *her* problem?'

'*Her* problem,' Gemma mimicked, 'is you.'

'I was only—'

'It might surprise you to hear this,' Gemma interrupted, 'but I'm not interested in what you were only. This whole operation isn't about you. And the sooner you stop treating it like your own private adventure and realise we're a team, the better.'

'Look, I'm sorry, OK?' Archie retorted, emotion strangling his voice. 'I was just trying to help that guy.'

'Well, you may have ruined everything in the process.'

'Don't you think I know that?' Archie shouted, tears smearing his vision. 'It's my father that's missing, you know. If I've messed up then I'm the one with most to lose.'

Gemma crossed the room slowly and stood in front of Archie. For a moment she said nothing. Archie drew a wobbly breath and wiped away his tears with his sleeve. Hesitantly he raised his eyes and looked into hers.

'Grow up,' she said coldly.

'Wh-what?'

'I'm sorry your dad's been kidnapped, really I am. But STINKBOMB's mission – your mission – isn't about saving him – it's about saving the world.' Gemma placed a firm hand on Archie's shoulder. 'I know it's tough but you can't base your decisions on rescuing individuals. You have to follow orders, simple as.'

'That's easy for you to say, but—'

'Look, I know what it's like to lose someone, OK?' Gemma's voice wavered. Taking out her purse she flashed Archie a snap of a teenage boy with bleached, spiky hair and a pierced eyebrow.

'This is my brother Jason. He went AWOL on Christmas Eve eighteen months ago. We haven't seen or heard from him since.'

'That's why you hacked into the police computer?'

'Well, I didn't find out anything I didn't already know.' Gemma shrugged. 'All I'm saying is this isn't all about you.' With that she walked into the bathroom and closed the door behind her.

Archie looked at Barney and returned his reassuring smile with a single nod.

227

Suddenly Finn looked away from the TV and scanned the room. 'Where did Gemma go?' he asked.

When Gemma returned from the bathroom, Barney and Finn were perched on the bed while Archie slumped in the easy chair by the window. He was reading the report of the previous day's kidnapping at the foot of page twelve of *Die Zeitung*, the German national newspaper.

'It says the victim was Karl Schumaker, aged seventeen,' Archie translated. 'He was an accomplished mountaineer – one of the youngest people ever to conquer Mount Everest and K2.'

'I wonder what Doctor Doom wants with a mountain climber?' Barney remarked.

'Whatever it is it's bound to be *summit* evil,' Archie said drily before continuing to read the paper. '*Police believe Mr Schumaker, who was a regular visitor at the gallery, had arranged to meet a friend at the time he was apprehended by two suspects. Police are also appealing for two witnesses who were seen engaging the suspects in a fight outside the gallery.*'

'Great work, guys.' Gemma rolled her eyes. 'How come you speak German anyway?'

228

Archie shrugged. 'My dad was stationed at RAF Laarbruch when I was younger. I went to school in Dusseldorf for a few years and just sort of picked it up.'

'Smarty-pants,' said Gemma.

'Not really,' Archie said humbly. 'German just came naturally. I had much more trouble learning Italian when we lived in Milan.'

'I see.' Gemma glanced at her watch. 'OK, Finn, I need you to jump in this laundry basket,' she announced. 'The police will be here any minute and we need to be at the end of the corridor when they arrive.'

'I don't get it,' Archie mused absently.

'It's simple,' Gemma said as if explaining something to a toddler. 'I wait to make sure you two clowns go with the police, then I wheel Finn into the service elevator and we leave the hotel through the back door where a British government official has orders to drive me to the airport.'

'No, I get *that*,' Archie said. 'I don't get how Doctor Doom knew Karl Schumaker had arranged to meet a friend in the gallery yesterday.'

'Text,' said Barney definitively.

'Sorry?'

229

'Schumaker probably made his plans via text message,' Barney theorised. 'Having identified him as a target, Doom would have hacked into Schumaker's phone network and remotely implanted some cyber spyware that echoes the activity on his mobile back at Doom's hideout.'

Archie looked at Gemma. 'Is he right?'

'May well be,' she said with a *who would have thought it?* expression on her face.

'My name was in the rucksack we left outside the gallery,' Archie recalled, feeling his heartbeat pick up like hurrying footsteps. 'If he knew my name, could Doom have tapped into my phone, read the text you sent me and found out that we're hiding in this hotel?'

'No way,' Barney said confidently. 'MI6 use highly sophisticated software to scramble outgoing messages to field operatives. The text is effectively jumbled up in the ether, remaining totally unintelligible until it is reassembled by the decryption software loaded on to the agent's handset. Isn't that so, X-ray?'

'Yes,' Gemma agreed. 'Except STINKBOMB doesn't exactly have access to all MI6 counter-espionage technology just yet so I sent you that message on my own pay-as-you-go.'

230

'And I don't have any decryption software on my mobile,' added Archie.

'In that case . . .' Barney nodded as if considering the situation, 'we're toast.'

Gemma shook her head. 'Not necessarily. It would take Doom considerable time to design the software tailored to latch on to your sim card's virtual fingerprint,' she said. 'By now all he could realistically have managed would be to hack into your network supplier's database. At worst he might have got your number.'

Remembering his phone had bleeped earlier, Archie pulled it out of his pocket. When he opened his inbox his heart broke into a frantic sprint.

'I got a text message this morning,' he exclaimed breathlessly.

'Ah, bless,' Gemma teased. 'I was excited when I got my first text too.'

'Really? And was yours from an evil mastermind as well?'

Barney and Gemma froze.

'That's right.' Archie nodded and tapped the screen on his mobile. 'It's from Doctor Doom.'

231

Chapter 30

Archie cleared his throat, pushed his glasses up his nose and read the message aloud.

'Master Hunt. Your father is alive . . . for now. By 2pm I will have my final specimen and I shall demonstrate my brilliance to the world by creating the genetic blueprint of the ultimate soldier. If you contact the police you will never see your father alive. The last thing I need is to have you snooping around my nice hideout in Caesar's Palace. Even if you find it you will need to enter a code to get inside. Take my advice – go home. You're way out of your depth.'

Archie read the text to himself twice more then looked

from Barney to Gemma.

'What do you think?' he asked.

'Unbelievable,' said Gemma.

'I know,' Barney enthused wildly. 'He's actually got his own hideout – how cool is that? He really is a full-on Evil Mastermind, isn't he? I bet it's on a tropical island somewhere or inside a volcano. At the very least it'll be perched on a rocky mountainside overlooking an ocean. I can picture him sitting in a leather chair behind a massive desk, stroking his cat and plotting.' As Barney's description gathered pace his eyes grew wider and his cheeks shinier. 'It'll be in a huge room – like the nerve centre in a nuclear plant or a NASA operations centre or something. There'll be banks of computer equipment everywhere operated by lots of blokes in boiler suits, and he's bound to have a computerised map of the world on the wall so he can monitor his quest for world domination. Ooh, and there's always a tank full of piranhas or shark-infested water under the floor with some sort of trapdoor that he operates from his desk. Whenever someone displeases him, or even just bores him, he'll press a secret button to open the door and they'll be gobbled up in seconds.'

'Thank you, Barney,' said Archie, adopting the

serious tone of an American news anchorman. 'That was our Overactive Imagination Correspondent, Barney Jones, reporting from Cloud Cuckoo Land.'

'Hey, Barney. I've got a message for you from Reality,' Gemma added. 'He says you really should get in touch.'

'But even *you* said his message was unbelievable,' Barney protested, his eyebrows dipping into a frown.

'Er, hello?' Gemma said loudly as though trying to get the attention of someone listening to an iPod through earphones. 'I meant Doctor Doom's *arrogance* is unbelievable. He's so sure Archie can't find him he's actually taunting him with clues.'

'Why's he contacted me directly though?' Archie wondered. 'Why not keep on showing off via his online profile?'

'Because he's got your father and he gets a kick out of torturing you,' Gemma suggested. 'He's probably punishing you for trying to stop him snatching Karl Schumaker at the gallery.'

Barney nodded knowingly. 'Anyway, this dude's so cocky he's sure no one can solve his riddle.'

'So let's prove him wrong,' Archie said defiantly.

'OK, Sherlock,' Gemma challenged, folding her

234

arms. 'If you're so smart go ahead and tell us what the message means. Where is Doctor Doom's secret lair?'

The most obvious starting point, Archie decided, was the reference to Caesar's Palace. Of course he'd heard of the famous hotel of that name in Las Vegas, but that seemed far too obvious and he doubted Dr Doom would kidnap people in Christchurch if his villainous hideaway was far away in Nevada.

Archie reckoned the next most logical meaning was something to do with a Roman emperor. His knowledge of ancient history was fairly sketchy but he was pretty sure there had been loads of Caesars who had presumably lived in a variety of palaces, not just one. Besides, he wasn't convinced of the likelihood that Dr Doom would have chosen to set up camp in some historic ancient ruins in Italy's capital city.

The phrase 'Caesar's Palace' had to have some other significance – but what could it be?

Archie gasped sharply as if he'd been plunged into icy water. 'Barney, who does Romario play for?' he demanded.

'The Brazilian? Lyons, I think. Why?'

Without a word Archie began tapping frantically at his mobile's touch-sensitive screen while Barney and

Gemma waited expectantly. For a minute the only sound in the room came from the TV, then –

'Gotcha!' Archie grabbed the air triumphantly.

'Do you have something you'd like to share with the class, Mr Hunt?' asked Barney.

'Yes! Doom's lair is in Caesar Romario's house,' Archie announced. 'Footballers always have really fancy pads, don't they? And Romario is well known for his lavish taste – that's what he meant by Caesar's Palace. I've just Googled his house and this website – stalkthestars.com – gives you its coordinates and everything.'

'Er, excuse me for spoiling the party,' Gemma interjected, 'but why would Caesar Romario get involved with Doctor Doom?'

Archie bit his lip and scrunched up his face.

'Gambling debts,' Barney said emphatically. 'Romario's probably blown all his cash and Doom's renting his house off him for mega bucks. Or he's got himself mixed up with a South American drugs cartel.' Suddenly Barney's eyes were as wide as an owl's. 'Or – what if Romario himself is one of Doom's genetic experiments? I mean, he is freakishly quick on the pitch.'

236

'OK, Zulu,' Gemma muttered sternly. 'Let's try not to get too carried away. Assuming we go to Romario's place, what about the code to get in?'

'I don't know.' Archie was almost dizzy with the thrill of the impending chase. 'Can't we can work it out on the way?'

Gemma shook her head. 'We've got our orders. You two wait here for the German fuzz, I'll take Finn back to base as planned. I'll report your theory about Doom's text to Highwater when she's out of her meeting. She can decide if we pursue the lead or hand it over to MI6.'

'But we haven't got time!' Archie's voice was shrill with exasperation. 'Barney and I will be in the police station for hours. Highwater might be stuck in her meeting all day. By the time we get out Doom will have taken over the world and our chances of saving my father will be smoke.'

'We have our orders,' Gemma growled, glancing anxiously at her watch. 'Finn – I really need you to climb in the laundry basket now. There's only two minutes until show time.'

'Which show are we going to see?' Finn enquired, turning away from the TV to face her.

'Just get in the basket.'

Finn obliged without further objection and Gemma draped a bed sheet over his head.

'If we follow orders we have no chance of stopping Doom,' Archie pleaded. 'You are the only chance my father has. You have to try and help him.'

'And you have to stop telling me what I can and can't do,' Gemma snapped. 'We have orders to follow.'

'You can't stop us leaving,' Archie said impudently as Gemma pushed the chambermaid's trolley towards the door.

'Is that so?' Gemma said, raising one eyebrow. 'Well, this can of floor polish is actually pepper spray so I wouldn't do anything stupid if I were you. Besides which, if you don't follow orders MI6 will seriously have you on an RAF plane to the Falklands before you can even blink.'

'Well, maybe that's a risk I'm willing to take,' Archie argued. 'As Highwater herself said, national security is more important than any individual's welfare – mine included. If you walk out on us, you're walking out on your whole country as well as my father.'

'How many times do I have to remind you,

STINKBOMB's mission is not to rescue your father?'

'You're right.' Archie nodded. 'Our mission is to save the world – so how are we going to do that from inside a police station?'

Chapter 31

One wheel on the housekeeper's trolley squeaked as Gemma pushed it to the end of the hotel corridor. Its hidden cargo weighed the trolley down and she had to lean into it, using all her strength just to keep it moving. Stopping at the service elevator, she pushed the button and waited for the lift to arrive. As the double doors slid open, Gemma saw two uniformed police officers appear at the far end of the passageway, stopping outside Archie's room and banging on the door. Quickly turning and lowering her head, she pushed her trolley into the lift and pressed the button for the ground floor.

Her mouth was dry and her heart was fluttering and, as the doors closed, she prayed she had made the right decision.

240

'The police have just arrived,' she said to the bed sheets in a low voice. There was no response.

When the lift doors opened on the ground floor, Gemma heaved the trolley into a hotel corridor. The short passage led to a room piled high with freshly laundered towels and sheets as well as huge plastic bins containing dirty laundry. Two doors led off the laundry room. Through one she could see the hotel kitchens, through the other a small external courtyard. Gemma rammed open the swing doors with the trolley and let if freewheel down a short ramp and into the warm morning air.

Agent X-ray immediately identified the vehicle waiting to take her to the airport. It was a silver VW saloon – the type of car commonly used by British Embassy staff on the continent. The driver stepped out of the car and approached her. He was about twenty-five years old, with short, neatly-parted dark hair and smartly dressed in a plain grey suit. Judging by his nervous expression, Gemma reckoned he was new to field ops – probably still in training.

'It's warm for the time of year,' he said.

Gemma nodded and recited her pre-arranged response. 'One swallow doesn't make a summer though.'

241

Without another word the driver grabbed one end of the trolley and helped Gemma haul it over to the passenger door of the car.

'It's a heavy package,' he observed.

'There's been a slight change of plan,' Gemma announced matter-of-factly. 'I'm invoking agency protocol seven-six-alpha.'

'Seven-six-alpha?' the driver repeated anxiously.

'Yes. Basically I'm changing our destination.'

'But my orders—'

'Listen to me,' Gemma said with quiet authority. 'As you know, seven-six-alpha gives an active field agent the power to change predetermined procedure provided it is done in the name of National Security. Now if you'd like to call your boss to check then be my guest – although I'm not sure your ignorance of manual Foxtrot Bravo Thirteen would reflect too well on your training record.'

The driver nodded vigorously. 'You're right. My mistake. OK – let's get the package in the vehicle. What's the new destination?'

Agent X-ray pulled aside the bed sheet covering the laundry bag. 'Tell this guy where we're going,' she instructed.

Finn's blank fish-like eyes stared out of the large canvas basket. His knees were pulled into his chest and his mouth hung open gormlessly. 'I don't know,' he said with a confused shrug.

'I wasn't talking to you,' Gemma sighed, yanking the bed sheet again to reveal two other figures.

Curled into tight balls, Archie and Barney raised their foreheads off their knees and smiled.

'Kirchdorfer Strasse,' Archie said, climbing out of the trolley. 'And hurry.'

Chapter 32

Hand-over-hand, Archie dragged the camouflage netting off the Dragonfly and bundled it into a ball before shoving it back into the small compartment in the plane's fuselage.

Agent X-ray admired the sleek silver jet with a long whistle. 'Wicked,' she murmured at last, a smile passing briefly across her lips. She had changed into a black T-shirt, jeans and a leather jacket in the back of the BMW. Slung over her shoulder was a rucksack containing her laptop, mobile phone and a few mobile earpieces, which had been stored in the boot of the car.

Barney helped Gemma and Finn into the cockpit, folding the pilot's seat forward so they could climb into the leather chairs behind. Meanwhile Archie made a quick circuit of the plane, checking the tyres and looking out for any stray twigs or leaves that might be sucked into the engines.

Within five minutes everyone was strapped in and Archie had started the two jet engines. He released the parking brake, allowing the plane to trundle out from under the cover of the tree towards the centre of the field.

'Are you sure you know what you're doing?' Gemma asked as Archie pulled the nozzle lever back to the hover stop.

Archie smiled at her over his shoulder. 'Don't worry,' he said, pushing the thrust levers forward. 'Flying a jet is child's play.'

'Fasten your seat belts,' Barney added. 'You're about to get the fright – I mean flight – of your lives.'

By the time the plane had climbed through ten thousand feet Archie had verbally filed a flight plan to Lyons with air traffic control and established a course to their first checkpoint. When the aircraft was maintaining its heading and speed steadily he quickly programmed the remaining waypoints into the navigation computer.

'This is pretty fly,' Gemma called from the back. 'It's like being in a really flash limousine that happens to be a jet plane. And your dad invented this thing?'

Archie glanced over his shoulder and nodded.

'He must be pretty cool,' Gemma surmised.

Archie nodded again, swallowing hard.

Barney turned in his seat and smiled approvingly at Gemma. 'Good work getting the driver to play ball back there,' he said. 'That's exactly what I would have done – invoke the old classic seven-six-alpha protocol.'

Gemma nodded, 'Is that so?'

'Yes siree,' Barney said with a wink.

'That's funny,' Gemma said absently, admiring the green countryside far below. 'Because there's no such thing as a seven-six-alpha protocol. I was just bluffing. I knew he wouldn't dare check it out in case it made him look stupid.'

'Oh yeah, of course,' Barney agreed hurriedly. 'That's what I meant. I would have *made up* something like a seven-six-alpha protocol if I'd been in your shoes.'

'Whatever,' Gemma mumbled.

Barney turned to face the front and noticed Archie struggling to stifle a smile.

246

'What's so funny?' Barney demanded.

'Nothing,' Archie said, pursing his lips.

The Dragonfly's navigation computer predicted Archie should start his descent in less than five minutes and his hands were beginning to sweat. Gemma had spent much of the hour-long flight surfing the Net on her laptop. Various celebrity gossip sites had photographs of Caesar Romario relaxing in his luxury residence and Google Earth offered sufficient external shots to identify their destination from the air. Finn was reclining in his plush seat, silently transfixed by the scenery passing serenely beneath him.

'So do we have any idea if Doom is working alone?' Archie asked.

'Almost certainly not,' Gemma replied, her fingers dancing over the keyboard. 'Just before Villenemi faked his own death a couple of years ago, a prison van carrying violent criminals was held up in London and there's evidence he financed the grab.'

'Why would he want to free the criminals?' said Archie.

'We don't think he freed them. In fact quite the opposite,' Gemma said, smiling grimly. 'The theory is that he used the criminals as human guinea pigs, experimenting on them to perfect his techniques. As well as meddling with their DNA he probably cloned them so that they could guard his hideout.'

'Sounds like an all-round nice guy,' said Archie. 'How do you think he's selecting his victims now?'

'We're pretty sure he has access to SPADE,' Gemma stated. 'Karl Schumaker and Henry Ulrik both scored inside the top one hundred from their year group, and when your dad was sixteen his SPADE score was the highest in the country.'

Archie allowed himself a brief moment of pride. 'So that reinforces the theory that Doom is an ex-government employee.'

'Exactly. The very existence of SPADE is top secret. There's no way Doctor Doom could get that information without insider knowledge of SPADE's programming protocols.'

'So why the long gap between hijacking the prison van and the recent abductions?' Barney mused.

'We don't know for sure,' Gemma admitted. 'One possible explanation could be that Villenemi has been perfecting his technique this whole time. Now he's

248

got the science bit sorted he's gathering top-quality specimens ready for the real thing.'

'Meanwhile his hideout's being guarded by horrible mutants,' added Barney. 'If they're anything like the dude in the gallery we've got our work cut out.'

'I dread to think what other sort of monsters he's created.' Gemma shuddered.

Her words hung ominously in the air as Archie eased the thrust levers back to idle and lowered the Dragonfly's nose to start its descent.

'Whatever they are, we're about to find out,' he announced. 'Everybody buckle up.'

Chapter 33

Caesar Romario's house was situated about fifty miles north of the city of Lyons, amidst endless acres of flat farmland and vineyards. The level terrain offered Archie plenty of suitable landing sites and he chose a ploughed field a few hundred yards behind the footballer's vast farmhouse conversion.

Archie, Barney, Gemma and Finn climbed out of the aircraft and stealthily approached the building, darting between the fruit trees that peppered the intervening field. Reaching the house's ten-foot perimeter wall, they skirted it to the front gate and crouched behind a statue of a lion to plan their next move.

'Why don't I just ring the buzzer?' Gemma

suggested, nodding towards the keypad inlaid in the stonework next to the iron gate.

'And say what?' Archie whispered.

'I don't know,' Gemma muttered, studying the house through the gate. 'How about, "Hi, I was just wondering if any evil villains live here"?'

'Negative,' Barney hissed. 'We must remain covert at all times. This is a black ops mission. I repeat, black ops.'

'Calm down, Agent Zulu,' Gemma whispered. 'I was only joking. You don't have to get your walkie-talkie in a twist. Now watch and learn.'

She pressed the circular button beneath the numbered keypad and waited.

'Oui?' The female voice sounded irritable.

'Oh, hello?' Gemma said pleasantly. 'I was just wondering . . .'

The voice on the intercom snapped, 'Ee eez not ere. Leave me alone.'

'Sorry?' Gemma said. 'Who is not there?'

'My 'usband,' said the woman. 'Ee eez playing away from 'ome. Again.'

'Oh, no, I'm not looking for your husband,' Gemma giggled sweetly. 'You see I've lost my cat and I think he may have wandered into your house. He's black and white and his name's, er, Skunk.'

Archie and Barney exchanged surprised glances.

'Just a moment,' said the woman crossly. 'I'm coming down.'

Gemma shoved her hands into her jacket pockets and scanned the scenery as she waited. After a few seconds there was a loud buzz and she grabbed one side of the ornate gate and pushed. With a sharp click the gate opened and the buzzing stopped.

Archie watched as Gemma turned and nodded briefly to him then strode confidently up the long drive towards the farmhouse, her feet scrunching on the gravel.

She looked tiny as she waited in front of the building's grand front door.

'She's so cool,' Barney whispered.

Archie nodded slowly. 'I told you so.'

'Who's cool?' Finn enquired, gazing dreamily into the distance.

The farmhouse door opened and a young woman wearing a pale pink velour tracksuit appeared. Gemma spoke for a while, gesturing to the nearby village and pointing to the wall at the side of the house, then she

252

hung her head and wiped her eyes with the back of her hand. The woman opened the door a little wider, said something to which Gemma nodded eagerly, then took Gemma's hand and led her inside, closing the door behind them.

'Bingo,' Barney mumbled. 'The hamster is inside the beehive.'

The boys waited in silence, occasionally peering round the statue in the hope of glimpsing Gemma. After forty minutes Archie and Barney were beginning to get edgy, while Finn remained blissfully unaware of the potential danger Gemma was in.

'Come on, where is she?' Archie said, glancing anxiously at his watch. 'It's gone midday. Less than two hours until Doom promised to carry out his final experiment.'

'I think Little Red Riding Hood has met the three bears,' Barney replied. 'I say we invoke phase two of Operation Trojan Horse.'

'Since when is this Operation Trojan Horse?' Archie asked. 'And as far as I know, there isn't a phase two.'

'If you say so,' sulked Barney. 'How about we just go and ring the bell and say we've lost our friend then?'

Archie was still considering Barney's suggestion when the farmhouse door opened and Gemma came out. Turning to wave at the woman, she retraced her steps down the driveway and through the gate.

'What happened?' Archie asked as they regrouped.

'Man!' Gemma sighed. 'I thought I was never going to escape.'

'Copy that,' Barney replied. 'Did you have to evade Doom himself or just some of his evil henchmen?'

'Neither,' Gemma said flatly. 'Just that woman. There's no one else in the entire house and believe me I should know – I had the full guided tour. I saw inside every wardrobe, examined every en suite bathroom. Even the wine cellar holds no mystery for me now. She is in there all on her own.'

Barney digested the information for a moment. 'So what you're saying is that Doctor Doom is actually a she and that she's plotting world domination all on her own?'

Gemma snorted and shook her head. 'No, genius. What I'm saying is that lady is a regular footballer's wife and she's so lonely she'd tell her life story to a donkey if she could get it into the house.'

'So . . . the trail to Doom has gone cold?' asked Archie reluctantly.

Gemma shrugged. 'Stone cold.'

The four friends returned to the Dragonfly and strapped themselves dejectedly into their seats.

'I can't believe we've come the wrong way,' Archie said. He thought of his father and remembered the final tense conversation they'd shared. He wanted to take back all his angry complaining and tell his father how much he looked up to him. Sensing the hands on his watch sweeping inexorably towards two o'clock he asked Gemma, 'Are you *sure* Doom's not hiding in there somewhere?'

'I promise I would say if there was any chance at all that we're on the right track,' said Gemma softly. She reached forward and placed a reassuring hand on Archie's shoulder. 'But we're not. The woman I spoke to is called Zoe Romario. She's French. She used to be in advertising but had to leave her job a couple of years ago when Caesar was transferred from Monaco to Lyons. Basically, she hates being stuck out in the countryside here – she kept going on about how much she missed the house and the life they used to have in Nice.'

Glumly, Archie sat with his chin on his chest, replaying Doom's text message over in his head. Something about the message had been niggling him all along, and as he listened to Gemma he suddenly realised what it was. Dr Doom had referred to his 'nice' hideout. This struck Archie as a really lame adjective coming from an odious mastermind bragging about his imminent world domination. Luxurious hideout – possibly, formidable – definitely, but *nice*? That just didn't ring true.

A whoosh of adrenalin coursed through him. 'Doom isn't staying in a *nice* hideout,' he yelped. 'It's a Nice hideout!'

'Huh?' asked Barney.

'When he played for Monaco he lived in a huge mansion in the hills overlooking the Riviera. Now I remember seeing it on MTV when we met you at the safe house. He moved to Lyons two years ago, so I guess that's when he sold his place in Nice.'

'That definitely ties in with the timing of Doom needing a new pad after faking his death,' said Gemma.

'So he bought Romario's house in Nice,' Barney stated.

Archie nodded as he fired up the Dragonfly's jet engines. 'And turned it into his "nice" hideout in Caesar's Palace.'

'Well, what are we waiting for?' asked Gemma. 'Nice – here we come.'

'Nice,' Finn parroted. 'That's nice.'

Chapter 34

The Dragonfly tore through the sky just a few hundred feet above the rocky mountain ridge and as Archie banked hard to his left, the ground fell steeply into the deep blue ocean far below. He carved a turn just to the east of the white crescent that was Nice's Promenade des Anglais.

Gemma had been busy searching the Internet for information during the short flight south from Lyons. One article she'd found revealed that the footballer had sold the property through an international agency called Lux Residence. Within minutes Gemma had hacked into its online classified property database and discovered that the house had a V-shaped floor plan, a swimming pool on the veranda and a helipad. She had also established the coordinates of the mansion, which Archie had programmed into his navigation computer. A green star on his moving map display now represented the location of what they suspected to be Dr Doom's lair.

Archie pulled the nozzle lever halfway back to the hover stop and allowed the airspeed to bleed off, raising the aircraft's nose to maintain its altitude. According to his navigation display, Dr Doom's hideout was three miles away, directly northward. Turning to head inland, he feverishly scanned the mountainside that was rapidly expanding in his windscreen.

Lurking among the lush undergrowth and rocky outcrops, houses of countless styles were strewn across the peninsula – from the traditional mock-Renaissance to ultra-modern glass boxes. Archie pulled the nozzle lever back to the hover stop and the plane slowed gradually until it wasn't moving at all.

'I can't see it anywhere,' he said, grimacing with frustration. Instinctively his eyes flicked to the clock on the instrument panel, which read 12:55. Time was slipping away fast.

'It must be here somewhere,' Gemma insisted.

'Up there!' Barney exclaimed, pointing through the glass canopy.

Archie followed his gaze and spotted a large V-shaped building perched just below the peak. Camouflaged against the rocky backdrop, it was difficult to make out. The point of the V seemed to be buried in the rock while the two arms protruded over the precipice of the cliff, supported precariously by criss-crossing stilts. The square ends of the arms were completely mirrored, making them look like a pair of giant sunglasses peering out from the hillside.

'Now there's an evil lair if ever I saw one!' gasped Archie.

He put on a handful of power and nudged the stick forward, driving the plane vertically upward and forward. When the Dragonfly was directly over the rooftop he throttled back and started a slow descent.

A black Bell Ranger helicopter was parked on the helipad. Apart from that, the roof was deserted. Archie deftly swung the Dragonfly to face out to sea before setting it down on the hard surface. Chopping the engines, he unfastened the red latch above his head and slid the canopy back.

Archie jumped on to the roof, turning slowly on

the spot to ensure he had not attracted a welcoming committee. He walked to the edge of the roof and cautiously peered down, immediately pulling back as a sudden wave of giddiness made his vision swim.

It was like standing on the very end of a giant diving board, with nothing but air between him and the rocky terrain sixty feet below. The hillside fell almost vertically for another hundred feet or so before easing into the slightly shallower, greener slopes peppered with exclusive mansions. Far below, the powerful waves of the Mediterranean crashed against the red sandstone cliffs.

'Are you OK?' Barney asked. 'You look a little queasy. Don't tell me our intrepid aviator is scared of heights?'

Archie swallowed and clenched his teeth into a smile. 'That would be ridiculous,' he said.

Gemma and Finn joined them on the roof and they took a moment to survey the building. A set of stone steps ran down the inside of its eastern arm, leading to a large triangular veranda nestled inside the nook of the V. Beyond the veranda was the vast pool Archie had seen Caesar Romario swimming in on MTV. Apart from the two huge squares of mirrored glass peering out to sea, the building apparently had no doors or windows and was completely clad in textured rubber, like the surface of a children's playground.

'Looks like Doctor Doom has fortified the place since he moved in,' Archie observed.

'I don't like it,' said Barney, squinting across the rooftop. 'It's too quiet. Where are the guards?'

'He doesn't need the guards out here,' Gemma suggested. 'What harm can we do stuck out on the roof?'

'Why are we stuck on a roof?' asked Finn.

The four figures stood in silence considering their options. Archie knew his father was close – probably not far below his feet – but if they couldn't find a way into the building he might as well be on the other side of the world. He checked his watch – it was just after 1 p.m. In less than an hour Dr Doom would start conducting his evil experiment that would spell the end for his father, the other captives and possibly the civilised world.

'There must be a way in somewhere,' insisted Archie weakly.

'Only by opening the trapdoor.'

He spun round and looked at Finn.

'What trapdoor?' he asked.

Finn looked at him blankly.

'You said something about opening a trapdoor?' said Archie gently.

Finn thought for a moment then shook his head. 'Impossible.' he pursed his fishy lips apologetically. 'The only trapdoor round here is locked by three thousand p.s.i. of hydraulic pressure and the only way to open it is by typing a code into the keypad in the rock face next to that sapling.'

Archie caught Gemma's eye then broke into a sprint towards the apex of the building's two arms. The others followed him and they regrouped next to a gnarled sapling that was somehow growing out of the cliff.

'Where is it?' he asked, scanning the rugged wall in front of him.

'Where's what?' Finn said. 'Are you looking for something?'

'The keypad,' Gemma said firmly. 'You said the keypad to open the trapdoor was on the cliff next to this tree?'

'Did I?' Finn's mouth opened vacantly. 'But if Doom had put the keypad here then anyone could see it.'

Archie, Barney and Gemma let out a collective

groan. Finn continued, 'That's why the keypad is hidden behind this secret panel.'

He placed his scaly hand on a rocky nodule and twisted his wrist. A small rectangle of the stone receded into the cliff face and slid down out of view, leaving a neat hole. With a mechanical whirr a telescopic metal arm extended out of the opening. Attached to the end of the arm was a small box with twelve buttons in four rows of three.

'Finn, you're amazing.' Archie high-fived Finn, who seemed at a loss as to why his companions were so excited. 'You had us all thinking you had no recollection of being here, but all you needed was a little time to Mullet over.'

'Exactly,' Barney chipped in. 'A Snapper decision is no use to anyone if it's way off Bass.'

'Were you teasing us on Porpoise?' Archie giggled.

'Excuse me,' Gemma announced sternly. 'If you two Clownfish have finished . . . we've got an Odious Mastermind to thwart and we don't have a hope if we can't work out the cod – I mean the code – to this door.'

Archie nodded seriously and checked his watch again – it was one fifteen. They had forty-five minutes left.

264

Chapter 35

Archie took out his own mobile and read aloud part of Dr Doom's text message.

> 'The last thing I need is to have you snooping
> around my nice hideout in Caesar's Palace.
> Even if you find it you will need to enter a
> code to get inside.'

'Nobody touch the keypad,' Barney whispered urgently. 'In my experience of megalomaniacs a device like this is always booby-trapped with fingerprint recognition software. If anyone outside of Doom's inner circle touches it, it'll set off a remotely activated ultrasonic pulse that will throw us all over the roof edge to our certain death.'

'Last time I read your file,' Gemma whispered, 'your experience of megalomaniacs was confined to the pages of kids' books or the local cinema.'

As Gemma reached out to examine the keypad Archie place his hand gently on her wrist.

'Wouldn't Finn's prints be logged in Doom's database?' he suggested. 'Maybe we should let him touch it. You know, to be on the safe side.'

For a moment Gemma's eyes bored into Archie's from behind her fringe, then she lowered her hand with a nod. 'Can't do any harm,' she conceded.

'Any ideas as to what the code might be?' Barney asked Finn, who had turned his back on the cliff and was gazing out to sea.

'Hmmm?' Finn mumbled, turning round. 'Sorry, I was miles away. Hey, look at that keypad! Where on earth did that come from?'

'Looks like the Finn we know and love is back,' Gemma whispered to Archie.

Archie beamed. 'That's cool,' he said. 'I think I've cracked it anyway.'

'You have?'

He nodded. 'The code is two, zero, two, six, three, three.'

'Really?' enquired Gemma.

'Of course! It's simply brilliant,' Barney enthused. 'And indeed brilliantly simple, as all the best ciphers are if you ask me.'

'If it's that simple, Agent Zulu,' Gemma's voice was tight, 'perhaps you can explain it to me?'

'Well, it's simply, er, simple . . . I'd even go as far as to say it's *simplistic*.'

'Yeah – simple – I get that part. Would you like to tell me *how* it's so simple?'

Barney nudged Archie. 'Doesn't she remind you of Moore the Bore when she's like this?' he giggled.

'Agent Zulu,' Gemma snapped. 'Do you understand the code for the keypad – yes or no?'

Instantly Barney's cheeks slackened and his mouth was suddenly small. 'Negative,' he whispered.

'In that case perhaps you'd let Agent Yankee explain?'

'Barney's right, actually,' Archie said with a smile. 'It really is simple.'

'Told you so,' Barney muttered very quietly.

Archie continued, 'Doctor Doom said in his message that I would have to enter a code to open the door.'

'Uh-huh.'

'And how did he send me the message?'

'By text.'

'Exactly.' Archie handed Gemma his phone, which was set up to send a message on predictive text. 'What happens if you type in the numbers two, zero, two, six, three, three?'

With a sceptical frown Gemma typed the digits with her thumbs. When she had finished and read the words on the phone's screen, her expression softened and a smile danced around her lips. 'You could be right,' she conceded. 'I'm beginning to see why SPADE rated you so highly, Agent Yankee.'

'Can I see?' Barney asked.

Gemma held up the phone to show the two words she'd written in the outgoing text field.

A code

'Cool! Let's try it and see what happens,' suggested Barney. 'But we have to be ready to roll as soon as the door opens.'

'I'll stay out here and work the comms,' Gemma offered, unzipping her rucksack and fishing out four tiny rubber earpieces. 'If we all wear these we can stay in touch. I can use my laptop to try and give you some sort of tech support. I'd better contact IC in her meeting – break it to her that we haven't exactly followed her orders to the letter.'

'So what's the deal?' Archie asked, working the rubber bud into his ear. 'Are we still operating on a surveillance-only basis?'

Gemma smiled wryly. 'As Holden Grey might say, there's a time for surveillance and a time to engage, and this is one of those.'

'Sorry, which one?'

'Do keep up, Agent Yankee.' Gemma winked. 'It's time to engage.'

'OK,' Archie said resolutely. 'Let's do this.'

'Yes!' Barney gave the air a furtive uppercut. Touching his earpiece, he mumbled to himself, 'We have a go situation. I say again, we have a go.'

'Finn,' Archie called gently, distracting him from the view, 'can you enter some numbers into the keypad for us?'

Finn turned and smiled pleasantly. 'What keypad's that?'

*

When Finn had entered the final number, the four companions held their breath.

'*Pssshhhht.*'

It sounded as though someone had popped open a giant can of Coke but when Archie spun round he saw where the pneumatic hiss had come from. A short distance from where he stood, a large round logo about four metres in diameter was painted on the roof. The black circle was bisected by a golden flash of lightning with the words 'RALLY Against the World' written down the zigzag design in red letters.

As he watched, his mouth dry and his palms wet, he saw a jagged fissure open up along the edge of the lightning. With silent elegance the zigzag crack yawned open like the mouth of a hungry shark. Within seconds the two halves of the circle had glided out of sight, leaving a large round hole in the roof.

Archie crept forward and peered tentatively into the opening. A flight of glossy white stairs led down into Dr Doom's hideout.

He turned and saw a look of utter joy on Barney's face.

'I know it's a silly question,' Archie said, feeling sick

with nerves, 'but are you sure you want to go through with this?'

Barney grinned. 'Does James Bond drive a fast car?'

'OK. I'll go first. Finn, you come behind me, and Barney, you bring up the rear.'

'Copy that,' said Barney.

'Stay in touch,' said Gemma.

Archie nodded grimly then turned and put one foot on to the staircase leading into the hideout. 'Everyone stay close,' he muttered. 'Let's go and let off a STINKBOMB right under Doctor Doom's nose.'

Chapter 36

Archie crouched low as he descended the short flight of stairs, ducking his head under the roof to check no one was waiting for him below. Finn and Barney followed, all three pausing to assess their surroundings when they reached the metal grille floor. They were standing in a long straight corridor that was octagonal in section, its walls constructed of smooth white epoxy.

'I can't believe there aren't any guards here,' Archie whispered, but as he spoke he understood why. Attached to the ceiling just above his head and painted white to disguise its presence, a security camera was trained on the entrance.

'We're busted,' he said, pointing to the surveillance

272

device. 'It's looking straight at us – its little red light is blinking and everything.'

'Don't worry,' said Barney confidently. 'That'll feed into a security suite somewhere nearby where a lone guard will be monitoring about ten screens. At least that's what he's supposed to be doing – he'll actually be reading the paper or snoozing and paying no attention to what's happening on the monitors in front of him.'

'That would be pretty convenient,' Archie said dubiously.

'Do you hear a warning siren?' Barney asked. 'Or a computerised voice going, *Intruder, intruder?*'

Archie paused for a moment. 'Er, no.'

'So we're good to go,' Barney concluded. 'All we need to do is find the security suite, overpower the inattentive guard, and put on the spare boiler suits that will be hanging up in the room.'

'Boiler suits?' Archie repeated, wrinkling his nose.

'Yuh.' Barney looked at Archie as though he was totally clueless. 'All evil masterminds' henchmen wear white boiler suits. Everyone knows that. It'll be a piece of cake, I promise.'

'I hope you're right,' Archie whispered, leading the way down the corridor.

273

As they neared a T-junction at the end of the passageway Archie heard voices accompanied by the metallic clang of approaching footsteps.

'Guards!' Barney hissed. 'Hide!'

'That's easier said than done,' Archie whispered, scanning the empty corridor. 'It's not like there's a handy sofa to duck behind.'

For a second the three companions froze helplessly in the middle of the passage. Then Archie noticed something out of the corner of his eye.

There was a small alcove in the wall right next to where he was standing. He ducked into it, pulling Finn and Barney with him. The three friends pressed their backs to the wall and held their breath as two figures clad in white boiler suits passed the end of the corridor.

'Looks like you were right about the outfits,' Archie whispered when the footsteps had receded out of earshot.

'Don't sound so surprised,' Barney smiled. 'I know my stuff.'

'OK then, Einstein,' Archie said, raising one eyebrow. 'Where do we go from here?'

Barney narrowed his eyes as he peered down the

274

corridor. 'My instincts tell me we should proceed and surveil our options from the junction up ahead.'

'If you ask me,' Finn offered, 'I think the security suite might be through this door.'

'You remember the layout?' Archie asked urgently.

Finn shook his head. 'No,' he said with an apologetic shrug.

Archie pursed his lips into a tense smile. 'So what makes you think the security suite is behind this door?'

'It says so right there.' Finn pointed one stubby finger at a small sign on the door.

SECURITY SUITE
UNAUTHORISED PERSONNEL – KEEP OUT

Archie edged out of the alcove and ducked against the wall next to the door. Holding a finger to his lips he tugged Finn's sleeve, and the fish boy shuffled back and crouched behind him. Barney stepped into the corridor and pressed his back against the wall on the other side of the doorway.

'What now?' Archie mouthed.

Barney responded immediately with a series of

275

briskly executed hand gestures. When he had finished he stepped in front of the doorway, grabbed the locking lever and began to turn it anticlockwise.

'Wait!' Archie hissed, gripping his friend's shoulder and hauling him back. 'I didn't understand any of that.'

Resuming his position next to the doorway, Barney sighed and shook his head patronisingly before repeating the sequence of signals, this time at a slightly slower pace. 'Did you copy *that*?' he whispered when he had finished.

'I don't think so,' Archie replied. 'Unless you actually want me to poke myself in the eyes while you arm-wrestle someone before commanding their dog to sit?'

Barney rolled his eyes before repeating the gestures in super-slow time, explaining what each of them meant. 'You keep a lookout (Barney pointed a finger at Archie then jabbed two fingers of one hand towards his own eyes) while I open the door (he mimed rotating the lever) and take down the inattentive guard with a single karate chop to the neck (he sliced his hand downward from his ear to his side). They're standard field signals, you know.'

'Really?' mused Archie. 'They actually have a field signal for *I'm going to take down the inattentive guard with a single karate chop to the neck*? Because if you ask me, it really looks like you're telling a dog to sit.'

'I suggest you check your manuals, Agent Yankee.'

'OK.' Archie exhaled, letting the air flap his lips. Then he continued tentatively, 'Are you sure you can take down the guard with a karate chop anyway? I mean, I'm not being funny but you're not exactly a highly trained unarmed-combat specialist. I'm not even sure you could take down a teddy bear without back-up.'

'Trust me, it's easy,' Barney assured his friend. 'You just sneak up behind them and . . . *Hiiiyyaah*.'

'Hiiiyyaah?' Archie grimaced quizzically.

'Hiiiyyaah.' Barney nodded. 'You chop them right where their neck meets their shoulder and they keel over like a sack of spuds. I've seen it done loads of times.'

'Yeah, in *films*.'

'Was I right about the boiler suits?'

'Yeah, but . . .'

Before Archie could protest further, Barney got hold of the locking handle and, with a movement

277

that did actually resemble an arm-wrestler levering his opponent's hand on to the table, opened the door.

Archie and Finn crouched in the alcove to monitor the empty corridor but Archie couldn't resist turning to watch Barney enter the security suite. Behind the door was a small windowless room in which a single figure wearing a hooded white boiler suit was sitting at a plain desk. Mounted on the wall beyond the desk were ten flat-screen TVs showing assorted sections of corridors.

Barney crept towards the guard, who was slouched in his chair with his back to the doorway. When he was no more than a foot behind the figure he realised the guard was actually asleep on the job – just as he had predicted.

Raising his right arm, he brought the edge of his palm to within an inch of the guard's neck and took a few practice swings, each time stopping his hand short of its target. Confident he had perfected his aim, he raised his arm above his head and chopped his hand down on the guard's shoulder with all his might.

'HhiiiyyyaaaAAHH!'

Archie winced at the force of the blow then watched events unfold in a matter of seconds.

Barney took a step back as the guard rocked forward in his seat.

He's actually unconscious, Archie thought, giving Barney a surprised thumbs up.

Then the guard jumped to his feet and wheeled round, clutching his neck.

'OWWWW!' he groaned angrily. 'That REALLY hurt!'

Chapter 37

Barney and the guard stared at each other for a moment, each as stunned as the other by the turn of events.

'Who are you?' the guard demanded. 'How did you get here?'

'I could ask you the same thing,' Barney said suavely, if nonsensically.

The guard shook his head vigorously to throw off the effects of Barney's karate chop then, as if he'd just remembered the purpose of his job, he lunged at the intruder.

Barney danced backwards, dodging two or three punches before retaliating with a volley of crisp blows that left the guard unconscious. At least, that's how he imagined it.

In reality Barney's evasive footwork was so sluggish that he'd only retreated about a metre before the guard was upon him, hands wide apart. As the guard's arms began to close, Barney tried to duck under the embrace but he was too slow and the guard gathered him up in what looked like a powerful bear hug.

'He's got Barney,' Archie told Finn urgently. 'Wait here.'

Before he'd had a chance to formulate a plan, Archie leaped into the security suite.

'Drop him,' he ordered, 'or I'm going to drop you.'

The guard glanced over his shoulder at Archie. His features were masked by the hood of his boiler suit, which covered his head like a bag with just a narrow rectangle of blacked-out plastic to see through. Without a word the guard proceeded to squeeze Barney with greater force, squashing his fleshy pink cheek against his chest.

'OK,' Archie shrugged. 'Have it your way.'

Skipping deftly to one side so that he was behind the guard, Archie leaped high into the air and drove his right leg out straight, slamming his heel into the guard's back. The guard exhaled with a groan, stumbling forward a couple of steps and releasing his grip on Barney.

Archie raised his hands as the faceless boiler suit turned and lumbered towards him. Standing his ground, Archie cycled his arms like pistons. But to his surprise, his hands bounced off the guard's strangely squidgy body. As the guard towered over him, Archie threw punches to his stomach and chest but every time his fists just seemed to spring back uselessly.

'It's like fighting Jabba the Hutt,' Archie panted.

Grabbing Archie roughly by the shoulders, the guard drove him across the room, knocking the desk over and slamming him against the wall. Holding one forearm across Archie's face, the guard pinned him back with his considerable weight. Panicking, Archie found that he couldn't breathe. His enemy's spongy arm was suffocating him like a pillow.

'Put him down!' Barney ordered. He began throwing punches at the guard's back but they literally bounced off. Stepping back, he tried one of Archie's spinning back-kicks but he gave up after the fourth attempt, having failed to get both feet off the ground. Realising he would need some sort of weapon to defeat the guard, Barney turned his attention to the overturned desk, searching desperately through the contents of its drawers for a suitable implement.

Archie knew he didn't have long. His eyes were ballooning and his lungs were burning. Frantically flailing his hands, he slapped at the guard's hooded face and scrabbled helplessly against the wall. He could feel his vision and his hopes fading.

Then, as one arm flapped feebly above his head, his fingers brushed against something solid.

Maybe this fight wasn't quite over after all!

Blindly raising his other arm Archie gripped the object with both hands and, harnessing every ounce of fight he had in his body, yanked it with all his strength. He felt it come loose and, as it dropped to the floor, guided its trajectory and added a little energy of his own, smashing the TV screen on to the guard's head.

Archie felt the guard's grip on him relax and he thought his battle was won. But his opponent quickly recovered, angrily shoving him against the wall with more force than before.

Peering up from behind the forearm that was obliterating his nose and mouth, Archie reached up for another TV. Again he grabbed the screen and hauled on it for all he was worth, once again guiding its fall and supplementing its momentum as he slammed it on to the guard's head.

This time Archie didn't wait to see if he'd done enough. By the time the second television hit the floor he had already reached up for a third, yanking it from its mounting and listening to it come crashing down. Sensing victory, Archie stretched for one more TV set which he forced down on the guard with extra venom.

The guard's arms dropped to his sides and he stumbled backwards a couple of steps before dropping to his knees and toppling on to his front. Fighting for breath, Archie looked down at the huge white figure slumped on the floor, surrounded by shattered screens.

'Looks like the grown-ups were right after all,' he said. 'Too much TV really is bad for you.'

'Are you OK?' Barney gasped.

'I'm fine,' Archie replied. As he spoke he noticed his friend was brandishing a shatterproof ruler like a knife. 'Is that the best weapon you could find?' he asked. 'Were you going to use it to set him straight on a few things?'

Barney grinned sheepishly. 'I think I would have got the measure of him.'

284

As Archie glanced down he noticed one of the guard's gloves had come loose revealing a section of his arm that was covered in brick-red skin. Gingerly Archie reached down, gripped a fistful of the guard's hood and hauled it off. As the mask was removed the guard's head spilt out on to the floor like a big rust-coloured marshmallow. Archie felt faint. There was no neck or chin or indeed any discernible features, just an amorphous mass of squidginess, tapering slightly towards its rounded crown. Lifting the head with his foot, Archie could make out two beady black eyes and a tiny opening for a mouth in the middle of the spongy mass.

A sense of dread gripped Archie as he removed the guard's boots and gloves to discover that he had no hands or feet. Each of his thick, squashy limbs culminated in a blunt nub that was, apart from the absence of the eyes and mouth, identical to his head.

'What *is* it?' Barney asked.

'I don't know,' Archie replied, a shiver rippling up his back. 'It's like a giant starfish or something.'

Barney stared pale-faced at the creature they'd just knocked out. 'That's so creepy.'

'I know. But we need to hurry,' Archie said firmly,

forcing himself to focus on the task ahead instead of the mutant at his feet. 'We've got bigger fish to fry.' As he spoke he noticed three boiler suits hanging on hooks next to the doorway. 'Let's get our disguises on and get moving. Finn, come in and close the door.'

Archie handed out the suits and the friends started pulling them on. As Archie zipped himself up to his chin he noticed the pockets of Barney's hoody bulging with sweets and chocolate.

'Where'd you get them from?'

'The hotel minibar,' Barney beamed, patting the snacks now hidden under his disguise. 'Hunger is an agent's worst enemy.'

'Really?' said Archie, hauling on his boots. 'I'd have thought fighting Stickman again or a school of giant mutated starfish might be slightly more dangerous than a rumbly tummy, but there you go.'

When all three had finished dressing they checked each other out.

'Looking good,' said Archie, his hood bobbing enthusiastically. 'It's amazing the suits all fit so well, especially when you think about what a funny shape the starfish guy is.'

The other two turned their whole bodies to exchange shrugs.

'So here's the plan,' said Archie. 'We'll split up and go out on a recce. Finn, you come with me. If anyone finds Doom and his captives, let the others know.' He tapped his hood by his ear to remind everyone they were equipped to stay in touch. 'Any questions?'

When neither answered, Archie opened the door and stepped into the corridor followed by Finn and Barney. They headed along the passageway towards the T-junction.

As they neared the end of the corridor Archie's heart leaped into his mouth. Two large figures dressed in white boiler suits and carrying clipboards rounded the corner and started heading straight towards them.

Chapter 38

Remembering that he was disguised head to toe in the boiler suit, Archie straightened his back and strode confidently towards the oncoming enemy, flanked by Barney and Finn.

As they passed each other Archie caught his breath and his muscles tensed involuntarily, but Doom's two henchmen barely seemed to notice the three slightly smaller guards heading the other way. At the T-junction Archie paused to take a deep breath. It was hot inside the hood and he could already feel beads of sweat worming their way down his temples.

'X-ray to Yankee – what's your status?' Gemma's voice sounded in Archie's ear.

'We're under cover,' Archie murmured. 'One guard is down. We're going to split up and look around.'

'Copy that. I spoke to IC. She's furious with us, by the way. She's sending a task force but they won't be here for at least another hour.'

'So it's down to us.' Archie's tone was determined.

'Also, I've done some research on Doctor Doom's renovations since he moved in. He had a company that specialises in digging mine shafts on site for a year.'

'Mine shafts?'

'And another thing. He paid a firm called Splash Out eighty grand this time last year. I hacked into their company files and they billed a certain Y. Villenemi for installing an Olympic-sized swimming pool.'

'But that outside pool has been here since Romario lived here,' Archie said.

'I know, it's weird. I'll let you know if I find anything else. Out.'

Archie surveyed the corridor in both directions. It was empty.

'You go left,' he instructed Barney. 'We'll go right. Let me know if you find anything.'

Barney gave him a thumbs up.

A short distance along the corridor Archie and Finn

came across a door. Archie rotated the locking lever and nudged it open a couple of inches. It led on to a circular metal grille platform – the landing of a spiral staircase that descended through a vertical shaft into the rock. Remembering what Gemma had said about Dr Doom hiring the excavation specialists, Archie's curiosity was aroused. There was no one about so he pushed the door fully open and hurried down the stairs, urging Finn to follow.

After descending about twenty metres into the mountain they came across another door which led to a vast underground room containing three long marble workbenches laden with glass containers of every imaginable shape and size. There were Pyrex cylinders and spherical vases and conical jugs joined by wiggly glass tubes and rubber pipes. Some contained vivid liquids bubbling over a Bunsen burner while others were full of slimy gunk that seemed to be fermenting in its own gases.

'It's some sort of science lab,' Archie whispered.

Clusters of figures in boiler suits were studying their experiments, measuring viscosities and temperatures and noting the results studiously.

Archie and Finn ventured into the laboratory,

weaving slowly between the huddled figures without being noticed.

'That's funny,' Archie muttered. 'I'd have thought coming into a chemistry lab we'd cause a bit more of a *reaction.*'

Finn said nothing but Archie suspected that he was blinking at him vacantly.

When he reached the far wall, which was formed of a single sheet of blue glass, Archie rounded the end of a workbench to make his way back to the staircase. As he turned he thought he saw something move across the wall, a familiar torpedo-shaped silhouette that seemed to glide behind the glass. When he looked directly at the glass the shape had gone and he was left wondering whether he'd imagined it. But before he could process the information his attention was snatched by something altogether more horrifying.

The adjacent wall of the laboratory was lined with shelves that were stacked with large glass jars and oversized test tubes. Each vessel contained different amounts of a pink substance that looked like a cross between jelly and raw meat. It reminded Archie of a sheep's lung he'd watched being dissected in biology once. As if that wasn't revolting enough, the shelves were labelled with two words that traced an icy finger down Archie's spine.

GENETIC WASTE

He realised that the grisly pink blobs were samples of living tissue – the leftovers of Doom's twisted experiments. A few of the organisms throbbed with some helpless inner pulse; others still bore the trademarks of their original form – a beak here, a few scales there, the odd eye staring out ghoulishly.

Archie felt sick. All he could think about was his father being reduced to one of these pathetic samples. He *had* to get out of this lab and find where Doom was keeping him. Archie glanced at his watch – 1.45. In fifteen minutes Doom would put his evil plan into action. Feeling the frantic panic rising inside him, he marched towards the exit.

At the end of the shelf one particular test tube caught Archie's eye. Like the others it contained a dollop of gibbering tissue, but something in its midst was glinting in the harsh clinical light of the lab. As he stopped to study it more closely Archie recognised the shiny object and noticed that the tube was labelled with a series of digits.

24121600

He understood immediately what the numbers meant. Pausing to check no one was looking his way, Archie grabbed the test tube and slipped it into the pocket of his boiler suit. Then he led Finn smartly to the exit, trying to suppress the almost overwhelming urge to sprint for the door. He was within a few feet of escaping the lab when a tall figure dressed in the seemingly obligatory hooded boiler suit stepped across his path.

'Hold it!' the figure ordered.

Archie's stomach felt like a rock. Busted, he thought. It had only been a matter of time before somebody noticed two figures that were shorter and slighter than everyone else sneaking about the laboratory.

'Where are you going with that sample?' the figure demanded, gesturing at Archie's pocket.

'What, this?' Archie said, feigning surprise. 'Oh just to, you know, er . . . Gamma . . . Sector.'

'There is no Gamma Sector.' The figure crossed his arms resolutely.

Double busted, thought Archie. 'Didn't you read the memo?' he argued. 'The sectors have all been redesignated because of a possible code amber. Gamma Sector is the new secret identifier for the room Doctor Doom is in right now. He wants this sample and I don't want to keep him waiting because some drone isn't up to speed with the latest operational protocol.'

The figure's stance softened slightly and Archie stepped past him, hoping to make it through the door before the guard could analyse the plausibility of what he'd been told. Archie turned the locking lever and swung the door open.

'Stop!' the figure commanded.

Archie groaned.

'Where do you think you're going?'

Archie cleared his throat. 'Well, I . . . er . . . it's funny but . . .'

'Everyone knows the quickest way to Gamma Sector is in the lift. It takes you straight to the observation gantry overlooking the Transmutator itself. Then you can just take the stairs down to the operations platform, which is where Doctor Doom will be preparing the control deck for his ultimate experiment. Otherwise you'd have to go through bio screening and security, and you know what a headache that can be.'

'Tell me about it.' Archie nodded. 'Thanks for your help.'

'Well, we're all on the same evil team, right?' the guard laughed.

Maintaining a dignified pace Archie headed towards the elevator, followed by Finn.

When the lift doors slid shut Archie leaned against the mirrored side and blew out hard.

'Well, that was close,' he said.

'I know,' said Finn. 'It's lucky you knew they'd renamed all the sectors or we'd have been in serious trouble.'

As the lift glided smoothly upward Archie called Barney to update him on their progress. 'Yankee to Zulu,' he whispered. 'Come in, Zulu, do you read?'

There was a long pause before Barney's voice came into Archie's earpiece.

'This is Zulu.' He sounded strange. 'The clawed man has an unbreakable grip.'

'This is no time for codes,' Archie said sternly. 'What is your status?'

'I was given away by what I had hidden.'

'Seriously, Barney, cut it out.'

'The ant is strong but its weakness is sugar.'

'Barney!' Archie waited but there was no reply. 'Barney!'

Silence.

Chapter 39

The lift doors slid apart and two large figures dressed in white stepped into the elevator as Archie and Finn stepped out. They found themselves on a small metal balcony about fifteen feet above the glossy white floor of a huge rectangular room. The gantry ran along three sides of the room, excluding the far wall, and a gangway spanned the width of the room, connecting to another balcony directly opposite.

The footbridge passed above a large leather chair positioned behind a banked U-shaped control deck covered in knobs and dials. An imposing figure dressed in black was standing in front of the console with his square shoulders hunched and his hands behind his back like a bodyguard. Sitting in the leather chair about thirty metres away was a stout figure in a round-necked suit.

Archie could see that one half of his skull appeared to be covered in green scales, and although the front of his head was completely bald a tangle of grey hair sprouted wildly from his crown. A bulbous eye protruded from the scaly side of his face and every now and then a fat sticky tongue forced its way out of his mouth.

'Doctor Doom, I presume,' Archie whispered to himself. 'We meet at last.'

'*I'm* not Doctor Doom.' Finn frowned and jabbed a scaly finger at the figure below. '*He's* Doctor Doom.'

The room was brightly lit by numerous fluorescent tubes hanging from the roof and a holographic map of the world was projected on to the glass wall behind Doom's control deck.

The other three walls of the room were covered by banks of metal cabinets crammed with flashing lights, buttons, endless switches and a baffling variety of instrumentation. Archie guessed they housed the electronic operating systems of Dr Doom's experimental apparatus.

As Archie and Finn edged along the gantry they were

able to get a better view of the monstrous contraption that occupied three quarters of the space inside the room. At its centre was a giant glass dome filled with swirling smoke that glowed orange, its crest almost reaching the height of the balcony. Four thick silver ducting tubes fed from the upturned bowl, looping way above Archie before feeding down into large glass cylinders positioned vertically around the equipment at equal intervals. Archie thought he whole thing looked slightly comical, like some child's model of a spider missing a few legs, but as he crept closer he saw what was in the cylinders and he was gripped by terror.

Three of the vertical tubes contained *people*. With wires stuck to their temples, chests and wrists. They stared out of their glass confines as if in some sort of trance. Archie continued round the gantry, studying them one at a time. The first cylinder housed a blond teenage boy Archie recognised as Henry Ulrik and the next contained Karl Schumaker. As the third tube came into view Archie caught his breath.

'Look,' Finn whispered. 'There's Richard Hunt.'

'You know my father?' Archie asked.

'Your father? I don't think so,' Finn replied. 'But I pulled that man out of a car once. I can't remember

299

how he got there, but he was at the bottom of the sea. Come to think of it, I don't know why I was there. I suppose being able to breathe underwater has its uses every now and then.'

Archie was mesmerised by the sight of his father inside the glass cylinder. He looked weak and vulnerable, and Archie realised that he had been subconsciously reassuring himself with the notion that his father was indestructible. After all, Richard Hunt had survived countless war zones – what harm could one mad scientist do? But now it was obvious his father was only human, and just as helpless in this scenario as Doom's other victims. Archie hated Dr Doom for reducing him to such a feeble-looking specimen. What must he have been through to end up like this? Even his father's eyes looked full of something Archie had never seen before. They were full of fear.

'This can't be happening,' Archie muttered. 'We have to stop this experiment, Finn. Otherwise it'll mean total disaster.'

'I know,' Finn replied. 'It'll never work with your father in cylinder two.'

Archie turned to look at his friend, who was still transfixed by the scene below. 'What do you mean?'

'The transmutation doesn't work with grown-ups,' Finn said, as if stating the obvious. 'That's why all the criminals' clones are such freaks. Doom's plan only works on kids.'

His heart pounding, Archie turned and studied the captives. He remembered reading that Henry Ulrik was sixteen years old although he looked much younger now, strapped up and cocooned in glass. He couldn't recall Karl Schumaker's age but he had always assumed, mostly because of his beard, that he was well into his twenties. Archie could see now that the goatee on Karl's chin was distinctly wispy, the sort of fluffy growth sported by some of the boys in Year Twelve who were desperate to demonstrate their masculinity. It was apparent that Karl was certainly no older than Ulrik and quite probably younger.

By contrast Archie's father looked haggard. He was pale and thin, his silver hair reinforcing his age.

As Archie ducked low behind the railings of the balcony his mind started to race. The original coded message on Doom's website had warned that *Police will take care of Hunt this afternoon*, which could refer to Archie just as much as his father. Gemma had

301

mentioned the MI6 theory that Doom was using the SPADE database to harvest individuals with particular abilities for his experiment, and both Archie and his dad had scored highly. Archie thought about the text message Dr Doom had sent him and one phrase stuck in his mind.

The last thing I need is to have you snooping around.

On the face of it Doom had meant that Archie's presence would have been an unwelcome hindrance, but what if he'd meant that Archie coming to his hideout was the final thing, the final *ingredient*, he required to complete his experiment?

'He never meant to kidnap my father at all,' Archie whispered, taking a deep breath. 'All the time I thought I was tracking down Doom he was actually reeling *me* in, using Dad as bait . . .'

'Sorry?' Finn asked.

'I feel so stupid,' Archie mumbled to himself. 'I thought he was showing off but he *wanted* me to solve his riddle and find his hideout. He's been playing me all along.' As Archie silently rebuked himself for being so naive he realised that all was not yet lost. So what if he's been leading me into a trap? he thought. As long as he doesn't know I'm here, I'm the one with the upper hand.

Suddenly the room rang with the sound of a harsh eastern European voice blaring from ceiling-mounted loudspeakers.

'Hello, Master Hunt!' The figure in the leather chair was leaning forward and talking into a microphone. 'It's so nice of you to drop in on us unannounced. We found your friend wandering about and my soldiers are *taking care of him* as I speak.' A long corpulent cackle was followed by some laboured gasps before Dr Doom continued. 'Do you see what I did there? The phrase *taking care of him* could have one of two very different meanings. We might well be offering him lavish hospitality *or*, equally, we might be torturing him to within an inch of his pathetic life. I'll leave it to you to decide which.' Archie squeezed his hands into fists as he imagined his friend suffering at the hands of Doom's mutants. Meanwhile, the sound of smug laughter filled his ears for another thirty seconds. 'Anyway, I reviewed the CCTV footage from the security suite and saw you disabling one of my guards so there is no use hiding any more. Besides, I want to help you – you must be scared being all alone in a strange place.

'I know you are listening to me so pay close attention to what I am about to say. Don't worry. I am a reasonable person, Master Hunt, and I would never force you to do anything – I am simply going to let you make your own choice. Either you show yourself in the next thirty seconds or I will kill your father. That's all. Your time starts now.'

Filled with panic, Archie considered the impossible choice facing him. If he gave himself up he would be playing right into Dr Doom's hands. Then who would stop him from completing his evil experiment and pressing ahead with his quest for world domination? And even if Archie did hand himself in, he knew there was no guarantee his father would be safe. But then again, he couldn't hide up here on the gantry and do nothing while some mad scientist executed his father.

'Ten seconds, Master Hunt!' boomed Doom's voice.

Frantically Archie pulled off his hood and unzipped his boiler suit.

'Three . . . two . . . one . . . time's up, Master Hunt.'

'OK, OK,' Archie yelled. 'I'm coming down – just don't hurt my dad.'

304

Dr Doom watched the slight figure in the hoody and jeans slink down the metal staircase with his head bowed in defeat. His hood was pulled up as if to hide the disgrace he felt at being publicly paraded before the people whose lives had depended on him. As he shuffled despondently across the operations platform he made no eye contact with Richard Hunt or either of the other two human guinea pigs. He passed the huge glass dome and slouched towards the evil mastermind's control console.

'Well, well, Master Hunt,' Dr Doom chuckled. 'It's a pleasure to finally meet you at last.'

Archie smiled grimly. 'The pleasure is all yours,' he muttered.

'Now, now, Master Hunt,' Doom teased. 'Let's not be a sore loser. Admit it – I won fair and square.'

Archie swallowed. 'Whatever you say.'

Chapter 40

'Allow me to introduce myself,' Doom announced grandly. 'I am your evil enemy.'

'I know you're evil,' Archie replied. 'And I know you're my enemy. Tell me something I don't know.'

'Not *your evil enemy*,' Doom spat. 'Yuri Villenemi.'

'All I can hear is *your evil enemy, your evil enemy*,' Archie said blankly, enjoying Doom's frustration.

'Look, I am Professor Villenemi!' screamed the evil mastermind. 'And my first name is Yuri.'

'OK, keep your hair on,' Archie retorted, as confidently as he could. 'What's left of it anyway.'

'You won't be feeling quite so clever when I have finished with you,' Villenemi promised.

'Shall we get on with this then?' Archie asked. 'The suspense is killing me.'

'Not so fast, Master Hunt,' Villenemi soothed. 'I have been waiting for this moment for many, many years. Before I enjoy my triumph I want to show off – for quite a long time. I will brag to you about my incredible master plan in great detail so that you will understand just how brilliant I am. Now that I have you right where I want you I intend to savour my victory, safe in the knowledge that you have absolutely no chance of stopping me – none whatsoever.'

'We'll see about that,' Archie snorted.

'Well, well, I admire your fighting spirit,' Villenemi chuckled. 'But save your energy – I don't want you to be too tired to enjoy what I have in store for you.'

'And what might that be?'

'Only the culmination of a lifetime of genius,' Villenemi announced. 'For the last decade I have been studying the science of genetic engineering. I secretly developed my techniques while I was employed by the British government but they didn't share my passion or my vision for the potential benefits of cross-cloning. They had some *ethical* problem with me testing my procedures on humans.'

307

'Some people are so unreasonable.' Archie muttered.

'They tried to lock me up but I escaped,' Villenemi declared defiantly. 'One female agent pursued me with impressive dedication and she nearly caught me too – but unfortunately she came to an untimely end.' The evil professor allowed himself a devilish laugh. 'They came after me all guns blazing and thought they'd destroyed me. But I outsmarted them and started again from scratch. Using the groundbreaking techniques I'd developed in the government labs, I created the incredible equipment you see before you.' Dr Doom gestured grandly at the glass-domed contraption. 'With my revolutionary Transmutator I have the power to genetically isolate and extract particular attributes from individual samples and combine them to create a single superior human.'

'Your guards are far from human,' Archie countered.

'You're very observant, Master Hunt,' Villenemi sneered. 'I wanted my creation to possess some characteristics that don't occur in the realm of humans but can be found elsewhere in nature.' Pressing a button on the panel in front of him, Villenemi mumbled, 'Bring him in.' The door at the far end of the room slid open and Barney stumbled on to the operations platform, his hands bound in front of him. Striding in behind him, with a long bony arm resting authoritatively on Barney's shoulder, was the gangly stickman. He guided the boy roughly to a position just yards from the control deck where guard and captive stood side by side.

Barney gazed around, taking in his surroundings with hungry eyes. His face was a mixture of terror and wonder.

'You have already met Antony, I believe,' Villenemi said cordially to Archie, as if introducing guests at a party. 'He is ten times as strong as a normal man because he has been transmutated with an ant. Unfortunately he has also inherited an ant's impossibly sweet tooth – he simply can't help himself where chocolate is concerned. In one of my earliest experiments I cross-cloned myself with a close cousin of the chameleon in the hope of being able to blend in with my surroundings should MI6 ever catch up with me.' Villenemi touched his face involuntarily. 'I wouldn't say that procedure was a total success. I have some characteristics of the reptile but camouflage is not one of them.'

'In other words you failed?' Barney taunted.

'On that occasion, yes,' Villenemi snapped. 'But I have since perfected the process by trial and error.'

'Where did you find your guinea pigs?' Archie enquired.

'While working for the British government I secretly made contacts in the criminal underworld, mixing with all sorts of dangerous characters. It was easy to pay a group of hoodlums to intercept a prison van full of violent convicts for my purposes. You'd be amazed what these desperate criminals were willing to submit themselves to given the promise of money and power.'

'So all your experiments were carried out on dangerous criminals?'

'Nearly all,' Villenemi said with a smirk. 'I had some success with these procedures but I realised eventually that the strands of adult human DNA were too brittle to be modified satisfactorily. I acquired a young boy and discovered that his DNA was much more malleable.'

'When you say acquired . . .' Archie probed.

'OK, so I kidnapped him,' Villenemi boomed. 'But he was a miserable little scrap so I'm sure no one missed him. The animal quality I finally decided to include in my creation is most readily found in sea creatures and he was my first attempt at a transmutation of human and marine DNA.'

'Where is he now?'

'Oh that's very good, Master Hunt,' Villenemi laughed wickedly. 'Do you take me for a fool? I think you and I both know exactly where he is, don't we?'

Archie held his breath. Villenemi's laughter subsided and he continued, 'I know as well as you do that you captured Finn in Hamburg,' he said smarmily. 'I also know that an RAF Hercules was sent to fly him back to the UK for interrogation. The funny thing is they won't get anything out of him – he can't remember his own name some days.'

'Memory can be a funny thing,' Archie said. 'Some things are never forgotten.'

'I'm not here to talk about my specimens anyway,' Villenemi hissed impatiently. 'I want to talk about *me*, and tell you how I brilliantly devised a machine capable of genetically extracting up to two attributes from each of three separate donors, as long as the donor is a teenager, or indeed younger. As if that wasn't mind-bendingly clever enough, I have perfected the process of adding a single animal attribute to my genetic

311

super-being. I did experiment with adding multiple animal traits but my trials just ended up creating useless blubbering masses.'

Barney turned to Antony and whispered, 'Did you hear what he called you? I wouldn't stand for that if I were you.'

With a grunt the mutant shoved Barney.

'Why are you designing this super-being anyway?' Archie asked.

'This is Operation RALLY,' Villenemi declared. 'By creating the genetic blueprint of the ultimate soldier I am about to *rally* against those who rejected me. With this being's DNA I will clone the soldier hundreds of thousands of times. Then I shall sell whole armies to any despicable warlord who happens to have a grudge against Britain – oh, and billions of pounds to spare. My made-to-measure mercenaries will destabilise the balance of world power, bringing misery to the British government in the process. By retaining the blueprint of the ultimate soldier I will dictate who possesses military supremacy in the world and I will be rich beyond my wildest dreams.' Villenemi threw his head back and let out a laugh of pure evil satisfaction, 'Mwah, ha, ha, ha.'

'Why Operation RALLY?' asked Archie. 'Why not Operation ULTIMATE REVENGE or something?'

Villenemi dropped his shoulders slightly. 'That would have sounded a little more menacing, I agree, but we evil geniuses have to give our brainchild an acronym and I couldn't think of one for U.L.T.I.M.A.T.E. R.E.V.E.N.G.E.'

'What does RALLY stand for then?'

Villenemi cleared his throat and said, 'It's the operation to Reak Almighty Lawlessness Lots, Yahoo.'

Silence filled the huge room for a moment.

'Is that the best you could do?' Archie sniggered.

'That doesn't even make any sense, does it?' added Barney.

Yuri Villenemi shifted awkwardly in his seat. 'At least the word RALLY gets the message across.'

'Except you don't spell wreak like that,' Archie pointed out, trying to sound helpful. 'It's W,R,E,A,K, not R,E,A,K, so actually you've named your life's work Operation WALLY. Is that the sort of message you were hoping to get across?'

Villenemi didn't say anything for a while but the scales on his head changed from green to vivid red for about a minute before cooling down to their original colour.

Turning to his guard, Barney whispered, 'Honestly, these Odious Masterminds are so condescending! First you're a useless blubbering mass, now you're a wally.' Antony responded with another angry shove.

'Why have you chosen these samples for your experiment?' Archie asked.

'A-ha,' Villenemi exclaimed, grateful for the opportunity to show off again. 'Master Ulrik is a champion biathlete so he has been selected for his marksmanship and sheer endurance, while our young mountaineer, Master Schumaker, possesses extraordinary climbing ability and unparalleled courage. I will include my secret characteristic from the marine world but my final volunteer is not your father at all.' Villenemi allowed himself a moment's pause before announcing gleefully, 'It is you, Master Hunt.'

'Er, yeah,' Archie whispered. 'I gathered.'

Villenemi looked crestfallen once more. 'Oh, come now. Please don't try and pretend you knew already,' he chuckled uncertainly. 'Did you?'

'Of course I did,' Archie insisted. 'As soon as I saw my father next to those two kids I knew he didn't fit in. But even if I hadn't worked it out then, you just told me that adult DNA is too brittle for your crackpot procedure.'

'Did I?' Villenemi mumbled. 'Drat. I didn't mean to give that away so soon.'

'Don't feel bad,' said Barney, rolling his eyes. 'You've only had, let me see, your *whole life* to prepare this little speech.'

'Where was I?' Villenemi frowned at Archie. 'Ah yes, I intended to kidnap you and stage a car crash to kill your father, leaving no one who would care enough to come looking for you. When my fake police officers bungled the job I thought I'd have to make do with a substitute. But then you appeared in Hamburg determined to save Daddy dearest and I realised that I could use your ingenuity to my advantage.'

'So why didn't you grab us as soon as we landed on your roof?' asked Archie.

'Oh, I considered it when I saw your little plane approaching.' Villenemi smiled smarmily. 'But it seemed a shame to interrupt you when you were doing such a marvellous job of coming to *me*. Besides, I was enjoying the thought of you scurrying around like a little lab rat. It was really quite tantalising.'

'Why did you choose me in the first place?' Archie asked.

'From you I shall be extracting your ability to fly and your inherited predisposition to excel at all martial arts. No other child in the world has your proven skill at the controls of a jet plane, while your aptitude for hand-to-hand combat will make my soldier especially valuable in guerrilla warfare.'

Archie remembered his father telling him he would turn out to be a natural at martial arts and he felt strangely uncomfortable – like he was the last one to be let in on a secret.

'Why does everyone keep going on about me being some sort of kung fu expert?' Archie asked. 'Even *I* only just found out I can kick the living daylights out of people – so how come you knew?'

'By all accounts you handled yourself *exceptionally* well in Hamburg,' Villenemi argued. 'And the spinning back kick in the security suite was quite something. You have certainly inherited the potential to be almost unbeatable in hand-to-hand combat.'

'When he was in the forces my dad was trained in self-defence, but I don't think he was any kind of expert,' said Archie.

316

'My dear Master Hunt.' Villenemi's patronising chortle made Archie's skin crawl. 'I wasn't talking about your father. I was talking about your mother.'

'My mother?' Archie could barely breathe.

'Yes, your mother.' The evil mastermind's scales turned a brilliant shade of orange. 'As I'm sure you know, she was a highly trained government agent and an expert in a multitude of martial arts. She was the operative who tried so hard to track me down when everyone overreacted just because a few orphans didn't survive my genetic experimentation.'

'My mother was an MI6 agent?'

'Oh dear. I seem to have let the cat out of the bag.' Villenemi feigned embarrassment.

'Did you know her?' Archie asked weakly, although in his broken heart he already knew the answer.

'Oh yes – your mother and I played cat and mouse for some weeks. She nearly caught me too.' Villenemi drew a satisfied breath. 'That's why I had to kill her.'

Chapter 41

'Y- you killed my mother?' Archie stammered.

'I'm afraid I did. My bad,' said Villenemi. 'If it's any consolation, she was too good an agent to be killed in the line of duty. That's why I had to find out where she lived and run her over when she was off duty. It was the only way I could get her off my case.'

'You monster,' Barney snarled.

Archie was speechless, rage and hatred coursing through his veins. His head throbbed with an almost overwhelming desire for immediate revenge but fighting his instincts he said and did nothing. Clenching his teeth, he waited for his anger to subside. He knew he had to stay calm for his plan to work. Your time will come, Doctor Doom, he thought. Sooner than you think.

'Well, I think I've talked for long enough,' Villenemi announced. 'If I went on much longer you might get the impression I'm some sort of twisted egomaniac.'

'No chance,' added Barney. 'I mean, so far you've come across as being extremely well-balanced and humble.'

'Anyway, I rather fancy taking over the world now,' said Villenemi, as though he'd had a sudden yen for a cup of tea.

'Will the experiment hurt?' Archie asked.

'Absolutely not,' Villenemi replied reassuringly. 'I won't feel a thing. You, on the other hand, will experience searing pain like you never thought possible.' Everyone waited around awkwardly while Villenemi indulged in another peal of wicked laughter. 'Claws, wire up our final volunteer into cylinder four, would you.'

The figure dressed in black immediately snapped into action. As his arms came from behind his back Archie could see that instead of hands he had two giant crab's claws. He made his way across the glossy floor, shuffling sideways, holding his pincers out in front of him like a surgeon who's just scrubbed up. As he turned, Archie noticed a shell hump that grew from his tortuously hunched shoulders enveloping his whole neck and half of his skull, to which it was fused. With his head rendered immovable, the crabman had to stop every few yards and rotate his whole body to check he was progressing in the right direction. Finally reaching his target, he grabbed Archie firmly by the arm.

Except the figure standing on the operations platform with his hood over his head wasn't Archie. Archie was still hiding on the gantry, watching the whole scene play out beneath him, while feeding Finn his lines through his wireless earpiece.

Finn's instructions had been to simply repeat to the evil mastermind everything he heard in his earpiece.

Holding Finn with one pincer, Claws started dragging him across to the vacant cylinder, which Villenemi raised with a lever on his control deck. Instinctively Finn resisted, struggling desperately against the crabman's efforts.

'Don't fight him,' Archie whispered.

Finn turned to face Claws. 'Don't fight him,' he said defiantly.

'You what?' frowned Claws.

'Don't repeat this,' Archie urged Finn. 'I'm just telling you to let him wire you up.'

320

'Don't repeat this,' Finn sneered into the crabman's face. 'I'm just telling you to let him wire you up.'

Holding Finn's arm, Claws turned his body towards Villenemi. 'I think this one's lost the plot, boss,' he said.

'Just get him connected up,' Villenemi snapped. 'It's time to get this show on the road.'

Archie held his breath while he watched Claws connecting the wires to Finn's temples and wrists. 'Let's get you strapped in nice and tight,' Claws said menacingly as he attached Velcro belts tightly round Finn's chest and legs, securing him to a backplate. With mock concern he added, 'If you're not strapped in you could end up getting hurt, and we wouldn't want that now, would we?'

When his work was done Claws sidled back across the operations platform, resuming his post in front of the control deck.

'I have one last question,' Archie muttered and Finn echoed his request. 'Which animal trait did you finally select for your ultimate soldier?'

'Ah yes, I'm so glad you asked,' Villenemi replied smugly. 'As I said, I realised that many sea creatures possess this quality, which is why I experimented with starfish for a while, but everyone I created was just so *spineless*. Finn's transmutation was actually a huge breakthrough – apart from the memory loss. While potentially useful, his ability to breathe underwater was just a side effect. The great discovery was to see how quickly his scales grew back. Eventually I perfected extracting a similar genetic code from a crab and have used it to create Claws here. I'm sure he'll be only too happy to give you a demonstration.'

Archie watched the crabman hold his arms in front of him, grabbing one pincer firmly with the other. With a violent twist, accompanied by the sound of snapping shell and popping tendons, he wrenched off his own arm and threw it to the floor.

Within seconds the empty sleeve hanging limply at the crabman's side began to twitch and stretch. Archie's eyes grew wider as he watched a brand new pincer grow from the severed stump. It took less than a minute for the new claw to develop to the exact size of the original. In the same time, the exposed muscle on the elbow of the discarded limb had itself begun to regenerate, sprouting into a complete upper arm and shoulder.

Archie felt the blood drain from his face as he

considered the potential effects of Villenemi's discovery. He had isolated the gene responsible for tissue regeneration, which meant he was about to create the genetic blueprint of a totally indestructible soldier.

Sensing time was short, Archie crept along the balcony and edged out on to the gangway until he was directly above the evil mastermind's chair. Scanning the scene below, he noticed a badge painted on the glossy white floor immediately in front of the door. The logo was identical to the one on the roof – a black circle bisected by a golden flash with the same red lettering along its length. The logo was about four metres in diameter and as he studied it Archie thought he could see shimmering blue light through a zigzag crack along the edge of the lightning.

'As you see,' Villenemi continued proudly, 'my designer soldiers will be invincible. I will be able to name my price for my army and everyone in the British government who dismissed me as a crazy fantasist will rue the day they vilified me. Now I'm getting impatient. Claws, would you kindly take Mr Hunt's place in cylinder number two, please. Oh, and before you wire yourself up, do me a favour and kill him.'

323

'Not so fast, Lizard Features!' yelled Archie, who had climbed over the railing and was balancing on the edge of the bridge.

Yuri Villenemi spun round in his leather armchair and scanned the metal gantry above his head, his human eye blinking against the bright lights while the reptilian orb panned about wildly.

'Who's there?' he demanded, his fat forked tongue darting out of his mouth.

As Archie looked down on the scene below him he suddenly felt strangely woozy. You're not that high up, he told himself. Stay calm. But instantly he felt his vision getting blurry and his grip on the railing loosened. In the next instant Archie's feet slipped on the edge of the gangway and he toppled from the bridge.

Chapter 42

Archie hit the ground hard and sprawled across the floor. Villenemi was still growing accustomed to the glare when he heard the thud on the marble surface behind him. By the time he had swivelled his chair back round Archie was standing up, shaking his head to regain his composure.

'I knew it!' Barney whispered. 'I can't believe you all fell for the classic decoy manoeuvre. It's the oldest trick in the book.'

Archie tried to appear confident as he studied the evil mastermind up close for the first time. The scales over half of Villenemi's head comprised a myriad of tiny lumps, giving it a uniformly rough texture, while his shock of grey hair was bisected by a purple streak.

One cheek was smooth and plump but the reptilian skin over the other side of his face hung loose, gathering about his neck in folds and hanging under his chin in a pouch.

But Archie couldn't move his gaze from the single bulbous eyeball protruding from Villenemi's temple. The size and shape of an onion, it was wrapped in mottled skin that was puckered into circular wrinkles around a twopenny-sized hole, through which an unblinking eye peered hatefully at Archie.

'Allow me to introduce myself,' said Archie with a grim smile. 'The name's Hunt. Archie Hunt.'

Villenemi started to laugh but then stopped himself, looking with disbelief towards the hooded figure. 'If you are Archie Hunt, then who on earth is that?' he snarled, his scales turning from cool green to livid scarlet to an almost luminous aquamarine.

'Now, now, Doctor Doomed,' smiled Archie. 'Don't get too hot under the collar. You've just been chatting to an old friend. I believe you know him as Finn?'

'Seize him, Claws!' Villenemi commanded, his voice trembling with rage.

The crabman paused for a moment, unsure whether he was supposed to grab Finn or Archie. Deciding

Archie was the greater threat, he began shuffling rapidly sideways towards his target.

'Hold it right there,' Archie ordered.

Claws stopped and twisted to see that Archie had slipped one hand inside the pouch of his sweatshirt. The pocket was stretched around a long straight object that Archie was pointing in his direction.

'That's right,' said Archie. 'I've got a gun and I'm not afraid to use it. So why don't you go over there and stand against the wall, nice and slow, with your pincers in the air.'

The crabman sidled back across the room, stopping every few yards to check his orientation, and positioned himself against the wall where he fixed Archie with a furious scowl.

Archie turned and pointed his weapon at Villenemi.

'You as well, Doctor No-body.' Archie jerked his hand sideways in his pocket. 'Your friend seems a bit crabby – perhaps you'd like to go and cheer him up. You know, bring him out of his shell?'

Muttering words of defiance, Yuri Villenemi stood up and stepped out from behind his control deck.

'And you, Antony,' Archie ordered. 'In case you haven't twigged, this is a stick-up.'

327

Giving Barney an angry glare, Antony stepped reluctantly backwards, joining the other two villains against the wall.

'Barney, come and stand over here,' Archie instructed, leaping into the evil scientist's vacant chair and scanning the array of levers, knobs and flashing lights. His initial reaction was one of utter confusion but then he noticed that most of the major controls had been helpfully labelled. He began flicking switches and operating levers with one hand – the other remained in his pocket, training his weapon on his enemies.

'You don't honestly expect me to believe you would shoot me?' Villenemi sneered. 'You're just a kid.'

'Just try me,' Archie replied, giving him a steely stare. 'There's no telling what I'll do to you. You killed my mother in cold blood.'

'But Master Hunt,' Villenemi pleaded, 'I am part reptile – everything I do is in cold blood.'

Sliding three switches, Archie raised the three glass cylinders imprisoning his father and the two boys. Operating another slider brought a cylinder down around Finn with a pneumatic hiss.

Barney rushed over to free the three prisoners from the straps securing them to the machinery. Richard

328

Hunt and the two boys gathered into a trance-like huddle, their limbs trembling as if weakened by their spell inside the giant test tubes. Archie fought the almost overwhelming urge to run over and hug his father who seemed to still be in a deep stupor, oblivious to his surroundings. Instead he remained at his station, the keyboard on the console in front of him clicking feverishly beneath his fingertips.

'I will not be defeated by a bunch of . . . kids,' railed Villenemi furiously.

'If it's any consolation, we're not just any old kids,' Archie smiled. 'We're STINKBOMB – a team of undercover MI6 agents.'

'Why STINKBOMB?' Villenemi asked. 'Just out of curiosity, I mean.'

Archie looked up from the control deck momentarily. 'Simple. We're a secret team of intrepid-natured kids battling odious masterminds, basically.'

'Ooh, that's good,' Villenemi purred in spite of himself.

'Yeah,' Barney piped up. 'You won't see us coming and we'll get right up your nose.'

Archie selected 'Initiate Transmutation' and was immediately prompted to choose the number of specimens and their capsule identifiers. He requested a two-sample process then, glancing up from the computer to see that Finn was inside cylinder number four, he selected capsule numbers four and two.

Briefly the instruction 'Select desired gene identifiers' flashed before Archie's eyes, then the screen was a sea of letters and numbers arranged in countless rows.

Archie had no idea what the gene codes meant and he could feel his plan crumbling around him. Glancing over the control console he saw Villenemi watching him closely, the human half of his mouth curled into an evil smirk – the other side turned down in permanent froglike displeasure. Archie peered at the screen and scrolled through the rows of digits, desperately hoping to see something that made sense to him.

'Poor Master Hunt,' said Villenemi, his voice mockingly sympathetic. 'He looks confused.'

. 'I am,' agreed Archie. 'I can't decide. Should I shoot you now . . . or later?'

Just when Archie was about to despair of making any sense of the information on the screen he reached the last line of text. 'Allow Natural Genetic Realignment.'

'Bingo!' He selected this option and turned the

oversized master control dial all the way round to the setting labelled:

REVERSE TRANSMUTATION – CAUTION:
MAY CAUSE SELF-DESTRUCTION

Archie dialled in the maximum period of one minute on the 'Initiation Delay Control' and pressed the big green 'Start' button. Immediately a synthesised female voice echoed round the room. **'Reverse transmutation will commence in – sixty seconds.'**

'Oh man, the classic countdown finale,' Barney observed approvingly. 'Wicked!'

'You're crazy,' shrieked Villenemi, his air of supreme cool deserting him once again. 'The machinery has never been tested on a total reverse transmutation. The strain of realigning every genetic code will overload the mainframe and send the power core into meltdown. An energy release of that magnitude could blow up the whole mountain.'

'Great,' Archie smiled. 'I've always loved fireworks.' Then, holding his lab sample over the edge of the control deck, he said, 'Barney, put this in cylinder number two. Quickly.'

331

As Archie reached over the control deck to pass the test tube to Barney he turned away from his three hostages for a moment.

'Antony! Do something!' shrieked Villenemi.

Before Archie and Barney even had a chance to react, the stickman had covered the ground between them with long jerky strides and gripped Barney tightly by the throat.

'Drop your weapon,' Antony ordered. 'Or I'll snip your friend's head off like a dead rose.'

Instantly Villenemi's expression of infuriation eased into one of utter superiority. 'Oh well done, Antony,' he chuckled, his saggy cheek blooming with a purple hue. 'Well, well, well, this certainly puts a whole new complexion on proceedings now, doesn't it?'

'If anyone here is in need of a new complexion it's you,' said Archie, slipping the test tube back into his pocket. But as the stickman dragged Barney backwards towards the far wall he knew his options had narrowed substantially.

He couldn't bear to look at the victorious grin that curled half of Villenemi's mouth. His bulbous scaly orb swivelled jerkily while his human eye glinted with glee. The sight of the slug-like tongue darting out of his mouth as if savouring the whiff of victory turned Archie's stomach. Archie glanced at his father, who gave him a look that told him not to try anything stupid. But it was the expression of cold, wild terror in Barney's eyes that made his decision for him.

Slowly Archie raised both hands. Gripping something straight, black and shiny between his right thumb and forefinger he held it high above his head so that everyone could see the weapon with which he'd been controlling the room.

Villenemi's shoulders began to shake, then he threw his head back and emitted a deep patronising laugh, one side of his mouth opening wide in triumphant glee, the other retaining its glum downward curve. 'Is that – forgive me – is that . . . a *Mars bar*?' he spluttered.

'Enjoy it while you can, Doctor Who-ever,' growled Archie. 'You'll be laughing on the other side of your face in a minute.'

'Oh really?' Villenemi whimpered, wiping a tear from his human eye. 'Don't tell me you've got a secret weapon? Some jelly-gnite babies perhaps? Or maybe you plan to shoot us all with a wine gun?'

Again Villenemi's squat body convulsed with laughter that came in waves, each one reaching a higher peak than the last. This maniacal behaviour went on so long that Archie was beginning to wonder if some genetic malfunction had actually caused the odious mastermind to get stuck in a never-ending laughter loop. Even Claws and Antony, who had initially joined in with the hilarity, soon tired of the performance, exchanging weary shrugs as their mirth subsided. Then the computerised female voice brought Villenemi's amusement to an abrupt halt.

'Reverse transmutation will commence in – thirty seconds.'

'You made this far too easy for me, Master Hunt,' smirked Villenemi. 'It's like taking sweets from a child. Now drop the Mars bar and step away from the console. And do try not to cry about it. Nobody likes a sore loser.'

Archie gave Barney an apologetic shrug then, with a flick of his wrist, he threw the chocolate bar to the floor.

Chapter 43

Antony reacted instantly. Unable to resist the lure of the chocolate treat he darted forward, pulling Barney with him, and snapped up the bar. In no time he had torn open the wrapper and, in two hungry bites, devoured the snack.

'You'll have to excuse Antony,' Villenemi chuckled. 'He's a sucker for a Mars bar.'

'I expect he gets antsy if he doesn't get his chocolate fix,' Archie shrugged. 'Except . . . that's not an ordinary Mars bar. It's a Toxic Chocolate Stinkbomb.'

'A what?' Villenemi sneered.

'A Toxic Chocolate Stinkbomb,' Archie repeated slowly as though explaining it to a small child. 'It's laced with a powerful insecticide, so any second now . . .'

Archie was interrupted by a horrible choking sound. Antony had released Barney and was staggering from side to side clutching his throat. As the stickman dropped to his knees his frogspawn eyes were swollen and bloodshot and his mandibles thrashed angrily. Then he slumped backwards, sitting on his heels, his arms dropped to his sides and his lifeless mouth fell open.

'Well, that's one less irrit*ant* to worry about,' Archie said dryly.

'Good riddance,' said Barney, rubbing his throat. 'He was becoming a real pain the neck.'

'Bravo, Master Hunt.' Villenemi clapped slowly. 'A poisoned sweet – how very . . . sweet. What have you got for me – some toffee bomb-bombs?'

Archie smiled confidently, although he wasn't sure how the next part of his plan would go. 'As I said, that was a Toxic Chocolate Stinkbomb,' he said suavely. 'You have seen the lethal effect of the toxic part – and any second now you will feel the effect of the stinkbomb aspect.'

'What are you wittering on about?'

'As well as being laced with insecticide, that Mars bar contained a powerful canine pheromone that would have

336

been released into this room when Antony bit into it.'

'So what?' Villenemi snorted. 'Who's afraid of a doggy smell?'

'It's funny you should say that,' said Archie, hoping he'd remembered his biology lesson correctly. 'Because wolves, foxes and coyotes are all canines and natural predators of lizards, who smell danger coming using their tongues. Last I heard you were half reptile, so the answer to your question "Who's afraid of a doggy smell?" is you.'

'That's ridiculous,' Villenemi said. 'I've never heard anything so preposterous in all my life.'

'Is it?' Archie held the evil maniac's stare, waiting anxiously for the pheromone to take effect.

Suddenly Villenemi gasped as if he'd just seen a ghost. His tongue flickered in and out feverishly and his head snapped from side to side, as if searching for impending danger.

'What's the matter, Doctor Crank-enstein? Is something dogging you?'

Without replying Villenemi turned and ran for the exit. When he reached the closed door a computerised voice announced, 'State name and identifier code.' Villenemi was panting so hard he could barely speak and had to take a few long breaths to gather himself, glancing nervously over his shoulder with a hunted look in his lizard eye.

The evil villain was right where Archie wanted him – standing on the logo on the floor in front of the door. One panel of the control deck was labelled *Ejection Module*, consisting of a lever, a button and a small monitor that was displaying a blue screen. Archie pulled the lever, labelled *Snare*, and a glass cylinder descended over the evil professor in a flash, confining him to the spot with a *'shuck'*.

Villenemi pressed his hands desperately against the glass and looked down at his feet. He turned to look at Archie, his human eye pleading for mercy.

'Please,' he whimpered through the perforated glass. 'I can't swim.'

'I wouldn't worry about that.' Archie held his gaze. 'I shouldn't think you'll survive long enough to drown.'

'I'm a wealthy man,' Villenemi said frantically. 'I'll pay you whatever you want. Just name your price.'

'You murdered my mother, you evil freak.' Archie swallowed back his emotions. 'I'd say it's high time *I* paid *you* back.'

He pressed the button labelled *Jettison* and a saw-

338

tooth crack opened up along the lightning bolt beneath the villain's feet. Within a second the two halves of the logo had slid out of sight and Villenemi dropped through the round hole in the floor. He entered the water beneath with a satisfying *'ploosh'*.

On the screen Archie saw an underwater shot of Villenemi plunging into the pool, leaving a trail of white bubbles like a depth charge. Before he could even kick to the surface a sleek silhouette of a shark intercepted the figure like a missile. Immediately the water turned frothy white before blooming crimson.

When Archie had first noticed the logo on the floor he'd suspected the design was camouflaging a trap-door – as it had done on the roof. Connecting that with the shadow he'd seen behind the lab wall, he had concluded that Barney had been right all along – Villenemi's lair really was equipped with a trapdoor over a tank full of shark-infested water.

'You really dropped him in it,' said Barney.

Archie nodded, his face suddenly pale. As he switched off the screen he thought about how different his life would have been if that one crazy individual had not crossed his mother's path, and a wave of sadness swallowed him up.

Chapter 44

'Reverse transmutation will take place in – ten seconds.'

The computerised countdown yanked Archie away
from his thoughts. He looked anxiously over at his
dad and the others, who finally seemed to be growing
aware of their surroundings.

'Listen, Dad,' he called. 'Take Barney and the boys
up to the gantry. There's an escape hatch there that
should lead out on to the roof where Gemma is waiting – she's with us. Get everyone in the helicopter – I'll
use the Dragonfly.'

Archie's father shook off his torpor and appraised
the situation with a glance.

'I'm not leaving without you,' he argued, his voice
croaky.

'I just have to finish something here,' Archie insisted. 'I'll be right behind you – I promise.'

Richard held Archie's stare for a moment then gave him a single nod.

'OK, kiddo,' he said with a wink. 'You're the boss.'

Richard Hunt herded Henry Ulrik and Karl Schumaker up the flight of metal stairs to the gantry. Barney paused for a moment, considering how he was going to get past Claws, who appeared stunned by Villenemi's sudden demise but was awkwardly positioned between Barney and the staircase.

As if suddenly remembering his evil purpose, Claws scrambled sideways towards Barney, his pincers snapping threateningly.

'This way, Barney!' Archie's father urged from the balcony. 'Run for it.'

Barney hesitated for a moment, mesmerised by the creature scuttling towards him, claws spread wide.

'Come on, Barney,' Archie called. 'You can do it.'

Barney cowered against the wall and shook his head. 'I can't. He'll get me.'

Archie was so engrossed in Barney's plight that he didn't notice the sound of approaching footsteps accelerating to a frantic pace. Then through the corner of his eye he saw his father flash across the operations platform.

Richard Hunt pelted towards Claws, dropping his shoulder at the last moment and charging him into the wall next to Barney. The crabman slammed face first into the solid surface and fell flat on to his back, writhing around like a stranded turtle.

'Nice work, Mr Hunt,' Barney mumbled, stepping over the figure flailing at his feet.

'You can thank me later.' Richard Hunt grabbed Barney's wrist and dragged him towards the metal staircase.

As Archie watched them climb the steps a sudden realisation filled him with hopelessness and he slumped back in the chair.

'Archie!' Barney called from the gantry. 'What are you waiting for?'

'The reverse transmutation,' Archie said wearily. 'I'm too late.'

'Rubbish,' Barney said encouragingly. 'You've got plenty of time. Every Evil Genius's final countdown slows down when it comes to the crunch. The last ten seconds always takes like *forever*.'

'But . . .'

'Reverse transmutation will take place in – five seconds.'

'See,' Barney grinned smugly, then reached up for Archie's father to pull him through the manhole and on to the roof.

Relieved he still had a chance, Archie ran over to cylinder number two. Delving into his pocket, he grabbed the test tube and placed it on the base of the cylinder. He removed the airtight stopper and attached a couple of electrodes to the spongy pink mass inside. Hurrying back across the operations platform, he jumped up into the seat behind the control deck.

'Reverse transmutation will take place in – three seconds.'

Maybe Barney had been right? The countdown definitely seemed to be slowing down.

All he had to do now to set up the process was drop cylinder two over the sample. As he reached for the lever to do so he felt an incredible pain in his wrist.

The crabman's pincer was clamped round Archie's arm and squeezing so tightly that he felt as if his hand might get snipped off. Screaming in agony, Archie

343

swung his free arm across his body, driving his fist into Claws's nose. The mutant staggered back, releasing Archie's hand from his clamp.

Archie turned back to the control deck but as he leaned forward for the cylinder control lever he was yanked back by his hood. Standing up, he swung round and delivered an instinctive karate chop to his opponent's arm, snapping it off just below the elbow.

The bewildered crabman glanced at his stump but before he even had time to look back at the boy who was responsible, a size seven trainer smashed into the side of his head, knocking him out cold.

At that moment he heard Gemma's voice in his earpiece. 'What's happening, Yankee?'

'Just disarming a bad guy,' Archie murmured with an air of resignation.

'Reverse transmutation will take place in – one second.'

Ignoring the severed pincer still clamped to his hood, Archie frantically grabbed the cylinder control lever and slid it down the panel. With a pneumatic hiss the glass tube glided down over the sample and sealed itself with a loud suck.

344

'Reverse transmutation commencing.'

Accompanied by a growing hum from deep beneath the floor, the cylinders housing Finn and the sample of pink jelly filled with smoke and glowed bright orange.

Archie waited and crossed his fingers.

Chapter 45

The hum deepened to a rumble and the whole building started to vibrate.

The walls of instrument panels were awash with red lights of assorted sizes and brightness, flashing frantically as a klaxon sounded its deafening warning.

'**Danger, danger – system overload – meltdown imminent,**' the computerised voice announced, with a disconcerting lack of urgency.

Soon the magnitude of the building's vibrations had increased to such an extent that Archie was forced to cling to the control deck to avoid being thrown from his chair.

A shrill grinding sound overhead was followed by a long squeal – like a door opening in a haunted house.

Glancing up, Archie saw that one end of the sliding gangway had unhinged itself. Instinctively he ducked down and covered his head with his arms just as the heavy structure crashed to the floor. The bridge came to rest at an angle, stretching diagonally from the floor to the gantry above – miraculously missing his head by millimetres.

'Evacuate, evacuate – total destruction guaranteed.'

Archie ignored the computerised warning and intently watched cylinder number two. The violent motion of the building threw him roughly from side to side and the klaxon was now accompanied by a whole orchestra of different bells and sirens as more and more destruction warnings were set off.

Metal panels and sections of pipe began to rain down from the ceiling on to the glossy white floor. Glass dials exploded and cables snapped, spraying the equipment with sparks as the Transmutator threatened to shake itself to pieces.

'Stay calm,' Archie muttered to himself. 'Nothing serious – just a few peripheral items.'

Suddenly an almighty cracking sound echoed round the room. Archie spun his seat round to see a fracture about ten centimetres wide tearing through the floor as it snaked from one side of the room to the other. With a sickening jolt one end of the building dropped about a metre, leaving the floor sloping down precariously towards the enormous tinted windows.

'Yankee, this is X-ray.' Gemma's voice was shrill in Archie's headset. 'You have to get out of there now. The whole building's about to collapse.'

'In a minute,' Archie replied calmly. 'I just need to see if I'm right about something.'

'Get out now!' Gemma yelled. 'That's an order.'

The next voice Archie heard made him stop in his tracks.

'Archie, it's Dad. I'm coming to get you.'

'Just a few more seconds, Dad. I promise – just trust me!'

'If anything happens to you, my boy, there'll be no pocket money for a month.'

Archie smiled to himself. 'OK, Dad. I'll see you in a minute.'

Archie watched the cylinders glowing a deeper and deeper crimson. The floor jolted again. The split in the floor had crept halfway up the walls. If it spreads to the roof, the whole arm of this building is going to slip into the ocean, Archie thought.

348

He watched the cracks growing up the walls like poisoned ivy. He knew it was unlikely that he would escape unless he evacuated immediately, but he would not leave until he had done all he could for Finn. Without him, Archie's father would still be strapped into his Audi at the bottom of the sea.

The computerised voice said something.

Archie wasn't sure if he'd heard it right.

He replayed the announcement in his head. It had definitely said, 'Reverse Transmutation complete.'

By sliding the appropriate levers up the control deck Archie raised cylinders two and four then jumped down from his chair. As the floor rocked beneath him he battled his way towards cylinder number two, staggering from side to side. He waited for the thick column of smoke to clear, and as he waved it away he saw at last that by risking his own neck and initiating the disaster-inducing reverse transmutation he had saved the life of . . . a fish?

It was flapping about helplessly on the floor of the cylinder, eyes staring blankly as its thick lips opened rhythmically.

Archie felt a sense of immense anticlimax but it lasted only a split second. He had hoped to return someone who was part man and part fish to his normal self. If he had returned a fish to normal in one cylinder, then surely in the other cylinder . . . ?

He heard someone coughing and turned to see a boy staggering from the plume of smoke billowing over the base plate of cylinder four.

Archie grabbed the boy, pulling an arm over his shoulder and supporting his weight. Glancing sideways, he saw the boy's short bleached hair and a stud piercing his eyebrow, glinting as it had done in the laboratory, and he knew he'd been right.

'Come with me, Jason,' Archie instructed, pulling one of Jason's arms over his shoulder. 'I'm going to get you out of here.'

The boy's mouth snarled up on one side. 'How do you know my name?' he asked.

Archie smiled. 'Long story.'

Archie supported Jason's weight as the pair fought their way up the rocking stairs to the balcony.

Using the railing as a foothold, Jason clambered up and levered himself through the escape hatch. Archie pushed Jason from below then followed him on to the roof just as the balcony came away from the wall and crashed down below. Outside on

350

the roof, Archie could see the helicopter hovering about a mile out to sea. The thought of his father, Gemma, Barney and the other two boys anxiously waiting spurred him on as he ran across the rooftop towards the Dragonfly, still taking most of Jason's weight.

'Jump in!' he yelled to Jason as he stood in the foothold on the side of the plane and unlatched the canopy. Still looking dazed, Jason did as he was told and hauled himself into the Dragonfly's passenger seat. Archie's hands blurred across the instrument panels, flicking switches and buttons as he fired up the plane's jet engines.

Suddenly there was a crack like gunfire behind them and Archie knew immediately what had happened. With an agonising groan the whole arm of the building listed sharply downward, leaning towards the rocks at a terrifying angle.

Archie slammed the throttles forward but the plane didn't respond – its engines were still accelerating.

Suddenly the building gave way beneath them, dropping away like a trapdoor.

Archie felt his stomach flip as the Dragonfly went into free fall. The plane tipped forward as it plummeted towards the precipitous rocks waiting to smash it to pieces far below.

Just as it seemed all hope was gone, Archie felt the engines roar to life, cushioning the plane's descent then forcing it upward, away from certain destruction and straight up into the air. As the Dragonfly powered skyward he eased the aircraft back to an even keel, allowing it to climb a hundred feet above the ridge before speeding out to sea.

When he was sure the Dragonfly was far enough away from the destruction he'd left behind, Archie banked into a steep climbing turn and glanced over his shoulder. Through the glass canopy he could see the whole section of Villenemi's lair sliding down the mountainside. It was now broken into three pieces that bounced and skidded on the rough terrain before plunging into the ocean, sending sheets of water high into the air. Where one arm of the building had broken away a gaping hole offered a clear view of the inside of Villenemi's hideout. The Transmutator was now glowing an incandescent white while the ground around it was slowly caving in.

Then a vast fireball billowed high into the sky in eerie silence. A split second later the sound of an immense explosion filled the sky, violently shaking the Dragonfly as lumps of sandstone arced into the air like meteors.

'Whoo-hoo!' Archie immediately recognised Barney's voice in his headset.

'Hey, Agent Zulu,' Archie beamed. He could see the helicopter about three miles away in his twelve o'clock. 'You were right about the trapdoor to the shark tank after all.'

'I know.' Barney sounded hyper. 'But is it me or are Evil Masterminds' lairs really going downhill these days?'

'Oh, I don't know,' Archie replied. 'I think we just witnessed a property boom.'

'Zulu, this is X-ray, do you copy?' Gemma sounded stern.

'Go ahead, X-ray.'

'What kind of stunt were you playing back there? When I told you to evacuate, that was an order.'

'Sorry. I just had to do something that was important to me.'

'I thought we'd agreed you can't just do what *you* want? STINKBOMB is a team.'

'I know.' Archie levelled the plane at eight thousand

353

feet. 'That's why it was important to me to show you I've learned not to be selfish all the time.'

'How do you mean?'

'I've got something for you.'

'For me? What is it?'

'Oh, nothing special.' Archie glanced at Jason and smiled.

After a moment's silence, Jason spoke into his microphone. 'Hey, Sis.'

The squeal of delight that Gemma emitted was so loud and shrill that Archie had to remove his headset in case his eardrums burst. When eventually she had composed herself enough to speak she did so with mock annoyance. 'Jason, where on earth have you been? You were supposed to be home months ago. Mum and Dad are going to go mental.'

'I know, I'm sorry.' Jason shrugged. 'I haven't been myself lately. Thanks to Archie though I'll be home in no time. It'll be like I've never been away.'

'Archie, are you still there?' Gemma asked. 'How did you know Finn was my brother?'

'I started to get suspicious in the hotel in Hamburg,' Archie explained. 'He called you Gemma even though you'd been introduced as Agent X-ray.'

354

'Pretty sharp,' Gemma said.

'When I saw the sample in Doom's lab I recognised Jason's eyebrow stud from the photo you'd shown me,' Archie continued excitedly. 'And the test tube was labelled 24121600.'

'Which means?'

'Twenty-four, twelve is the date,' Archie said. 'And sixteen-hundred is the time.'

'Four o'clock was about the time Jason went missing on Christmas Eve last year,' Gemma muttered.

'That's what I guessed. It's the same code Doom used for the snatch at the gallery.'

'Quite the detective, aren't you, Agent Yankee?' Gemma remarked with a smile.

'Don't worry,' Archie said. 'You can thank me later.'

'Thank you?' Gemma laughed. 'I could kill you. He's always taking my stuff without asking and embarrassing me in front of my friends. Have you any idea how annoying a kid brother he is?'

Archie and Jason exchanged a high five.

'Listen, kiddo,' Richard chipped in. 'Nice work back there – I'm proud of you.'

'Thanks, Dad.' Archie paused and when he spoke

again his voice was quiet. 'Dad? I can't believe Mum was an agent . . .'

'I'm really sorry, Archie,' Richard replied warmly. 'I was going to tell you when I thought you were old enough. Looks like that time has come. Let's talk on the ground – we've been cleared to land at Nice airport. The wind's a tricky north-easterly so take it easy near the deck. I'll see you on the helipad.'

'Archie?' it was Gemma again. 'I've got IC on the phone. She knows what happened and she just wants a quick word. I'll patch her through over the RT.'

'Agent Yankee, this is IC. Well, it looks like following orders is hardly your strong point, doesn't it?'

Archie hesitated for a moment, unsure how to explain his actions.

IC continued, 'However, it looks like defeating odious masterminds certainly is. Well done, Yankee.'

'Thank you, IC,' Archie replied.

'Someone else here wants to have a word.'

He could hear her passing the phone over.

'OGM, Agent Yankee!' enthused Holden Grey. 'There is only one word to describe what STINKBOMB has achieved – *spectacular*. Oh, and brilliantly *swashbuckling*. Come to think of it, *intrepid* sums it up quite neatly

356

too. So I guess I'm saying there are a number of words to describe what STINKBOMB has done for the nation of our country. Mr Figo is suitably impressed by our monumental success and I made it quite clear to him that it was not all down to my technological je ne sais rein. Enough respect.'

'Thank you, Mr Grey.'

'FIY, STINKBOMB has been awarded official MI6 agency status so next time an odious mastermind comes knocking we'll be looming large and lying low – you get me?'

'I think so,' Archie said uncertainly.

'In that case you have a safe landing and we'll see you when you're on terra cotta. Laters.'

Archie sensed Jason staring at him, his mouth slightly ajar.

He grimaced and shrugged. 'Don't ask.'

Snapping the control column to the right he rolled the plane on to its wing tip and smiled to himself. The sea was glistening in the afternoon sunshine that was bathing the coastline in warm golden light. All of Dr Doom's hostages were safe and the madman's evil plot had been thwarted.

'Mission accomplished,' he said to himself.

357

Suddenly a blurred black shape flashed over his shoulder and he was slammed against the side of the cockpit. He immediately recognised the searing vice-like grip squeezing his wrist and an awful realisation dawned on him.

The pincer attached to his hood! he thought. It had regenerated into another crabman.

Chapter 46

The crabman was grappling with the aircraft's controls. Archie's face was buried in his attacker's body but he could feel the plane bucking and weaving as he battled to maintain a safe flight path. But it was no good. The crabman was too strong and Archie could feel his grip weakening.

He felt the plane lurch into a vertical climb and knew he had only seconds to do something before the Dragonfly ran out of energy and tumbled back to earth.

Wriggling one hand free, he reached up and twisted the red latch over his head. Easing the other arm under the crabman's body, he felt about until he'd located the control stick but he didn't try to seize it.

'Listen, Claws,' Archie grunted. 'You really should have your seat belt on, you know. As you told my friend earlier, if you're not strapped in you could end up getting hurt, and we wouldn't want that now, would we?'

Claws reacted to Archie's comment with a moment's confusion during which he inadvertently relaxed his grip on the control column. Seizing his opportunity, Archie grabbed the stick and shoved it forward immediately, slamming it to one side.

The Dragonfly's nose dropped sharply then it flipped upside down. When the plane was inverted Archie checked the roll and held the plane level, feeling the pressure on his shoulders as he hung in his harness.

In the blink of an eye the black mass pressing Archie to his seat fell out of his lap and tumbled through the open canopy above his head. He looked up to see the crabman flailing helplessly as he accelerated towards the sea, receding to no more than a speck at a blistering rate.

'That's what you get for being so shellfish,' Archie muttered, rolling the Dragonfly the right way up.

The plane's speed was dangerously low so he poured on full power but it was too late. The nose kicked up as

360

the Dragonfly flipped on to its back and corkscrewed earthward in a tightening spiral dive.

Archie cut the power and squeezed on the left rudder pedal to arrest the spin.

The aircraft plunged through eight thousand feet, rotating fast. The outside world was still turning as the altimeter wound past four thousand feet.

'Do something!' Jason yelped.

'In a moment,' Archie replied calmly.

One thousand feet. Finally the spinning stopped.

Archie pulled on the control stick, gently at first but steadily increasing the back-pressure. He felt the wings start to shake. The Dragonfly was dangerously close to a high-speed stall, but Archie had no choice but to maintain his pull. Reluctantly the aircraft raised its nose slightly but they were still plunging. More pressure on the controls made the plane judder like a car racing over a cattle grid.

At last the aircraft was showing signs of coming out of its dive. Shaking violently, its plummet began to flatten as it swooped towards the pebbly beach below.

'One hundred feet,' announced the radio altimeter.

Archie kept pulling.

'Fifty feet.'

There was nothing else he could do.

'Thirty feet.'

He screwed his eyes shut.

Silence.

Archie waited.

Then, 'Fifty feet . . . One hundred feet . . .'

'Yee-haa,' Archie screamed, gradually feeding on the power as the Dragonfly speared upward over the shoreline. 'We did it!'

Jason said nothing but a weary smile spread across his bloodless face.

'Archie, where are you?' It was his father on the radio. 'Is everything OK?'

'Coming, Dad,' Archie replied easily. 'I just had to drop someone off. Then I thought I'd take Jason for a quick spin.'

Archie banked the plane out to sea, beginning a wide circuit round to the helipad at Nice airport. He set the Dragonfly down about forty yards from the helicopter, killed the engines and slid back the canopy. As he and Jason crossed the tarmac, he saw Gemma's slight frame climb out of the helicopter and start walking towards them. Within a few strides she had broken into a run and Jason immediately ran off to meet his sister, who threw her arms round him and lifted his feet off the ground.

Archie kept walking, sharing a brief smile with Gemma over Jason's shoulder. He could see Barney beaming at him and giving him a thumbs up through the helicopter's rear window, then his father appeared round its nose.

Richard Hunt approached Archie and gave him a warm, tired smile.

'Good to see you, kiddo,' he said, placing a hand on his son's shoulder. 'Nice flying, by the way. I knew you'd turn out to be an ace.'

'Really?' Archie asked, wrinkling his nose. 'How come you grounded me then?'

'I didn't ground you,' Richard laughed. 'As I was trying to explain before we were run off the road – I couldn't take you flying while I was helping Cranfield with its study because they constantly monitor the Dragonfly's flight data recorder.'

'So they would have known you were letting me fly the plane,' Archie concluded, blushing a little at the thought of his tantrum. 'And you would have been in serious trouble.'

'What did you think? That I didn't believe in you?'

363

Archie studied the ground and shrugged.

'You wally,' Richard laughed, ruffling Archie's tangled hair. Then he pulled his son towards him and wrapped both arms round his ribcage, holding him tightly against his body. 'I'm so proud of you,' he whispered into Archie's hair.

Archie closed his eyes and squeezed his father as tightly as he could. Then he looked up at him. 'If you're really proud, you could show it by letting me fly the Dragonfly round here for a few days?' he said hopefully. 'The views are awesome.'

Richard gave his son a wry smile. 'Nice try, kiddo. Unfortunately, I think you're about to be debriefed by MI6, then we'll have to fly straight home.'

'Can't we even go for a pizza in town?'

'You know the rules,' Archie's father said, shaking his head apologetically. 'Even for STINKBOMB agents, bedtime is nine o'clock. Especially on a school night.'

Chapter 47

The classroom window was intensifying the afternoon sun and Archie was struggling to stay awake. He hadn't made it to bed until 1 a.m. and then he'd lain awake for hours having drunk too much Coke on the British Airways flight home from Nice.

As his eyes drooped he mentally replayed the events of the last few days. Moore the Bore's nasal voice was droning in his ears as he remembered his conversation with Highwater and Grey, who arrived at Nice airport about fifteen minutes after he'd landed the Dragonfly on the helipad. They had taken him, Barney and Gemma to a quiet corner of the Business Class departure lounge to debrief them on the mission.

They were told not to tell anyone else anything about their activities over the past few days, which seemed pretty obvious really. Highwater confirmed that STINKBOMB was to be made an official agency within MI6 and, given the success of its first assignment, its personnel were to remain unchanged.

As promised by the DG, Highwater had been offered a promotion to Head of Surveillance. But to Archie's surprise and delight she had turned it down – preferring to remain in her present position as Initiative Commander of STINKBOMB.

Secret training details were to be arranged after school and at weekends to sharpen the agents' trade craft in readiness for their next mission, whenever and whatever that might entail. On Saturday, Archie and Barney would spend the day at an MI6 safe house learning surveillance recognition techniques and taking part in memory training exercises.

'Mr Hunt.' Moore the Bore's voice was weirdly close and yet distant at the same time. 'Mr Hunt! Are you on the planet?'

Archie sort of knew his head was lolling and he could feel a string of saliva running down his chin but he couldn't bring himself to open his eyes. Only now was the stimulating effect of the caffeine in his system wearing off and he *really* needed a sleep.

THWACK!

The sudden stinging sensation in his right ear snapped Archie out of his cosy slumber and deposited him rudely back in the classroom, where every pair of eyes stared at him. Pressing his palm against his burning ear, he twisted to glare angrily at Harvey Newman, who was flexing a shatterproof ruler and grinning at him.

'There you go, Miss,' Newman giggled. 'Sleeping Ugly is awake now.'

'Thank you, Mr Newman,' Miss Moore said in her dreary monotone. 'Although I would advocate a slightly gentler approach to waking a fellow classmate in future.'

Archie turned and faced his teacher, who was now standing right in front of his desk. 'Mr Hunt,' she said wearily. 'I'm so sorry to keep you awake. You'll be relieved to hear it's just about home time and I would recommend you have a very early night.'

'Sorry, Miss,' Archie offered contritely.

'Why are you so tired anyway?' Miss Moore persisted. 'Spent the weekend flying your plane around

367

saving the world, I suppose.' The teacher allowed herself a small smile at her own witty comment.

'He's actually Buzz Light-thingummy,' Newman interjected, buoyed by the positive reaction to the ear-flick incident. 'He's probably been fighting off some sort of evil emperor or something.'

'Is this right, Mr Hunt?' Miss Moore enquired playfully. 'Are you really a secret superhero? Did you spend the weekend keeping us all safe from devilish individuals who want to take over the world?'

Yes I did, as it happens, Archie thought, nervously pushing his glasses up the bridge of his nose. 'No, Miss,' he said. 'I was just out playing with Barney.'

'Ah yes. Mr Jones.' Miss Moore turned, arms folded, and regarded Barney as if she was analysing a statue in a gallery.

Barney was slumped over his desk, forehead on his exercise book, snoring gently like a contented horse. Miss Moore tiptoed over to his side and leaned over so that her mouth was just inches from Barney's ear.

'Come in, Agent Jones!' she shrieked.

Instantly Barney sprang out of his seat and swung round, adopting a combative karate stance. 'Doctor Doom is dead,' he recited. 'Genetic disaster has been

368

averted . . . Mission accomplished. Stand down all units.'
As reality dawned on him his words ground slowly to a
halt and he stood in silence, blinking at the class.

'Well, well,' said Miss Moore with mock admiration.
'I can see you and Mr Hunt have had quite a weekend,
saving us all from the terrible Doctor Doom!'

'Yeah,' heckled Newman. 'They're a right pair of
Super Zeroes!'

When the wave of laughter had died Miss Moore
asked, 'So what's your next mission, boys? Any more
masterminds on the horizon?'

Archie said nothing but Barney couldn't quite stop
himself mumbling, 'That's classified,' to which the
class howled in amusement again.

'Well, as it happens I have a special assignment for
you,' said Miss Moore.

Archie groaned inwardly while Barney's eyes lit
up. The teacher continued. 'Your assignment is a one-
thousand-word essay entitled "Why I must not sleep in
Miss Moore's Biology Lessons" – to be on my desk by
Friday morning. Is that understood?'

'Yes, Miss,' Archie and Barney replied dejectedly,
although their replies were drowned out by the school
bell.

As he left, Harvey Newman made a point of accidentally swinging his rucksack into the back of Archie's head.

'Oops! Sorry, Buzz,' he laughed.

'Seeya, Hardly,' Archie mumbled, straightening his glasses. He went out into the corridor and jogged to catch up with Barney. Waiting until everyone else had pushed past them and they were alone, he whispered, 'I thought we weren't ever supposed to mention anything about our mission – especially not the names of anyone involved.'

'I know,' Barney replied coolly. 'That was just a little anti-intelligence psychology back there.'

'Oh right,' Archie smirked. 'Because it sort of looked like you accidentally blurted out a load of details from a top-secret assignment?'

'That's exactly how it was *meant* to appear,' Barney said mysteriously, adding through the corner of his mouth, 'but I think it's safe to say we threw them off our scent.'

'Oh, I agree,' Archie smiled. 'I don't think anyone even smells a rat – let alone a STINKBOMB.'

Name: Archie Hunt

S.T.I.N.K.B.O.M.B. codename:
Agent Yankee

Age: 12

Appearance: Brown messy
hair, glasses

Hobbies: Flying, reading,
swimming

Favourite food: Pizza, milkshake

Personality: Clever, single-minded and loyal.
Becomes competitive when his ability is
challenged or doubted.

Special skills: Talented (secret)
pilot, capable of flying Dragonfly
jet aircraft in challenging
circumstances.

Most likely to say: 'I'm not
exactly one of the in-
crowd. I don't play football
and I have a slightly
nerdy obsession with
aeroplanes.'

Name: Barney Jones

S.T.I.N.K.B.O.M.B.

codename: Agent Zulu

Age: 12

Appearance: Blue eyes, blond curls, stocky (i.e. tubby) build

Hobbies: Reading (anything to do with spies), watching TV (anything to do with spies) and going to the cinema (anything to do with spies)

Favourite food: Cheeseburgers, chicken nuggets, sausages, pizza (all with chips, please), ice-cream, sponge and custard, Banoffee pie, trifle, Mars, Twix, Bounty, Snickers, Maltesers, Monster Munch

Personality: Energetic and enthusiastic. Has the potential to become overexcited in the field.

Special skills: In-depth knowledge of spy fiction (see Hobbies), which may provide on-the-money intel on Odious Masterminds' secret lairs. Must try and limit his use of spy jargon to occasions when he actually understands what he is saying.

Most likely to say: 'All units, we have a code yellow – the badger has entered the stingray's cave.'

'Are you going to finish those chips?'

Name: Gemma Croft

S.T.I.N.K.B.O.M.B. codename: Agent X-ray

Age: 14

Appearance: Blue eyes, often rolled, straight dark hair with asymmetric fringe

Hobbies: Shopping, Facebooking, listening to music, reading (esp. Twilight novels)

Favourite food: Tuna salad

Personality: A sullen and often cynical facade masks a strong team ethic and motivation. Is naturally suspicious of strangers/newcomers, who will have to work hard to earn her respect.

Special skills: Mathematically gifted. Exceptional knowledge of computer technology – able to gain access to any website or mainframe.

Typical quotes: 'Keep your voice down, motormouth.'

'Whatever.'

Name: Helen Highwater

S.T.I.N.K.B.O.M.B. codename:
  I.C. (Initiative Commander)

Age: Claims to be 49 (official
  records show her to be 53).

Appearance: Brunette, angular
  bob. Grey, cold eyes.

Interests: Theatre, Renaissance
  art, the symphonies of
  Beethoven and Brahms. (NB
  Although she claims to detest the
  insipid emptiness of
  pop music, colleagues
  report that she is often overheard
  singing the songs of Westlife and JLS
  to herself.)

  Favourite food: Indonesian-French
  fusion

Personality: Businesslike, authoritative. Likes to
  win.

Special skills: Excellent leadership and
  management qualities. Thinks 'outside the
  box', as demonstrated by her
  suggestion to use kids as
  undercover agents.

Most likely to say: 'We have
  an E.M.U. on our hands.'
'Does anybody understand what
  Agent Zulu just said?'

Name: Holden Grey

S.T.I.N.K.B.O.M.B. position: Tech
  Branch Specialist

Age: 73

Appearance: White, neatly parted
  hair (although has recently
  started spiking it up). Thin
  silver moustache.

Interests: Listening to the wireless,
  watching *Antiques Roadshow*, *Coronation Street*,
  MTV Cribs, *The Hills*.

Favourite food: Steak and kidney
  pie, jam roly-poly

Personality: Infectiously
  enthusiastic. Sometimes a little
  overeager to connect with the young
  agents.

Special skills: Has a sharp mind but
  his knowledge of technology
is twenty years behind the times.
When it comes to designing
gadgets his record is somewhat
hit-and-miss.

Most likely to say: 'BWT, guys, the
  new Kaney West track is, like, so nasty? And by
  that I mean it's groovy.'

(Examining an iPod) 'Over a thousand songs? Surely
  not at the same time? How on earth do they get
  them in there? I can't even see the eject button.'

Name: Yuri (pronounced Yur-ee) **Villenemi**

A.K.A: Dr Doom

Location: Somewhere in Europe

Appearance: Strange. One human eye (brown), one reptilian (bulbous and green).

Interests: Evil genetic experiments, world domination, cricket (the game)

Favourite food: Cricket (the insect)

Personality: Psychotic in his determination to take over the world. Constantly feels the need to be appreciated. A keen blogger.

Special skills: Cackling for long periods of time. Genetic science.

Most likely to say: 'Ah, Mr Hunt – I've been expecting you!'

'Do excuse my friend. His name is Mr Claws but I'm afraid he's no Santa . . . and I will take over the world, mwahh ha ha ha ha ha ha ha ha ha ha ha ha ha ha ha ha ha ha ha ha ha ha ha ha ha ha ha.'

Name: Evelyn Tension

Age: 42 (approx)

Eyes: Green, piercing

Hair: Long, flame orange

Background: An ex-MI6 Scalpel (assassin) with a history of overstepping the limits of her mission. Thought to bear a grudge against the British Prime Minister after he revoked her licence to kill. Suspected to have her heart set on personal revenge, possibly leading to world domination.

Favourite food: Steak tartare

Personality: Vain, charming, dangerous

Special skills: Expensively educated, multilingual, with a sky-high IQ and a black belt in numerous martial arts. An exceptional master of disguise and impersonation, having perfected instantaneous spray-on-liquid-latex-face-mapping technology. All agents beware – she could be the old man in the bus queue or the schoolgirl in the park.

Deep Trouble
By Rob Stevens

If there's an evil mastermind
In a secret lair
Who you gonna call?
Team S.T.I.N.K.B.O.M.B.

The Secret Team of Intrepid-Natured Kids Battling Odious Masterminds, Basically (phew!) is BACK! And this time they're in deep . . .

As London prepares to host the annual Student Games, MI6's team of child agents has a new mission: to protect the Prime Minister's son – who is competing in the games – from the vengeful and villainous Evelyn Tension (say it slowly). With her face-mapping-quick-drying-liquid-latex-mask gun she has the power to change her appearance with a squeeze of the trigger. Will S.T.I.N.K.B.O.M.B. be able to keep her at (bionic) arm's length?

Look out for the next adrenalin-fuelled
S.T.I.N.K.B.O.M.B assignment – coming in March 2012!